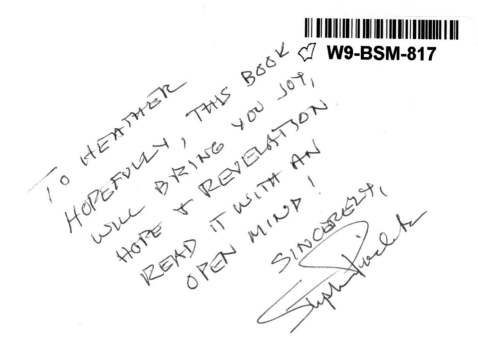

To HEATHER

HOPEFULLY, THIS BOOK ♡
WILL BRING YOU JOY,
HOPE & REVELATION

READ IT WITH AN
OPEN MIND !

SINCERELY,

The Cleansing Reign

ISBN-13: 978-0-9819478-5-3

This book is printed on recycled paper

Printed in the United States of America

The Cleansing Reign

by

Dr. Stephen Piechota

Dedication

This book is dedicated to
my loving wife Reine
and my children
Jon Christian and Lara Christine.

Acknowledgements

To Betty, whose devoted efforts in typing the manuscript made it possible to complete this work.

To Jon Christian Piechota, whose brilliant cover design and intellectual insights added so much to the presentation of the book.

To all the great Theologians, Philosophers, Avatars and Writers who sought to enlighten humanity.

To Bill Bradley, whose spiritual insights provided invaluable advice in finalizing this story.

To Beth Bruno, whose expertise in editing helped bring this story into a more readable form.

To Dan Uitti, whose knowledge in publishing was paramount into bringing this story into book form.

Preface

This book is like no other. It may even rank as the second greatest story ever told. Not only will it entertain, but it will also teach universal principles that apply to everyday life. It will explain sacred mysteries, the global conspiracy theory, the true nature of reality, and the purpose in life.

The first idea for this story was actually spawned in the early 1970s when the author read a book called, *They Dare Not Call It a Conspiracy*. Although an outline and brief sketches of the plot were initially written out, the main body of the work was not undertaken until 2005 AD. The impetus for getting serious about embarking on the arduous journey of writing a novel was provided by global events that were occurring at a bewildering rate. It became obvious that many of the warnings and predictions found in the book on the conspiracy were coming to fruition. After reading a second book, *The Handbook of a New Paradigm*, which mentioned that a book in novel form had never been written to explain how great changes were about to occur, the author dedicated himself to the completion of *The Cleansing Reign*.

It is my hope as the author that this book of revelation will provide a thorough understanding of life's mysteries and prepare readers for man's ascension and life in a glorious future.

Dr. Stephen Piechota

Chapter One

- Jon Corbett's Early Years and Education

The dirt and grime of a winter time were being washed away by a cleansing spring rain. This was the scene on an April day in 1954 when Jon Corbett sat at his bedroom window watching and pondering this change in nature along with a simultaneous change in his life.

Jon's spell of deep thought was interrupted by the sound of his mother's voice. "You up yet, Jon? Breakfast is ready."

Wonderful aromas of coffee, bacon and his mother's fabulous crepes wafted up the stairway to his room.

"Coming, Mother," Jon replied. He descended to have breakfast and to begin a very important discussion.

Jon was a lad of thirteen. To the casual observer he would have appeared no different than thousands of other boys during the 1950s. He was the product of loving, hardworking parents who inculcated a strong sense of values, virtue and reverence in him. The Corbett family's only connection to notoriety and fame stemmed from Jon's great grandfather, James J. Corbett, a former world heavyweight boxing champion. Gentleman Jim, as he was affectionately known, had dethroned boxing legend John L. Sullivan by employing techniques of boxing skill that were heretofore unknown, such as the left jab and right cross. Jon took pride in his heritage although he remained humble about it, too, as his parents discouraged boasting or displays of self-importance.

Jon loved baseball and was fiercely devoted to the Boston Red Sox, evidenced by the team banner hanging over his bed and the baseball cards of the entire team tacked on the wall. The names and stats of Williams, Doerr, Goodman, Zarilla, Tebbetts, Stephens, DiMaggio and Dropo were second nature to Jon. He ate, lived, and slept BoSox, exulted in their triumphs, and overlooked their losses and shortcomings. He sought to emulate their excellence in his sandlot and organized baseball play, valuing his personalized Williams glove and Goodman bat above all things. This ardor and dedication were also evident in other aspects of his life in that simpler time back in the 50s. Jon was the kind of kid who polished his bike weekly, shined his Shell Cordovan Shoes to a mirror-like finish, coordinated his dress for school and church and took pride in the way he mowed a lawn or washed dishes.

By all appearances Jon was a normal American boy of the 1950s except for one characteristic: he was much more intelligent than his peers. Not only had Jon been at the top of his class at St. Joseph's grammar school but he had also accomplished many notable feats of mind for a lad so young. His papers on literary geniuses such as Melville and Shelley were so well written that they were used as illustrations to students in the third and fourth year of high school. Two of his exhibits at science fairs on meteorology and genetics were afforded national recognition. It was this latter acknowledgment that was to become the causal agent for a gross change in the life of Jon Corbett.

A seemingly incredible stroke of fortune brushed Jon's life when a certified letter arrived at his home. Within that letter was an offer to provide a free higher education, which had but two requirements: first, within three years of completing his college education Jon must give five years of his life in service to the organization that offered this scholarship; and second, no questions were to be asked as to the identity of the benefactor.

Jon's early childhood was a joyous and comfortable time. He often reflected on the wonderful, secure times when as a youngster his father would read classic stories to him, such as Treasure Island, Kidnapped, Huckleberry Finn, Red Badge of Courage, Lord Jim and a variety of other books dealing with sport and historical heroes. For Jon the most exciting stories were those involving his notable great grandfather, the former world heavyweight boxing champion James J. Corbett.

James John Corbett was born September 1, 1866, in San Francisco, California, and passed away on February 18, 1933, in Bayside, New York. Because of his good looks and classy boxing style he was dubbed with nicknames such as Handsome Jim, Pompadour Jim and ultimately Gentleman Jim. He was college educated and had performed as an actor in a variety of theaters. He was known in boxing circles as the father of modern boxing because of his scientific approach and innovative boxing technique. He was credited with changing prizefighting from a brawl to an art form. James J. Corbett represented the new age of boxing in which fighters honed their skills in a gym under the guidance of a coach rather than on the streets. He began his boxing career in 1886 after attending college and working as a bank teller. Because he wore his hair in a full pompadour, dressed tastefully, and employed fine grammar when he spoke, he earned the Gentleman Jim moniker.

Young Jon always felt a real affinity for his great granddad. Maybe it was the fact that Jon had inherited the good looks and ruggedness of his famous ancestor.

In 1891 James J. had fought a four-round exhibition with the legendary champion John L. Sullivan, who was considered unbeatable. This encounter was a prelude of things to come. On September 7, 1892, the famous Sullivan-Corbett championship battle took place in New Orleans, LA. It was the first heavyweight championship fight in which gloves were used; and it was fought under the Queensbury Rules.

Jon most enjoyed his father's reading from James J. Corbett's autobiography, The Roar of the Crowd. Jon's dad had read the account of the fight out loud several times, but Jon never tired of hearing it. J. J. Corbett described the match with John L. Sullivan as follows: A crowd of over 10,000 jammed the arena. Sullivan weighed in at 212 lbs., 25 lbs. heavier than Corbett. The betting was heavy. Two thousand miles away, beacon lights atop New York City's Pulitzer Building alerted the fans below as to which fighter was winning—red for Sullivan, white for Corbett. Corbett describes the fight: "Now, I knew that the most dangerous thing that I could do was to let Sullivan work me into a corner when I was a little tired or dazed. So I made up my mind that I would let him do this while I was still fresh. Then I could find out what he intended doing when he got me there. In a fight, you know, when a man has you where he wants you, he is going to deliver the best goods he has.

"From the beginning of the round Sullivan was aggressive—he wanted to eat me up right away. He came straight for me and I backed up and backed up, into a corner. While I was there I observed him setting himself for a right-hand swing, first slapping himself on the thigh with his left hand, which was sort of a trick to balance himself for a terrific swing with his right. But before he let the blow go, just at the right instant, I sidestepped out of the corner and was back in the middle of the ring again, with Sullivan hot after me.

"I allowed him to back me into all four corners, and he thought he was engineering all this, that it was his own work that was cornering me. But I had learned what I wanted to know; just where to put my head to escape his blow if he should get me cornered and perhaps dazed. He had shown his hand to me.

"In the second round he was still backing me around the ring. I hadn't even struck at him yet, and the audience on my right hissed at me for running away and began to call me 'sprinter'. Now I could see at a glance that Sullivan was not quite near enough to hit me so suddenly I turned my side to him, waved both hands to the audience and called out, "Wait a while! You'll see a fight!" So far Sullivan hadn't reached me with anything but glancing blows, and it was my intention when the third round started, to hit him with my first punch, and I felt that it must be a good one! If my first punch didn't hurt him, he was going to lose all respect for my hitting ability.

"So with my mind thoroughly made up, I allowed him to back me once more into a corner. This time I didn't intend to slip out, even though my actions indicated that I was going to, just as I had before. As we stood there fiddling, he crowding almost on top of me, I glanced as I had always done before, first to the left, then to the right, as if looking for some way to get out of this corner. He followed me and thinking I wanted to make a getaway, determined that he wouldn't let me out this time.

"For once he failed to slap himself on the thigh with his left hand, but he had his right hand all ready for the swing as he was gradually crawling up on me. Then, just as he set himself to let go a vicious right I beat him to it and unloosed a left hand to his face with all the power I had behind it. His head went back and I followed it up with a couple of other punches and slugged him back across the ring and into his corner. When the round was over his nose was broken.

"At once there was pandemonium in the audience! All over the house, men stood on their chairs, coats off, swinging them in the air. You could have heard the yells clear to the Mississippi River!

"But the uproar only made Sullivan more determined. He came out of his corner in the fourth like a roaring lion, with an uglier scowl than ever, while bleeding considerably from the nose. I felt sure now that I could beat him, but I made up my mind that it would take a little longer, and I would play it safe.

"From that time on I started doing things the audience was seeing for the first time, judging from the way they talked about the fight afterwards. I would work a left hand on the nose, then a hook into the stomach, then a hook up under the jaw again. I delivered a great variety of blows, using

5

such quick sidestepping and footwork that the audience seemed to be delighted and a little bewildered.

"In the twelfth round we clinched, and with the referee's order to break away, I dropped my arms. Sullivan let go a terrific right-hand swing from which I barely got away; as it was it grazed the top of my head. Some in the audience began to shout 'foul' but I smiled and shook my head to let them know I could handle myself.

"When we came up for the twenty-first round it looked as if the fight would last ten or fifteen rounds longer. Right away I went up to him, feinted with my left and hit him with a left-hand hook alongside the jaw pretty hard, and I saw his eyes roll. Summoning all the reserve force I had left I let my guns go, right and left, with all the dynamite nature had given me, and Sullivan stood dazed and rocking. So I set myself for an instant, put just a little more in a right and hit him alongside the jaw. He fell helpless on the ground, on his stomach and rolled over on his back! The referee, his seconds and mine picked him up and put him in his corner, and the audience went wild."

The reading of his great grandfather's own words had significant meaning for Jon. It certainly allowed for a real bonding with his dad as he reverently read this account to Jon. Jon also developed a wonderful sense of connection and appreciation for James J's intelligence, courage and thoughtful strategy in defeating the seemingly invincible John L. Sullivan. Jon took pride in knowing that he was a descendant of such a great champion. He determined at an early age that he would dedicate his life to living up to the high standards of his great grandfather, Gentleman Jim.

Even though Jon's ancestry was of such high quality the economic status of his family was no more than middle class. The family's modest wealth had been lost in the Great Depression of the 1930s. It was only through the diligence and hard work of his father, who ran a fairly prosperous hardware store, that the family had achieved some measure of material comfort.

Jon's parents were common folk of modest economic status. Their ability to provide Jon with anything but a public high school and state university education was highly doubtful. Therefore, the offer of a free prep school and Ivy League education was considered to be the most fortuitous of events.

As Jon descended the stairs to have breakfast with his parents and to discuss the prospects of this monumental change, several thoughts raced through his mind. He realized that some major changes would have to occur if he were to adapt to life with people of higher class. He would have to forego his DA haircut, pegged pants, blue suede shoes, and the rhythm 'n blues music he so loved. He wondered if he could make the transition to a preppy appearance and attitude without any serious psychological damage.

After a delicious breakfast and serious conversation with his parents, Jon decided that accepting the educational proposal was a no-brainer and he would embrace the idea wholeheartedly.

Jon's last summer at home was a joyful experience. He had a very successful pony league baseball season and enjoyed hanging out with his friends at the downtown soda shop, the Koffee Korner. He spent the last week of that summer saying goodbye to his friends with the promise that he would always value their friendship and the many memories of their shared experiences. On the next to last day before his departure to attend Taft School in Watertown, Connecticut, Jon had his hair shorn at Frank's Barber Shop and went down to Tony Calbi's Clothing Store to buy a new wardrobe.

Jon's years at Taft School were fantastic. Taft was and still is one of the finest prep schools in the United States. The school was known for its long list of graduates who distinguished themselves in later life. Not only did Jon find the academic environment fulfilling, but his prowess on the athletic fields of Taft also gave him an equal amount of satisfaction. Jon's baseball and golf achievements were legend at the school and may never be matched. His batting and pitching led the baseball team to three consecutive New England Prep School Championships. Jon's career batting average of .630 and a 28-1 win-loss pitching record were phenomenal and even spurred the interest of several major league teams. His golf career was unparalleled as well. A scoring average of 72.5 and an unbeaten match play record helped the school to another three New England crowns.

Those carefree years in the quiet New England town of Watertown, Connecticut did much to shape this extraordinary young man into a quintessential human specimen. The incredibly beautiful campus with the best instruction imaginable, and the friendly townspeople could have nothing but a positive effect. Most memorable were nightly visits to the soda fountain at Post Office Drug Store, which was just a leisurely walk from the campus dormitory. Not only were there ice cream sodas like none he had ever tasted, but also the conversations the students had with an erudite pharmacist named Richard Sagin were both inspiring and memorable. Discussions included topics such as the existence of God, economic theories, egalitarianism versus elitism, the nature of the universe, absolute values, true reality, eastern philosophies, vibrational medicine and myriad other subjects. It was fascinating! The engrossing discussions often extended well past the drug store closing time of 9 p.m. and were an education in themselves. Never before had Jon's mind been exposed to such exciting ideas. These revelations of truth and knowledge did much to inspire him to dedicate himself to his absolute fulfillment as a student.

Jon graduated with the highest academic honors and was readily accepted into Yale University. Jon's college years were equally fulfilling as he continued to broaden his intellectual foundation with exposure to a wide variety of experiences and new knowledge. Much of Jon's growth could be attributed to his college roommate, Fred Martin. Fred was a black student who had grown up in humble social circumstances, in an area of Hartford, Connecticut known as Bellevue Square. Despite being raised in an extremely disadvantaged section of Hartford, Fred overcame those circumstances and went on to become an exceptional student, cellist, and track, tennis and football star at Weaver High School. These accomplishments were a direct result of his mother, Mattie, who dedicated her life to instilling absolute values into her son along with providing him with exposure to great literature, music and art. Remarkably, she did this without state assistance but by working two jobs as a cleaning lady. Jon had met Mattie on several visits to Fred's home and had grown to admire this amazing lady. He often thought that Mattie's story should be told and retold as an example for all Americans to follow.

In addition to his cello skills and appreciation for classical music, Fred possessed exceptional improvisional talents, which were evident in his jazz playing as a bassist. Being Fred's roommate allowed Jon exposure to both the magnificence and grandeur of classical music as well as the soulful expressionism of jazz. He would oftentimes accompany Fred to classical concerts and jazz gigs. Many of the gigs were either in small jazz clubs or at college parties.

Jon had a rather interesting encounter at one particular fraternity party that would have strong implications many years later. It so happened that this one evening a fellow student named G. W. Plante had purposely bumped Jon as he walked by. Jon let the first nudge pass but when Plante bumped Jon a second time while sneering at him, Jon became angry and slapped the young man and threw him across the room. This obviously inebriated buffoon slid under a table where he remained in a drunken stupor for the rest of the evening. Jon didn't know G. W. Plante personally but he knew of him. Plante had a reputation as a ne'er-do-well who was a very poor student and a perpetual drunk. He came from a wealthy and influential family and was a brat who only got into Yale because of his family's wealth and influence. Plante was somewhat of a mystery to the other students because for some inexplicable reason he had been tapped to be a member of the highly mysterious and secretive organization known as Skull and Bones. Little did Jon know that decades later this individual would play a major role in the future of America. The incident was quickly forgotten and played no role in Jon's remaining time at Yale.

Many of the jazz clubs that Jon visited as he accompanied his roommate were located in the more sordid areas of New York and Connecticut cities. It was in these clubs that Jon learned about some of the negative influences in the world, such as the deceitfulness and amorality of people; the unscrupulous behavior and greed of club owners; and the racial hatred and distrust harbored in the minds of both the black and white races.

Another significant incident occurred at a small jazz club in Hartford, Connecticut, where Fred was playing. Jon was approached by a young, hip, black fellow.

"Hey man, what's happening? My name is Killer Joe Spivey," he said as he offered to shake hands.

"I'm just here listening to my friend Fred play the bass," Jon replied.

"That's cool! Are you telling me you actually have a true Negro friend?"

"I sure do. I've never had a more trusted friend."

"That's quite unusual. I really appreciate your reaching out to us black folks. To show you my appreciation, I am going to offer you an opportunity to make a few bucks. Just give me $50 and I will return $150 to you by the end of the night. You can trust me. I give you my word." Jon naively dug into his wallet to give Killer Joe $50.

"I'll be back within an hour with your $150."

Jon felt fully confident in the wisdom of his investment. Shortly thereafter the band took a break. Fred sat down next to Jon and asked him, "You didn't give Killer Joe any money, did you?"

"Yes, I did. I gave him $50 to make a quick $100," replied Jon.

"Well, I hate to tell you, Jon, but you'll never see your $50. Killer Joe is known for his scamming ability and he took advantage of your trusting nature. I hope you learn from this experience."

A period of enlightenment followed for Jon and did much to accelerate his thrust toward maturity. No longer was he just aware of the saccharin world of his younger years; gone forever was his tendency to view life through rose-colored glasses. Fred's friendship was of great importance to Jon and it not only provided the internal rewards of such a relationship but also allowed him to understand the manner in which black society existed. Jon became heavily involved in the civil rights movement in the early '60s. It was his thought that many of the inequities of life were due to prejudices and not to inferior talent or lack of intelligence. As is most times true, youthful exuberance leads to liberal ideas, which many transfer in later life to become far more conservative. Whether or not such a change would ever occur within Jon would remain to be seen.

Jon completed a well-rounded education at Yale with a double major in political science and philosophy as well as a minor in biochemistry. Even with this heavy load of study Jon managed to graduate with summa cum laude honors. Such a broad foundation of knowledge gave Jon a uniquely balanced view of life. It seemed that he had a total comprehension of man's pragmatic needs as well as appreciation of man's scientific and evolutionary destiny. Jon was well aware of his commitment to those who had financed his education and was determined to fulfill his obligation to them. He chose to wait three years before actually joining the ranks of this organization, which assigned him to a think tank in Rome, Italy. Jon was convinced that he should gain some experience in the real world before he could be fully effective and contribute something of value in his work assignment at Egalitaire, a liberal think tank under the auspices of the Club of Rome.

CHAPTER TWO

- On the Road
- Smuggling and Export
- Falling in Love

To gain more life experience, Jon decided to enter into a small business enterprise, one that imported Mexican and Native American artifacts into the New England states. He had first entertained this idea during the summer between his junior and senior years of college. During this period Jon toured the western United States and Mexico by motorcycle. It was on a stopover in southern New Mexico that Jon first encountered the beautifully crafted work of the Navajo Indians. He was enthralled at the masterful way in which artisans could incorporate turquoise and silver into such beautiful creations. It was then that Jon thought he might enjoy the challenge of starting a business venture of buying native artwork and reselling it in the northeastern area of the United States. Jon began this operation with a small bankroll of $850, which he smartly invested in the purchase of Navajo jewelry. He then had the goods transported to the Boston area where he could distribute these wares to various exclusive gift shops in the New England States. Jon's first foray into these areas was a great success and he managed to nearly quadruple his initial investment of $850 into $3,000. With this enlarged bankroll he returned to the Southwest to purchase a new shipment of goods. This process of buying, selling and accumulating an ever-growing amount of cash went on for several cycles until Jon had amassed a small fortune of nearly $100,000. It was this incredible amount of new wealth that was to influence the next chapter in Jon's life.

The love of money was beginning to change Jon's nature and erode the solid foundations of his earlier life. As is usually the case, when one travels extensively, Jon encountered all sorts of people, of both high and ill repute. On one particular visit to Tijuana, Mexico, Jon met up with another enterprising young American, Nelson Demerit, who had amassed considerable wealth as a smuggler of marijuana across the Mexican border into the United States. The outcome of their first and subsequent encounters was a new friendship that was to grow into an eventual business partnership of a new kind for Jon, the illegal trafficking of drugs.

Nelson Demerit was striking in appearance. He was tall and slender with a handsomely chiseled face, which was topped by a bountiful head of dirty blond hair styled in a modest Afro. He was a product of a liberal education, having graduated from Antioch College, and his attitudes typified the youth of that time. Nelson not only exemplified the concept of moral relativism but he was a very articulate spokesperson for this nihilistic approach to life. He welcomed the challenge of debating anyone who held to absolute moral values and most times would come away from these intellectual sparring matches feeling he had vanquished his adversary. Jon admired Nelson's innate intelligence and enjoyed his company; however, he did have some concern for Nelson's lack of appreciation for universal truths and principles. Despite these doubts he decided to team up with Nelson and accept the challenge of a new business.

The combined talents of these two young men overwhelmed other competing marijuana smugglers in northern Mexico with their resourcefulness. They developed an intricate and efficient network of smuggling drugs across the border and distributing marijuana in U.S. cities. Jon's imagination led to the creation of a communications system within the trucking system that was so covert that detection by law enforcement was virtually impossible. With this great advantage the export of drugs became a great deal easier and profits exploded accordingly. The influx of vast amounts of money had changed Jon into someone who was unrecognizable from the young man of only one year previous. He became immersed in hedonism and prodigality, looking only for the materialistic and external pleasures so characteristic of that type of person. Gone were his high ideals, which were replaced with the desire for power, wealth, and pleasure. Jon used his newfound wealth to fund several expensive vacations to glamorous Mexican resorts and was looking to parlay his money into even greater wealth by investing in an Acapulco resort venture. While inspecting a prospective site for a hotel Jon met an intriguing Native American woman who was to have a profound effect on his life.

Luz Barca, or "Apache" as Jon called her, was a lady of mixed Apache and Spanish ancestry. She was the product of an Apache mother and a Spanish father. Luz's Spanish ancestry stemmed from the Barca family in Barcelona, which was directly linked to the great Carthaginian leader, Hannibal. She bore the dignity and nobility of the Spanish and the vital strength and spiritual awareness of the Apache. This engaging woman, who was 46 years old, was to become not only a love interest but also a teacher of the most meaningful and penetrating view of life and reality that Jon had ever known.

The first meeting with Luz occurred rather innocently when both were in attendance at a meeting of potential investors in a new resort in Acapulco, Mexico.

Jon arrived just as the presentation was beginning, so he sought the nearest available seat. He politely asked a lovely lady sitting in the adjacent seat for permission to sit.

"Can I sit here?" Jon queried.

"Yes, you can, but you may not," she replied.

"Are you serious?" Jon quizzically asked.

"Of course I'm not serious. I was just being flippant. It was a bad joke about the proper use of the language. Please, take a seat."

As Jon took his seat, he briefly glanced at Luz and was taken aback by her astonishing beauty and her stylish presence. She was dressed in a crimson, gaucho style outfit, trimmed in gold. The crimson tone of the outfit was complemented by a pure white blouse. It was a look that evoked an image of a perfect "lady in red".

At the end of the presentation all those in attendance were invited to a luncheon buffet. Jon courteously asked Luz if she would like to join him at lunch. Luz was gracious enough to accept.

As the two were enjoying the exceptional cuisine and fine wine offered by Resorts International, their conversation was polite but superficial. It wasn't until Jon asked a few questions pertaining to Luz's heritage that the discussion took an unexpected turn onto a path of incredible profundity and depth.

Luz presented her story and background in a lucid, concise fashion that began with a focus on her Spanish heritage and the connection to the great Carthaginian family of Barca, which gave the world the city of Barcelona and such leaders as Hasdrubal, Hamilcar, and, most notable of all, Hannibal. Hannibal was famous for his prowess in military strategy and his many defeats of Roman legions in the Punic Wars two millennia ago. He had conceived of invading the Italian Peninsula from the north by traversing the formidable Alps with a vast army of men and elephants. He consistently outsmarted the Roman generals and scored dramatic and decisive victories in several major battles. His ingenious battle plans have been studied by military students throughout history and are testament to his greatness. It was immediately obvious to Jon that Luz reflected such Barcan greatness in her grace, dignity and intelligence.

Luz Barca was a woman of stunning beauty. Although she was in her 40s, her youthful looks belied her years. Her jet black hair was beautifully coiffured in a shoulder length style that framed an olive skinned face so wonderfully sculpted that it presented an image unparalleled in feminine grace and beauty. In addition to her lovely face Luz possessed a figure that was equally impressive. Standing at 5'5" she had an ample, yet firm bosom with a derriere that would even turn the head of Rubens.

As Luz delved into her native Indian background, she explained how her Spanish father had married a young Apache maiden some years ago. She was the only child born to that union. Jon was thoroughly engrossed as he listened to Luz weave her tale of living her early years in a tribal setting. Especially interesting were her stories of the gatherings the Indian children had with the elders and the Shaman who described their tribal origins, their relationship with the Great Spirit (God), and the eventual destiny and purpose of life.

Jon found the fervent sense of spiritual awareness held by the Apache to be somewhat unsettling. He felt somehow threatened in that he had lost much of his early religious belief and had fallen into a solid rejection of anything beyond the material world. He was committed to secular, pragmatic humanism and based his behavior on a morally relativistic philosophy. All of this discussion on the possibility of something beyond the physical universe pushed Jon towards a sense of doubt concerning his belief system. Was everything he had learned in the hallowed halls of Taft School and Yale University a falsehood? Jon felt a compulsion to seek more knowledge in this area of spiritual insight and asked Luz if she would be willing to mentor him. Luz agreed and welcomed the opportunity to engage Jon in a teacher/student relationship.

Jon reacted with gratitude and the two made arrangements to begin sessions at Luz's home in Scottsdale, Arizona. As the two shook hands to cement the deal they were the only two remaining in the dining area. They had been so engrossed in conversation that three hours had passed before either one of them realized it.

Jon returned home and made arrangements to leave his apartment in Albuquerque, New Mexico, and to relinquish his ties with Nelson DeMerit and their smuggling business so he could begin what would become a life-changing period of learning.

As Jon drove to Scottsdale his mind was filled with great anticipation and a new appreciation for the stark beauty of the desert region of the southwestern United States. The miles flashed beneath the wheels of his Jaguar XKE as he sped toward Scottsdale and his rendezvous with Luz.

Jon found Luz's home without difficulty and was not surprised to find a home of exquisite design and charm. The home was styled in an unpretentious hacienda style and was situated on a hill overlooking a golf course. Seeing the golf course reminded Jon of his former golfing prowess and thoughts of possibly getting in a round or two flashed through his mind.

Luz welcomed Jon with a reserved embrace as a lady should and invited him into her home. The interior of the house reflected the wonderful esprit of Luz Barca, for it had a sense of nurturing warmth and balance. The appointments and furnishings were of exquisite taste yet not at all excessive or pretentious. The house had an eastern face and a central core to it. Jon marveled at the beauty and atmosphere of Luz's lovely home. Luz told him that the house had been designed on ancient Vedic principles known as Sapata Veda, similar to the Chinese Feng Shui concepts. The tasteful musical sounds of jazz vibraphonist and composer, Gary McFarland, penetrated the air. The music in combination with the elements of the room created a perfect setting for the first page of a new chapter in the life of Jon Corbett.

After a light lunch of tomato, mozzarella and basil salad with a Chianti wine Luz asked Jon to follow her to a room in the rear of the home that was ostensibly used for reflection and meditation. The room seemed perfectly designed for such a purpose: the lighting was just right; the texture of the room exuded quiet comfort; and the aromatic atmosphere seemed to satisfy some deep-seated mental requirement. Jon asked Luz about the aromatics and she explained that certain essential oils stimulate the pineal gland (third eye), which is conducive to deep contemplation and a sense of spiritual awareness. She further iterated that frankincense has been used for this purpose in religious ceremonies for thousands of years and that aromatherapy was the medicine of the ancient Egyptians. She added that aromatherapy was in reality a vibrational type of medicine with great healing qualities that would play a major role in the holistic medicine of the future. Jon was greatly impressed by the wealth of knowledge that Luz possessed and couldn't wait for the lessons to begin.

Lesson I: Introduction

The first session was essentially an introductory lesson and involved Luz explaining the general structure, goals, and time frame of the whole program. Luz detailed the early sessions as being ones that would involve basic teachings on the true reality of the universe, man's multi-dimensional anatomy, and the ultimate meaning and purpose of life. This foundation of knowledge was a requirement for transformation to occur and Jon had to be firm in his openness to a new belief system if he was to evolve towards his true potential. Luz explained that once Jon developed an appreciation for knowledge of the true reality, she would begin to teach him the way within through meditative techniques.

Luz outlined and defined the program as follows:

1. The program will consist of five four-hour sessions a week, Monday through Friday, from 9 a.m. to 1 p.m., lasting a total of two months.
2. Each session will begin with the creation of a vibrational frequency generated in a large crystal "heart chakra" bowl. The vibrations will be created as Luz runs a cylinder-like device slowly over the edge of the bowl. The purpose of this opening ritual will be to create an atmosphere conducive to serious intellectual conversation and contemplation.
3. Proper attire consists of clothing that is non-restrictive and light in weight and color. Luz mentioned that what she was wearing was a good illustration of the idea. She was wearing a white gossamer tunic made of translucent linen with narrow gold embroidery around the neckline, sleeves, and the hem of the gown. Luz appeared buoyantly light and angelic and Jon felt stirrings deep within himself as he admired her incredible allure.

4. No external distractions will be allowed because contemplation requires peace and quiet.
5. One must maintain personal freedom and responsibility, for they are the keys to transcendence of the individual.
6. The ultimate goal of a serious student is to increase vibrational quality until pure potentiality is reached, which is a condition known as "ain soph".
7. One must understand the four secret laws that govern our galaxy and current dimension; the four laws are: attraction, deliberate creation, allowance, and balance.

Luz and Jon had a long conversation after the initial session. They both recounted their life histories, which helped them assess and understand one another. Jon's history was, of course, shorter and much less interesting than Luz's fascinating life story.

Luz had spent her early years living in a tribal setting on an Apache Reservation until her teen years when she left the United States to live with her parents in Spain. While attending the University of Seville she met a brilliant young American exchange student, James Lawton, who was studying political science and economics. They fell in love and eventually married. Her husband began work for the government in the international aid program, which forced him to travel to various stations around the world. James had assignments in Benin, Chad, the Congo, and Rhodesia. While in Rhodesia he was the unfortunate victim of an ambush and was murdered by rebels who were seeking independence. Luz escaped from Nairobi with her young daughter, Zadia, and returned to Spain.

A large life insurance policy had been taken out by her husband and Luz was the sole beneficiary, which resulted in an award of a half million dollars, a vast sum of money in 1950. Luz decided to return to Arizona where she established herself as an astute real estate investor and a well-respected lady in the intellectual and social circles of the Phoenix area.

Once she became independently wealthy, having taken full advantage of the phenomenal growth in the Phoenix and Mesa areas, she decided to move to Scottsdale and pursue a quieter life style, which would allow her the time to participate in deeper intellectual pursuits. Although she had always held a keen awareness of the spiritual side of life, it wasn't until she went to visit a certain monk she had heard about that the course of the rest of her life would shift toward an appreciation for true reality. Luz learned of him via a stream of coincidental developments that unfolded as follows:

When Luz was vacationing on Cape Cod one summer in 1956 she had frequented a donut shop in Eastham. The shop had a certain uniqueness, personality and atmosphere that made it enchanting. She met several native Cape Codders there who sat at the counter and engaged in good down-home conversations, which displayed their pragmatic wisdom, wit and knowledge of local and world politics. Luz particularly loved another popular feature of the donut shop, which was a daily trivia question written on a small blackboard. One morning the question was: What were the priests of the Celtic people called? Luz knew the answer-- the Druids--which led her into a dialogue with a priest who happened to be sitting next to her. They engaged in a discussion of several religious topics.

The priest was especially interested in Luz's tale of an old Apache legend. She detailed the story of how back in the 1600s a Lady in Blue appeared to the Apaches for the purpose of teaching them about the life and message of Jesus Christ. The lady taught them to revere the symbol of the cross and to utilize the rosary while in prayer. After several visits over several years she informed them that her visits would end. However, for them to continue learning about the Christian faith they would have to trek from their home in the Texas Panhandle to New Mexico where missionaries would complete their education. On her last visit, the Lady in Blue lifted into the sky and departed forever. The fields around her transformed into a blanket of lovely blue flowers, which later became known as "Blue Bonnet" flowers.

When a contingent of fifty Apaches arrived at a mission in New Mexico, the missionaries were amazed to see the Indians carrying a cross and crude rosary beads. When asked how the Apaches knew of these religious symbols, they recounted the story of the Lady in Blue. Several years later, church authorities interviewed a Spanish nun, Mary of Agreda, who corroborated the Apache story. The nun confirmed the fact that she could bi-locate and travel astrally. She described the natives' appearance, dress, culture and environment. Mary of Agreda later became an iconic figure in church history and wrote an important book, The Mystical City of God.

The priest sat in stunned silence for a few minutes and finally said, "What an incredible story. I will definitely investigate it further and use it as a foundation for what could be a great sermon. Luz, I appreciate that story and wish to relate a story that will rival the one you just told me. It's the story of a monk of incredible spiritual presence.

"This monk was staying at St. Joseph's, a monastery in Spencer, Massachusetts. The story goes that Brother Vladimir had been a hermit in a certain order of Russian Orthodox monks. Each of the monks spent five years living in a cave with nothing more than a small meal and water, which were left for them each day. This particular monk, Vladimir, left a written message stating that he wished to do a second five-year stint and that he would no longer require a meal. All he wanted was a communion wafer and a glass of water each day. After the second five-year period of isolation and prayer he emerged from the cave totally radiant with auric power. In addition, he had developed prophetic ability. His monastic order's hierarchy decided that Brother Vladimir would be of great benefit to mankind if he were allowed to counsel individuals. To this end, he was sent to St. Joseph's monastery in Spencer, Massachusetts.

When Luz heard this story she was so intrigued that she decided to drive to Spencer on the spur of the moment to verify the existence of Brother Vladimir. The drive from Eastham was a comfortable two hours. Luz drove with a heightened anticipation of meeting a true mystic. When she arrived at the monastery she asked to see the monk. She was told that Brother Vladimir was in the chapel praying and that she could find him there. As she opened the front door of the chapel and entered the vestibule, she was startled by the sight before her. Brother Vladimr was in actual levitation about three feet off the floor. Luz watched the scene in total astonishment for approximately thirty minutes. When the monk descended to the ground he said, without turning around, "Luz Barca, I've been expecting you."

Since Brother Vladimir had no prior knowledge of Luz and she had driven to the monastery without forewarning, it seemed inexplicable that this could be happening. After a cordial handshake Luz introduced herself and requested counsel with the monk. During their discussion, which took place in an herb garden at the rear of the chapel, Brother

Vladimir told Luz she was being propelled by a celestine force that would lead her to eventual enlightment. He reminded her that those who seek will find and those who ask will receive. He encouraged her to continue her search for truth and once she found it to share and teach others that very same truth.

This experience had an enormous impact on Luz and impelled her on a serious quest for her own spiritual growth. Many years of study and meditation provided the result before Jon's eyes—a woman beyond beauty.

So it was on February 2, 1965, that the transformation of Jon Corbett began in earnest. It would be a change from a mere ignorant human with an existential approach to life, much like a seagull whose sole purpose is to grovel after fish heads, to a being in a relationship with the God presence within him that would set him on a path towards perfection, pure potentiality, and enlightenment.

Luz had structured the lesson plans to commence with discussion of the histories of ancient civilizations such as Lemuria, Atlantis, and Egypt. Once a thorough understanding of past advanced societies was established as a foundation then she could begin to build a structure of knowledge by adding one brick at a time. The bricks would involve: the nature of the universe; the spiritual reality; the multi-dimensional anatomy of man; the law of one; reincarnation; the five rites exercise system; yoga and meditation; astral travel; Gnosticism; Kabala; Chi; the four galactic laws; and spiritual healing.

In addition to the daily lessons Jon was given a list of readings as a means of reinforcing the teachings of Luz. The list included the following: Secret Teachings of All Ages by Manly P. Hall; Freemasonry by C. W. Ledbetter; History of Atlantis by Spencer; Yoga, Key to Life by J. McCartney; Book of Urantia; Kabala by Adolph Franke; Secrets of the Great Pyramid by Spencer. Luz also presented Jon with a dozen past issues of the Rosicrucian Digests.

Jon realized that his commitment to learning the mysteries would be a daunting task and would require total dedication and sacrifice. It was with this attitude that he began his quest for truth.

Lesson 2: Lemuria and Atlantis

This is what we know of Lemuria and Atlantis. The Legend of Atlantis is significant to modern civilization because it contains the earliest seeds of holism, which are sprouting in the present age. It warns about the misuse of technology and the dangers of materialistic thinking, and gives us knowledge of crystal power, so important in computers and electronics and a possible source of alternative energy to power our civilization.

Luz introduced Jon to the legends and mystery of the lost continents of Lemuria and Atlantis. She explained how the memory of these ancient civilizations has persisted in the minds of many, ever since Plato wrote about Atlantis nearly 2,500 years ago. The indigenous peoples of the world have similar stories in their mythologies. Evidence, although not concrete, points to the existence of Lemuria in the Pacific Ocean and Atlantis in the Atlantic Ocean. Knowledge of Lemuria stems from ancient texts of India, called the Vedas. Plato's information came from the writings of the famous Athenian lawgiver, Solon, who was given the account of Atlantis by Egyptian priests in the 7th century BC. With the destruction of Atlantis a great migration occurred and survivors went east to the Pyrenees and Egypt and west to the Americas.

Lemuria, also known as Mu, was a large continent, which existed in the Pacific Ocean for several hundred thousand years until its destruction about 50,000 years ago. It extended 3,000 miles from just north of Hawaii, south to Easter Island and Fiji, and 5,000 miles from east to west. This is knowledge taken from sacred tablets in India. The inhabitants of Lemuria were highly spiritual and recognized the God force in all things. They lived in harmony with the Creator's law. They were healthy, psychic, and telepathic and lived a joyful existence until the fall of Adam and Eve. The fall occurred in Lemuria where the Garden of Eden existed on the eastern side of the continent. This catastrophic event resulted when the people succumbed to the temptations of the carnal mind, which is personified in the serpent. This unfortunate decision is a contradiction and counters the logic of the heart and man's inclination to do God's will.

The term Karma has a Lemurian root. The derivation comes from the following: KA (cause, the will of the Creator), RA (Ray, the word), and MA (manifestation in matter). Karma is God's energy in action. It is reflective of man's actions and deeds and man's relationship to Cosmic Law.

Upon the destruction of Lemuria, which was coincidental with the first cataclysm of Atlantis 50,000 years ago, survivors went west to India and east to South America.

The Hawaiian Islands are thought to be remnants of Lemuria, as are Easter Island and the Fiji Islands.

Lesson 3: Atlantis

Atlantis was a continent in the Atlantic Ocean at least as large as North America.

The civilization began about 150,000 years ago and lasted until around 10,000 BC when a third and final cataclysmic event destroyed Atlantis forever. The climate was warm and tropical. The inhabitants were known as the red race because of the color of their skin. Atlantis was whole until the first destruction, which resulted in a breakup, which left five major islands. The event is thought to have been caused by the misuse of crystal power, which resulted in massive, destructive explosions. Many Atlanteans fled and migrated to other areas, such as the Americas, Ireland, Spain and Egypt.

The second destruction took place around 28,000 BC, which left Atlantis with three large islands and several smaller ones. This cataclysm was the result of a conflict between two groups, the believers in the Law of One (deists) and non-believers who were materialists (the Sons of Belial). Many experts in esoteric history believe the flood of Noah equates to this event.

The third and final destruction occurred in 9600 BC as a result of a negative imbalance, which was created by the dominant group of non-believers, the Sons of Belial, who held power. It is thought that survivors established three halls of records, which store Atlantean history in crystals, in the Yucatan, the Bahamas, and in Egypt. These sites have yet to be discovered. The ocean became impassible because of "shoal mud," which persisted for many centuries.

The capital city was known as Center City and was located on Poseidon's Island. It was spectacular in its beauty and design, which was reflective of the genius and character of its people. The Temple of Poseidon occupied the center on Acropolis Hill. Surrounding the Temple were three concentric canals separated by two strips of land, which held the buildings of commerce and the residences of the citizens. Three walls guarded the city: the first was of stone and brass; the second of tin; and the third of a substance called orichalcum, which sparkled like fire. The continent was governed by a confederation of ten kings.

In the early years of Atlantis the people were closely attuned to the God force and held strong religious convictions. As time went on and the sophistication of the people and technology evolved, materialistic thinking crept into the society. This degenerative development led to severe conflicts between the deists and the materialists, which eventually caused the disintegration of Atlantis.

In the formative period and the subsequent years when Atlantis grew in power and wealth the belief that all of life is in unity with the God force was prevalent and the Atlanteans recognized that God exists in each cell of matter. This belief system was known as the Law of One and still remains the basis for all monotheistic beliefs. Science and religion were integrated and existed in a symbiotic relationship.

The priesthood and mystery schools preserved the knowledge, which was only disseminated to initiates within the schools. These schools are the foundation of the major religions of the world. It is thought by some that Jesus Christ actually studied these very same mysteries when he spent his childhood in Egypt. A large six-sided white crystal was used by diviners to communicate with the divine god mind, much like communicating with an oracle.

A group of non-believers, the Sons of Belial, gradually grew to be the dominant force, which resulted in evil, debauchery, and perversity being rampant in the final days of Atlantis. These self-possessed power-mongers and pleasure seekers misused the technologies of crystals and their great knowledge and power to wreak havoc on the continent. The Sons of Belial sank to such depths of depravity that they actually created a mutant race of slaves known as "things;" they achieved this through genetic engineering. Such dissolution and evil occurs in any society that places its personal will above the universal will. The lesson to be learned is that when man detracts from the creator all his structures will fall into an entropic welter of turmoil.

Atlantis was highly advanced in a technological sense because they had discovered how to make use of higher dimensional energies of consciousness and the vibratory life force, the forces of chi and prana. They also discovered and made extensive use of crystal power. Crystals focus solar energy found in sunlight to create gases to turn turbines for power. Crystals transform and use negative space and time energies, which are magneto-electric versus the electro-magnetic energy of positive space and time as in our reality. The power created was a free energy source and powered transportation systems, homes, manufacturing, and communication. Unfortunately, the misuse of crystal energy led to energy imbalances and caused major earthquakes and the eventual break up of the continent.

The Atlanteans were well advanced in the areas of medicine and healing. They employed vibrational medicine, flower essences, homeopathy, gem elixirs, and aromatherapy. They used harmonious sound and color for healing as well. The therapeutic use of color was produced by passing sunlight through prisms as well as creating higher octave rays. As the materialistic view of life became more dominant, allopathic medicine became more popular and pushed the holistic approaches to healing into the background. We see this conflict even in the present age as holism and allopathy still are in conflict over which is the best means of reversing illness. It must be appreciated that this struggle is a microcosm of the larger, age-old battle of God-oriented philosophies versus the godless, materialistic views.

The Lords of Darkness (the fallen angels) have infiltrated every civilization including Lemuria and Atlantis. The Golden Ages of these civilizations came to an end when man preferred self-love to the love of the creator. The abuses of freedom led to destruction and slavery in Lemuria (Fall of Man) and Atlantis (The Great Flood).

Lesson 4: The Great Pyramid

The Great Pyramid of Giza in Egypt still evokes a sense of mystery and wonder because its construction and grandeur are still not explained by modern science. The majesty of this structure as it looms over the Giza Plain has captivated the minds of mankind for as long as 12,500 years. The Great Pyramid, Khufu, and its smaller companion pyramids, Khafre and Menkaure, were built to configure with the alignment and size of the stars Mintaka, Al Nilam and Al Nitar in the belt of the Constellation Orion. Some experts believe there may be a spiritual connection with the Orion Constellation. Could it be that our human biology originated in that star system?

The Great Pyramid was not built as a tomb, as is commonly believed. It was built as a site of initiation into a society of enlightened individuals, and as a temple, which was intended to interpret that which had been, that which is, and that which will be. The King's chamber concentrates cosmic energies, which facilitate a mystical union with the God mind.

The pyramid was built by levitation of huge blocks of stone weighing sixty tons in or around 10,500 BC. The Atlanteans who migrated to Egypt after the destruction of their home continent were the actual builders. Supernatural forces and individuals in possession of knowledge greater than modern man guided them. The structure was built with phenomenal precision beyond the capability of today's technology and it embodies an advanced knowledge of geometry, geodesy (science of earth measurement) and astronomy. It can be considered to be a permanent monument to universal knowledge because it contains symbolic measurements, which could only be known by higher intellectual beings. Some examples of symbolic measurements and other significant characterizations:

- Sixty ton blocks of granite aligned with four cardinal points (North, south, east, west) more accurately than any other structure in the world
- Base length in pyramid inches x 43,200 is equal to the circumference of earth at the equator

- Height in pyramid inches x 43,200 is equal to earth polar radius
- 4320 is the number of years it takes for earth to move through two signs of the zodiac, or 1/6th of the complete cycle of 25,000 years
- The perimeter to height ratio is precisely 2 pi
- The pyramid is located at the exact center of the earth's land mass
- The sides are concave and exactly match the curvature of the planet
- Four walls when measured are 36,524 pyramid inches, which is reflective of our solar year (365.24 days)
- Dimensions of the inner passages have been diligently studied and it has been theorized that they are an encoding of the years of significant world events, including the birth of Jesus Christ—the most important figure in human history.

According to Egyptian mythology, the Great Pyramid was built by a supernatural being from the sixth density named "RA". (There are actually eight densities or vibrational frequencies in the universe, the last being the Godhead itself. Mankind of this time and space are living in the third dimension. RA incarnated as Ra-Ta and took human form. He became Pharaoh and ruled for hundreds of years. The early Egyptians constructed their religion based on this scenario. The ceremonies and ritualism continued through the centuries and became the foundation of monotheism. Ra gave mankind the "Law of One." Unfortunately, many secret occult societies have restricted accessibility to these mysteries and used their knowledge of the law of one for their own gains in power and wealth.

Free will means that man can choose to do God's will or to defy it. Our planet is at the end of a cycle and is going from the third to the fourth density. This is a cosmic evolutionary process that occurs as the solar system orbits the galaxy center. Ra explains that third dimension realities for a planet occur in cycles of 25,000 years. This period is relative to the length of time it takes our sun to travel through an energy zone as it circles the galactic center. After three 25,000 year cycles the vibrational energy of the planet moves into the next density and transforms the DNA of life forms to a higher level of development and spiritual awareness. In essence, it's God's way of returning all that exists to eventual oneness. Our planet is about to enter the last stages of this cycle, which will culminate in a full dimensional shift or ascension in or about the year 2012 AD. The ancient Egyptians, Mayans, Hindus, Hopi Indians, and many other indigenous peoples have knowledge of this event.

Luz concluded this lesson by telling Jon, "You are becoming aware of little-known mysteries, and I hope you use these insights to prepare yourself and your fellow man for this future event."

Lesson 4-A: Meditation

Luz decided that before delving too deeply into the lesson series, it would be prudent to expose Jon to a conceptual understanding of meditation and the methods of achieving deep contemplative states.

The initial exposure to meditation was a rather simple technique based on a method known as Silva's Mind Control. Although it didn't take Jon into deep self-realization levels it did demonstrate the basic nature of meditation. The technique was presented as follows:

- Step One: Take a deep breath. Envision a large screen with the number 3, then 2, then 1. Take deep breaths between each numbered step.
- Step Two: Count down from ten to zero and tell yourself that you are getting more relaxed with each descending number.
- Step Three: Focus on your feet and imagine your mind to be present there. Then relax your feet. Gradually work your way up to your calves, thighs, abdomen, chest, shoulders, neck, and head.
- Step Four: Imagine a place where you are most at ease and relaxed. Take yourself there mentally. Feel your presence there.
- Step Five: Count down from ten to zero again.
- Step Six: Imagine a room that will be your laboratory. Now enter the room and use it for creative thinking, telepathy or healing.
- Step Seven: Return to normal consciousness by counting back slowly from ten to one.

Luz instructed Jon to practice this technique every day for twenty to thirty minutes during the next few weeks. He would gradually improve the technique and find it easier and easier to get into deep relaxation. Once accustomed to the concept of altering his consciousness, Luz taught him techniques that would transcend his external being and bring him into the outer reaches of cosmic consciousness. She further explained that only through deep meditation could he ever know his real nature and achieve oneness with the universal creator. Luz provided Jon with several basic ideas that he should understand before embarking on the road to enlightenment.

- Deep meditation transcends the sensory mind, subconscious mind, and the super conscious mind and takes one into cosmic consciousness.

- True yoga is the union of the soul with God or the Spirit. The terms God, cosmic consciousness and universal creator are considered synonymous. Jesus Christ fully understood yoga as evidenced by the following quote attributed to him, "Take my yoga upon you and learn of me for my yoga is easy." Jesus was telling us that by discovering the Christ consciousness within us we could return to the Father and that his way was the easiest of all.

- Learn how to meditate by shutting out external sensory input and keeping your consciousness focused on the spiritual eye.

- To restore Christianity, emphasis should be placed on quiet meditation and inner communion, and not with homilies, ceremony, ritual, Bingo and social gatherings. "Be still and know that I am God."

- Just worshiping the Body of Christ is not the way to know him. The Christ consciousness can only be realized by awakening the spinal chakras through meditation. The soul cannot be fulfilled through the senses but through peace and calm from meditation.

- The real secret of religion is found within oneself in the so-called cave of intuitive wisdom and the cave of the spiritual eye. The term religion has a Latin derivation and refers to the ability of man to join with the divine. Think of the ligament, which joins muscle to bone.

- During meditation attention is focused on the area between the eyebrows. This is the location of the third eye, also known as the spiritual eye. It is our link to the divine and is related to the brow chakra. Jesus said, "If therefore thine eye be single, thy whole body will be full of light."

- The seven cerebrospinal centers (energy vortexes), known as chakras, must be awakened if one is to find the way to God. St. John the Evangelist in the biblical book, Revelation, refers to these seven centers as the seven seals, stars, churches, angels and candlesticks.

- No one can reach the Father (cosmic consciousness) except through the Holy Ghost (cosmic vibration) and the Son (Christ consciousness).

- Prodigal sons have left the home of their parental divine consciousness by placing emphasis on the external needs of the body.

- In meditation learn to focus on the aum (om) and the sacred vibration of the Holy Spirit will be heard. Meditation on aum brings baptism with the Holy Spirit and the Christ consciousness is revealed, which takes the soul home to the Father.

- As one concentrates on aum, by chanting in the mind, one will actually hear that sound and the mind will leave its attachment to physicality and perceive the sounds of vibrating life. The consciousness then proceeds to the harmonic vibrations of the astral body from whence it will expand into vibrations of consciousness in the causal body and the Holy Spirit. The causal body is the highest and least dense of the seven bodies that comprise the multi-dimensional anatomy of a human being; it houses the soul, Christ consciousness, and the I am or God presence. At this point if one feels the aum vibration in all finite matter, he will become one with the Holy Spirit. Through the power of the Holy Spirit, the consciousness is then baptized with the Christ consciousness. This event brings inner peace and joy and results in health and a sense of well-being. The healing power held within this type of individual can also be transferred to those in need of divine help. Thus is a healing presence created and a healer born.

- The real teaching of Christ tells us: only that person who can see his spiritual eye and perceives God can achieve enlightenment and salvation. He can then spiritually baptize others with the vibration of the Holy Spirit and incorporate in them the means to ascend to the Father. This is how salvation is achieved for the many.

- The basic concept of true religion is triune in design and is characterized by the mystic division into threes. The Christian Trinity of Father, Son and Holy Spirit and the Hindu Trinity of Brahma, Vishnu and Shiva are perfect illustrations of this belief. The union of three parts—the two polarities of masculine and feminine held together by the third unknowable element (God)-- are infinite in the triune principle.

- White light is the secret key to opening one to truth. It contains the one pattern upon which all truth is based. When one "sees the light" it is indicative that one's potential has been reached and the person has returned to Eden.

- The "voice" is an inner vibrational language that communicates with the world of spirit and connects to the other world. It holds divine spark.

- Life is a learning experience for the soul's development. The soul climbs higher with each lifetime.

- Sin is action against one's soul and universal will. It shows disrespect and lack of faith in our real nature. Sin creates a Karmic debt, which must be paid off for salvation to occur.

- The religion one chooses in a lifetime is dictated by his spiritual evolutionary state. One path is not right for all. Everyone is at a different level of approaching salvation and oneness.

- We are the product of past lives, but are none of them.

- The roots of one's past nurture the seeds of destiny.

- Spiritual power results from living in a sacred manner.

- Man has spiritual guides (ascended souls) that seek to help man unlock the door to one's higher nature.

- To find freedom one must submit to intuitions and inner knowledge. The ego and a focus on externalism prevent this from occurring.
- Belief imparts reality. Beliefs are real when supported by faith. Cultures and nations decline and fall into dissolution without a belief system.
- Those that are wise know that legends hold the essential truths.
- Just as we cannot comprehend infinity we are unable to see God as infinite and without origin.
- The law of duality applies in both the material and spiritual realms. In the spiritual world like forces attract and allow for growth. This explains the law of gender separation, which governs religious orders and is the reason for gender separation. In the material world opposite forces attract and when combined lead to wholeness.
- When the student is ready, the teacher will appear.

Golfing Experience

After Jon's first session in learning meditative technologies he decided to take a ride over to the Yellowbird Golf Club, which was situated near Luz's home. Jon had not played much golf in the last two years and realized how much he missed the joy of playing what he regarded as the ultimate game.

The practice area beckoned as Jon walked on the beautifully manicured grounds of the golf club. He had decided that rather than rush out to play a round it would be more prudent to spend a few hours just hitting shots, working on chip shots, and getting a feel with the putter. It was about 3 p.m. and only three other golfers were using the range. Every once in a while as Jon would take a brief break in his sequence of going through the various clubs, he noticed the other three golfers and found some interest in the sights before him. Two of the golfers were working on some strange techniques, which really drew Jon's curiosity. The third golfer, a stocky black fellow, was striking the ball beautifully off to the far side of the practice tee.

After about one and one-half hours of practice Jon decided to take a breather and relax with a refreshing lemonade at the small concession area adjacent to the practice area. Coincidentally, the other three golfers came over shortly thereafter and all four sat and started polite conversation. Jon introduced himself to the others and they returned the courtesy in kind. The black fellow's name was Elton Woods. He was a career army sergeant stationed in the area as a recruiter for the US army. He admitted that he had a two handicap, which is indicative of a highly accomplished golfer. The other two golfers were real characters. Not only were they striking in appearance, but also their opinions on golf were quite unique. The first of the two was a slender, sinewy olive skinned man, obviously with great golf talent, and his name was Raul Castaneda. He was the resident teaching pro. The other fellow, Sven Davidson, was his student. The four engaged in a lively conversation that became even more interesting when Jon asked Raul about what he and Sven were trying to accomplish. Raul explained that he was trying to get Sven to be less concerned with the mechanics of the swing and to focus on the mystical aspects of playing golf. It was Raul's feeling that if you abnegate your ego and your external nature and deeply impress the image of the perfect ideal in your mind your subconscious will dictate the necessary movement to your muscles to achieve the desired result. Jon and Elton Woods found Raul's ideas to be quite a revelation and both agreed that there was definitely something to what he was saying. Both Jon and Elton had experienced being in the so-called "zone" at some point in their past, but never fully understood how that occurred. They thanked Raul for his elucidation of golf in the kingdom and told him they would try to incorporate his methods into their golf games.

Jon was rekindling his ardor for the game and decided he would try to devote a few afternoons a week to playing again. Elton Woods seemed amenable to the idea of getting into a regular routine of meeting Jon at the club and playing in friendly competition.

After several weeks of playing together Jon and Elton developed a real friendship and appreciation for one another. The two were about equal in ability, which allowed them to have highly competitive matches. They had great fun attempting to employ the egoless, mystical approach to the game that Raul Castaneda had introduced to them. Both were amazed at how easily their games improved without the psychological impediments of fear and negativity.

It was a great surprise to Jon when Elton proposed the idea that they team up to play in an international four-ball amateur tournament in Mexico City. Elton was a well-known, respected figure in amateur golf circles and had often attracted invitations to major tournaments, but he seldom accepted them because of work obligations and other constraints. He had evidently decided that he and Jon could be competitive even against some of the best amateur players in the Americas.

The Mexico City tournament, known as the American Four-Ball Classic, was a very prestigious event, and an invitation was highly prized by serious, talented amateur players. Invitations were only given to golfers of considerable ability and a history of some achievement. Many of the invitees were state amateur champions, club champions from important golf and country clubs, or winners of noteworthy tournaments. All of those invited had to have handicaps of two or lower.

Elton Woods had always contended well in Arizona State tournaments and was certainly deserving of an invitation. The tournament directives allowed anyone who accepted an invitation to select a partner who had an appropriate handicap. Thus, Elton decided to ask Jon, who had earned a handicap of one at the Yellowbird Club. Jon thought it would be something of a lark for them to participate; he never expected them to actually contend for the championship.

The tournament was a best-ball seventy-two-hole affair, meaning the lowest score of the two players on each hole would count as their score. For example, if one player had completed a hole in five strokes and the other in four strokes, their score would be a four.

After two uneventful rounds, Jon and Elton stood well off the pace, trailing by five shots with a four under par score of 140. Something magical began to happen in the third round when Jon inexplicably entered "the zone" and reeled off four consecutive birdies on holes nine through twelve, which propelled the team to a seven under par score of sixty-five. That round, which was the lowest of the tournament, moved them into second place, just one stroke behind two other teams that were comprised of four New England champions from Connecticut, Massachusetts, Vermont and Rhode Island. This group was formidable competition for

Jon and Elton, but for some reason they entered the final round with absolute calm. Maybe it was the fact that they had embraced the teaching philosophy of Raul Castaneda and had found a way to eliminate the ego and anxiety from their play.

While Jon was warming up on the practice range prior to the final round, he noticed the player hitting balls next to him had an image of the Blessed Virgin emblazoned on his golf bag. Jon inquired as to the purpose of such a statement on a golf bag and was told that the figure represented Our Lady of Guadalupe, who had appeared in a miraculous event back in 1531 AD. The golfer, a Mexican named Juan Diego, stated that he always found strength and courage from this saintly personage when he found himself in situations of challenge. Jon made a mental note that he would try to pay a visit to the shrine of the iconic figure of Mary, which was located in a nearby suburb of Mexico City.

The final round of the tournament began with Jon and Elton playing in the next to last group. The pair played steady if unspectacular, two under par golf through the first seventeen holes. As they stood on the eighteenth tee preparing to hit their tee shots, a spectator informed them that they were tied for the lead. Jon and Elton were totally shocked because they never expected their modest play would have been sufficient to place them in such a position. Normally, such information might unnerve someone, but Jon and Elton accepted the challenge without a hint of trepidation and played the final hole perfectly; they both made easy pars. The final group followed them with one twosome making par and the second a spectacular eagle, which resulted in three teams tied with the same score of fourteen under par, a 274 total. A three-way playoff ensued. Jon and Elton played the first hole beautifully--a lengthy par five--but unfortunately both missed relatively short birdie putts. On the second hole Jon hit a spectacular three iron to about six feet. But again, the putt was missed and they had to settle for a tie, although making a bogey eliminated the third team. On the third hole Elton was faced with a twenty-foot putt for birdie. Once again something strange happened. Jon knew without a doubt that Elton was going to make that putt. As the ball dropped into the hole, Jon ran to Elton and embraced him with a giant hug. They jumped together as one bounding bundle of joy. When the jumping finally stopped, they stared momentarily at one another then burst out simultaneously with the shout, "My God, this was it, it was golf in the kingdom."

Jon and Elton celebrated by spending a few hours at the clubhouse bar. They just couldn't believe that they had overcome insurmountable odds by outplaying some of the best amateur players in the world. "It was a miracle, indeed," said Elton.

"Speaking of miracles, Elton, what do you say we visit the Shrine to Our Lady of Guadalupe tomorrow before our flight back to Arizona?" Jon asked. "I am intrigued by the story of that miracle and would love to see the evidence of it."

A lovely young lady named Leonella took Jon and Elton on a guided tour, which was highlighted by viewing the original garment displaying the image of the Blessed Virgin. Leonella related the incredible story of the appearance of the Virgin that took place on December 12, 1531.

The story goes that after Hernando Cortez, the Spanish conqueror, had subdued the Aztecs in 1520, the Spaniards attempted to convert the Indians to Christianity. The attempts at conversion largely failed as very few conversions occurred. The Bishop of Guadalupe was dismayed and as a result sought the guidance and help of the Blessed Virgin. In his prayer he stated that if his supplication were heard he would like to see a sign signified by roses. It just so happened that a young convert who was walking to the church was hailed by a voice, "Juanito, Juanito come here." Juanito followed the voice and came upon a vision of the Virgin standing on a small cactus-covered hill. As Juanito approached her, the hill became filled with roses, which the Virgin instructed Juanito to pick. Juanito filled the front of his tunic with the roses and was told to take them to the Bishop. Juanito informed the Bishop of his experience and was met with skepticism until he dropped the front of his garment to reveal the roses. The Bishop was amazed at the sight of the roses and then viewed the formation of a representation of the Virgin on Juanito's garment. The figure was interpreted by the Aztecs as a sign to them because the Lady's cape was a certain bluish green color that held special significance to them. In addition, Aztec symbols covered the front of her gown. In just a short time Aztecs by the thousands began their conversion. The Bishop's petition to the Virgin had most definitely been answered.

Several additional facts astounded Jon and Elton: the burlap-like material used to make the Indian garment was derived from cactus and

37

had a short life expectancy of around ten years—this garment had lasted nearly five hundred years without a sign of aging or deterioration; science could not explain how the image was imprinted or the nature of the coloring agents; it was not paint or any other known coloring dye. When looked at face on it appeared to be opaque; however, when viewed from the rear it was transparent. If one examined the right eye with a microscope, a scene of the Virgin and Juanito could be seen; if the same eye was viewed through an ophthalmoscope, the eye would appear as a normal eye.

"Truly, truly a miracle," declared Elton. "I never would have believed it, if I hadn't seen it."

"Hey, Elton, would you believe two miracles on consecutive days?" said Jon. "I can't wait to share this experience with Luz. I'm sure she'll look at me and say, 'I told you so!'"

Lesson 5: Nature of the Universe

The total universe exists in two different polarities or realms: the physical and the spiritual. The physical universe is actually comprised of seven universes, which encircle the God Head (Hovana). It exists in positive space and time, which is associated with electricity and electromagnetic radiation. This is in contrast to the spiritual universe, which is in negative space and time and is associated with magnetism and magneto electric radiation.

Based on Einstein's view, energy and matter are essentially the same thing. The equation $E = MC2$ explains that the energy within a particle is equal to the product of its mass (m) and the speed of light (c) squared. One can think of matter as being energy in a lower vibrational frequency and density. It is a specialized energy field described as frozen light. Modern physicists do not yet understand negative space and time and the idea that accelerating particles beyond the speed of light will bring you into that unknown realm.

Negative space and time demonstrates negative entropy, which is order within a system. Remember, entropy is disorder or chaos. Without the vibratory life force of God and subtle energies influencing the physical, systems will fall into chaos. This applies to all types of systems, be they political, economic, social, medical, or educational. Physical life apart from the influence of the spiritual force cannot exist in harmony and order.

The pantheistic view explains that God is all that is and that we as individuals are fragments of that whole. Each human fragment is made in the image of the universal creator and its structure reflects the patterns of order throughout the cosmos. God as the cosmic hologram is in contact with all of creation and that includes all of us. Each of us has a personal hologram, which must be completed by doing God's will. Once the personal hologram is completed and one's Karmic debt has been paid, oneness and salvation result. This goal is one's ultimate purpose in life. Remember, every piece contains the whole, and the "part is the whole."

Lastly, the universe is multidimensional with many frequencies and forms, just as the human being is. There are theorists who claim that the past, present and future exist simultaneously but in different vibrational time frames.

Lesson 6: The Multidimensional Human Anatomy

- A new model of the human anatomy is now being understood.
- The new perspective describes matter as a substance composed of particles, which are points of frozen light.
- The solid nature of matter is an illusion of the senses.
- A continuum exists between our physical system and higher subtle energy systems.
- The physical body is only one of several systems, which are in dynamic equilibrium and are superimposed upon one another. These subtle bodies are seven in number and are composed of matter in different vibrational frequencies.
- The seven bodies are as follows: physical; etheric; astral; mental (instinctive); mental (intellectual); mental (spiritual); and the causal

body, which houses the soul, the cosmic Christ consciousness, and the I am presence of God.

- Such knowledge is known to ancient Egyptians, Atlanteans, Hindus, Druids, Chinese, Tibetans and many other indigenous peoples.
- The physical body cannot exist without the etheric body because the etheric determines the cellular activity of the physical body and provides energizing nourishment.
- The upper four bodies survive physical death. This is the spiritual reality of things.
- The causal body has its first impact on the mental bodies, which then cascades down the scale to the astral, etheric and finally the physical.
- The higher self is in the causal body, which is of the highest frequency. The causal body consists of the soul, the cosmic Christ, and the I am presence of God. It is the essence of one's being.

Lesson 7: Teaching of RA

The entire universe is made up of spiraling light energy, which comes from the one infinite creator, God. This spiraling torsion energy is the basis for all that exists, from the structure of the spiraling electrons of the atom, to the spiraling DNA, to the spiraling planets around their suns, to the spiraling solar systems around galactic centers, to the spiraling galaxies around their universe centers, to the seven spiraling universes around Hovana, the source of all.

The universe is divided into eight dimensions or densities. All life moves through these densities as part of an evolutionary process. Once an entity achieves the seventh density it is preparing to become one with the ultimate density---God-- and the pantheistic "all".

Each galaxy is a part of the Creator with its own personality and set of natural laws for the planetary systems within its domain. Soul evolution occurs within each galaxy until oneness with God is reached.

Timelines are set for each planet as it progresses through each density. Humans are given free will and can therefore choose to do God's will or to defy it. Our planet is at the end of a major cycle and is going from the third to the fourth density.

DNA is formed by spiraling energy as we pass through high-energy photon belts. DNA will be altered and life forms will ascend to the fourth dimension and become sons of God and ultimately Christ-like. Remember the words of the cosmic Christ who said, "You can do all that I do, and things even greater." This occurrence will be the actual second coming, when all of man will become as Christ was and is.

Luz reminded Jon of the Lessons on the Great Pyramid which discussed the fact that this process is a perpetual movement throughout the cosmos. She also reiterated the idea that an evolution into the fourth density would occur soon as predicted by the ancient Egyptians, Hindu Vedas, Hopi Indians, Mayans and indigenous natives around the world.

Luz told Jon, "You are becoming aware of uncommonly known "mysteries," and I hope you use this knowledge to prepare yourself and your fellow man for this future event. Luz also warned Jon about evil forces that are aware of the evolutionary process, forces that will do all in their power to prevent the ascension of mankind. She did not elaborate on the so-called Lords of Darkness but told Jon he would someday become aware of who they are.

Lesson 8: Secrets of Water

- Water at the cellular level is imprinted with the energy and emotion that surround it.
- Experiments were conducted exposing water to various thoughts and then freezing it after 24 hours. When prayerful and loving thoughts or words were focused on the water, incredibly beautiful crystal patterns would form. When exposed to negative thoughts and words, the water patterns were irregular and disordered.
- The human body is 70% water so the energetic nature of the water plays an important role in the overall health of the

individual. If someone lives in fear and has constant negative emotions, negative effects will be seen.

- Psycho-neuro immunology is a new science that is forming. It links the mind (psyche), nerve (endocrine) system, and the immune system. It explains how all three systems interact, which may result in the formation of illness.
- The science and spirituality gap is narrowing with each passing day. Eventually science will explain the true nature of reality.

Lesson 9: Numerology

- Numerology was founded by Pythagoras, a member of the Greek 6th Century BC mystery schools. He theorized the vibrational and mathematical nature of the universe.
- The vibration of the day you enter this reality influences your destiny.
- The date of birth and the letters of your name at birth are very significant. The name is actually determined by the source through the mother.
- Luz developed a numerology chart for:

Jon Tad Corbett	Date of Birth: 7/9/41
Destiny No. 11/2	Psychic
Avoids conflict	
Life Path: 22/4	One who manifests
	Spiritual
Soul No. 9	Selfless Service
Maturity No. 33/6	Healer, nurturer
Here to teach unconditional love	
Master teacher of enlightenment	

Luz commented that this was the most extraordinary chart she had ever seen. Jon could be destined to be a most important figure in human history.

Lesson 10: The Druids

Much of the knowledge we have of the ancient Druids stems from the most famous of Druidic books, the Book of Pheryllt. The Pheryllt were the legendary priests of Pharon, an ancient God whose worshipers were, according to legend, inhabitants of Atlantis. When Atlantis was destroyed many survivors and priests found the shores of Wales. Wales is referred to as the homestead of Druidism and it was here that the Pheryllt reestablished their advanced religion.

The Druids were actually the priests of the Celtic people. The Celts were a vast nation of peoples sharing a common culture and were dominant in nearly half the known world in ancient times. Celtic culture came to Britain in the Fifth Century BC following the Battle of the Trees. The Celtic culture was matriarchal in nature; whereas, the priestly Druids were patriarchal. It could be considered that this difference is a further example of the dual nature of realty: the worlds of matter (feminine) and spirit (masculine). The term Druid refers to "Oak Men" – the oak tree being the king of all trees.

Druids were primal mystics and were the mediators between man and God. They drew their power and authority from supernatural sanctions. They were the doctors, scientists, lawyers and ministers to the Celtic tribes. Because their doctrines were not recorded, much of what we know is a result of Roman accounts. Even though the Romans sought to destroy the Druids they had high respect for them. Some opinions of famous Roman observers follow:

"Druids could intervene and stop warring armies from fighting. Thus, even among the most savage barbarians anger yields to "wisdom."

--Strabo

"They profess the immortality of the soul and share Pythagorean beliefs; above all they strive to explain the high mysteries of nature."

--Ammianus Marcellinus

"The Druids were held in much honor above all other priesthoods and had authority in peace and war."

--Possidonius

"They discuss and impart to their youth many things reflecting the stars and their motions, respecting the extent of the universe and of our earth, respecting the power and majesty of the Immortal Gods."

--Caesar

"The Druids are generally freed from military service, nor do they pay taxes with the rest... Encouraged by such rewards many come to their schools, as they are sent by their friends and relations. They are said to learn by heart a great number of verses; some continue twenty years in their education: neither is it lawful to commit these things to writing, though in almost all public and legal transactions and private keepings they use Greek characters."

--Caesar

Druids were famous throughout Europe for the excellence of their schools, libraries and colleges. Hundreds of schools existed and the best were at Tara in Ireland, Oxford and Iona. Only the best were considered for study. The approach was a blending of natural philosophy and religion into one. The Druids were scientists, both of the visible (physical) and invisible (spiritual) worlds and they knew specific laws ruled in each world.

The various concepts were taught in Triadic Verse because all manifestation occurs through three and all learning takes place in threes. This technique was used for ease of memorization and its mystical connection.

Examples of the Triads:
    Three things a Druid ought not reveal:
        Injurious truth
        The disgrace of a friend
        The secrets of the Druids
    Three things a man is:

> What he thinks he is
> What others think he is
> What he really is

Luz explained to Jon that this triad was very similar to the modern concept known as the three-circle concept. This concept explains that for someone to avoid internal conflict and disharmony, the three circles of how one sees him, how others see him, and how God sees him must be in agreement and on one plane.

Three keys of Druidic mastery:
> To know
> To dare
> To keep silent

Three things that make rebirth necessary for man:
> His failure to obtain wisdom
> His failure to attain independence
> His clinging to the lower self

Three things to break the cycle of rebirth:
> See all
> Study all
> Suffer all

Dualism was a Druidic conceptual belief and Druids were segregated by gender. Gender-specific systems were characteristic of Druid society as exemplified in gender separateness in school and religious communities. According to Druidic thought gender energy differs, with the masculine being expansive and the feminine being absorptive. For each gender to grow spiritually they must be separate because in the spiritual realm like attracts like. This is in contrast to the material realm wherein like forces repel.

The Druids did not eat the flesh of any animal. Instead they ate fruits and grains, which are the gifts of Mother Earth. It was their belief that by eating another creature one absorbs the energies and qualities of that creature. By absorbing these qualities a human retards his evolution beyond the animal kingdom into the higher realms. Eating in a vegetarian way will encourage growth rather than decay.

Mastery over the physical world was the single most important aim of spiritual evolution.

Some additional facts and beliefs concerning the Druids.

- Druids established many sacred sites throughout Europe, which were selected because of powerful magnetic forces formed by Ley Lines. Many Christian churches were later built on the very same sites, because these sites are access points to the other world.
- The Druids may not have built Stonehenge and several other megaliths in Britain, but they studied and understood their meanings. The Atlanteans were thought to be the original builders.
- Truth must be kept secret and the masses need a teaching proportioned to their imperfect reason.
- Balance is a result of opposites being existent, not by their union.
- Time is a man-made invention and a concept that enslaves man. One must be free of such untruths to grow.
- Respect for truth measures the quality of one's soul.
- A Druid's quest in life is the knowledge of truth.
- There is nothing in creation that is bad in itself, for everything plays a role in the balance of nature.

Customs, traditions and legends that originated with the Druids:

- Adoration of the cross
- Sacrament of communion
- Worship on Sunday; Druids spoke to the people once a week on the Day of the Sun
- Priests not allowed to marry
- Three-stemmed peace symbol
- May pole
- Valentine's Day hearts

- Easter Bunny
- Halloween pumpkin carving
- Bobbing for apples
- Kissing under the mistletoe
- The Christmas tree
- The Yule log
- Awarding stars as marks of excellence

Christian saints who are versions of Celtic deities:

- St. Anne – Celtic Water Goddess Ana
- St. Bridget – Celtic Fire Goddess Bride
- St. Brendan – Celtic God Bran
- St. Corneille – Celtic Forest God Kernunnos

English legend has it that Jesus visited Britain in his youth to be taught the ancient wisdom and mysteries. His Uncle Joseph of Arimethea was a prominent merchant/trader and evidently brought him there.

Rites of Assumption

Druidic visualization exercises are aimed at tapping into natural archetypal realms (the "other world" of spiritual reality), which are memories that remain after the originating individual or group no longer exists. C. G. Jung, psychologist and mystic, described the archetypal world as a sea of symbols shared by all of mankind, usually accessed through dreams or altered states of consciousness, and from which cultures draw images to found their religions. Jung's views closely resembled Druidic beliefs. Luz suggested that Jon read Jung's Gnostic Treatise "The Seven Sermons to the Dead" to gain a better understanding of these concepts.

Druids placed heavy emphasis upon prose, poetry and verse as a means to express archetypal realms. A technique known as the illumination of rhymes was a means of intense imagery and visualization, which allowed an individual to become one with the forces of nature. To achieve this level of meditation requires careful practice under proper conditions. The first of these conditions is environment, which should resemble the ritual site. The thought processing thus encourages assumption, e.g. matching the meditative spot and the image being described in prose or poetry.

The second condition involves external atmosphere. The contemplative person creates an atmosphere that is conducive to attracting like forces, thereby deepening the assumptive process. For example:

- Use of proper type of incense for a particular thought frame
- Use of aromatic essential oils to create an atmosphere for contemplation
- The environment should reflect the nature of prose or poetry facilitation toward communion with a particular archetype.

The third condition is the internal environment, which explains the need. Your emotional state should match the prose or poetry being worked on.

The book of Pheryllt outlines nine different rites of assumption, which are classified in three sets of three. Each set denotes a past, present, or future relationship.

Jon was given the assignment to study these rites because, as Luz explained, it would promote his understanding of deep meditations.

Lesson 11: The Four Universal Laws

Four universal laws allow for the creation and support of the galaxy. The term galaxy refers to the flow of manifested reality around a center of focus.

The four laws of the third dimension in which we presently exist are: attraction, deliberate intent, allowance, and balance.

For man to be in harmony with the galaxy he must live according to the four laws, which are immutable.

1. Law of Attraction

Positive thought attracts more energy to bring form (manifestation). If you hold the desire, the law will take over.

2. Deliberate Intent

Creation in co-operation with God's will is how to create purposeful experience.

3. Allowance

The most difficult of the laws, it allows the process toward transcendence to go forward. The ego and attachments to it must be surrendered without resistance. One must be non-judgmental and exhibit forgiveness and unconditional love.

4. Balance

Occurs when a still point between the conscious and subconscious is found. The result will be the co-operation of others.

Employing the first three laws--attraction, intention, and allowance-- leads to balance through the application in experience. This is the way to ascension. Balance is needed to enter the higher dimensions. For man to achieve the second coming, when all of mankind will become Christ-like, large numbers will have to be brought into balance. The spiral energy of evolution occurs within the positive and negative polarities. The Law of Intention in cooperation with the Creator's expansive mode leads to purposeful manifestations or new paradigms of experience.

Lesson 12—Sacred Geometry

Sacred geometry has been called the "blueprint of creation." It is an ancient science and belief system that affirms that there are fundamental forms of space and time. The geometry is considered sacred because it is the basis of all things.

Sacred geometry can be seen in great architectural designs and inspired art. There is the conviction that mathematical ratios and geometry underlie music, cosmology, harmonics, astrology and other features of the universe.

Pythagoras discovered the relationships of geometry and mathematics to music. He discovered octaves, fifth intervals, and fourths in music, and believed that music could promote healing of a body that was out of homeostasis and balance.

Medieval European cathedrals and other holy places incorporate sacred geometry in their designs. The Knights Templar, who built many cathedrals, were thought to possess knowledge of sacred geometry, which they had discovered during the crusades. The ancients believed the experience of sacred geometry was essential to educate the soul.

Sacred geometry seeks to explain the energy patterns that create and unify everything and demonstrates how energy of the created universe is organized. Every natural pattern of movement or growth is influenced by one or more geometric shapes. All life forms emerge out of geometric codes, which direct the patterned beauty of creation. Examples of these geometric forms can be seen in the following: spiraling helix of DNA; Buddhist mandalas; Hindu designs of the cosmos; hexagonal shapes in the honeycomb of bees; snowflakes; crystals; cornea of the eye; flower petals; crop circles (coded messages of the cosmos) and the Great Pyramid of Giza.

Sacred geometry has been described as "meditation for the logical left hemisphere of the brain."

Lesson 13—The Kabala and Gnosticism

Kabala is the mystical religious philosophy of the Hebrews, which is rooted in origins that are pre-Christian, and Zoroastrian. It is a system that imparts wisdom to man and attempts to explain man's relationship to the universal creator.

Its study is reserved for the wisest and most deserving disciples. Kabala can be described as a speculative science, which claims to unveil the secrets of creation and of divine nature.

The Kabalistic system is based on two books: The Sefer Yetzirah (Book of Formation), which contains a cosmologic explanation of phenomena, and the Zohar (Book of Brightness), which focuses on the spiritual world. Zohar is considered more important, whereas the Sefir Yetzirah is the more ancient. The Zohar explains the ten attributes of God, which are subdivided into three trinities, all in different planes (frequencies): supernal, spiritual, astral and physical.

All that exists came from non-being. For example, pure consciousness can manifest in form, which is the basis of the dualist explanation of all that exists. It becomes obvious that a similarity exists between this idea and the beliefs of the Gnostics. The Gnostics (searchers for knowledge—gnosis) were the foundation of early Christianity and borrowed heavily from the Zohar. Gnosticism teaches that the totality is based on the opposite polarities of principles: gnosis/ignorance; masculine/feminine; yin/yang; light/dark; wisdom/intelligence; active/passive; spirit/matter; alpha/omega; life/death; monk/warrior; Sufism/Islam; Gnosticism/Christianity; Kabala/Judaism. Gnostics believe all springs from the divine and that man has the ability to reunite with the divine through annihilation of self (ego).

Lesson 14 – Isms of Destruction

The following isms or belief systems foster dissolution of human structures, be they political, social, economic, medical, or moral. This negative, entropic effect results because these beliefs do not reflect the true nature of things and ignore the spiritual reality. For any system to flourish it must be able to receive the life-giving divine energy from the creative source, God.

Materialism, egoism, atheism, agnosticism, feminism, egalitarianism, pragmatic humanism, secularism, liberalism, meism, hedonism, narcissism are all isms of destruction.

Luz explained to Jon that he must fully understand the concept that these isms are destructive and prevent us from evolving spiritually. She expressed the view that these philosophies represent the anti-Christ and are a great threat to human advancement.

Lesson 15 – Reincarnation

Each lifetime is an opportunity to explore the dimensions of our true nature. Through experience on the material plane we grow in knowledge and we learn to deal with life's situations into which we have incarnated.

Our perception of reality on the physical plane is an illusion, for the true reality is in the spiritual plane. Life in space and time is a teaching mechanism. Our thoughts, attitudes and actions program our spirit component and continuously generate our individual beliefs by such behavior.

Reincarnation explains the function of our various energy bodies and the way we express ourselves upon the physical plane in the world of experience.

Our limited physical perceptions create an illusion of the world of appearance. True reality is beyond the five senses.

Of the seven energy bodies of the human anatomy the outer four-- mental-instinctive, mental-intellectual, mental-spiritual and the causal bodies--survive physical death, for they are eternal. These four bodies are reinstilled into physical forms until their karmic debt is paid and salvation into the oneness with God is reached.

It is the energy fields that generate the physical form as a vehicle of expression for our higher consciousness.

The energy channels in the body, known as meridians, develop before the organs. The etheric body is a template and actually guides the development and structure of the body. At conception the etheric body is a projection of an archetype as modified by karma. The physical form is a representation of the etheric mold and the currents of energy perfusing it. Each part of the body fits the incarnated one's energies.

The belief in reincarnation is not antithetical to Christian beliefs. For that matter, early Christians had a firm belief in this concept. It was not until the sixth century that purgatory replaced reincarnation as a major tenet of Christianity. This change occurred because church leaders at the Second Council of Constantinople decided purgatory was more easily understandable.

Lesson 16 – The Five Rites
The Ancient Secret of the Foundation of Youth

A series of five ancient Tibetan exercises that can be done daily in a short time can be used to revitalize the human body. The system is based on the fact that the body has seven energy centers known as chakras. These chakras are associated with the seven endocrine glands, which regulate body functions, including the aging process.

The energy chakras revolve at high speed allowing the life force of chi (or prana) to move up through the endocrine system. If the flow of energy is impeded the health of the individual will suffer. To restore health one must initiate the spinning of the energy centers to more normal speed. The ancient monks of Tibet developed five simple exercises known as rites, which produce the desired result.

Rite Number One

With arms outstretched, palms facing downward, spin in a clockwise direction a dozen times.

Rite Number Two

Lie flat on back with arms at your side. Bring your chin to your chest. Lift legs to a vertical position. Precede each repetition with deep breathing and do several repetitions.

Rite Number Three

1. Kneel on the floor with your body upright. Place hands against thighs.
2. Bring your chin to your chest.
3. Arch your back and move head as far back as you can.
4. Do deep breathing prior to each repetition and do several repetitions.

Rite Number Four

1. Sit on the floor with legs stretched out, feet slightly apart, and hands on the floor.
2. Bring your chin to your chest.
3. Pull your head back as far as you can.
4. Keeping the arms straight and your hands and feet in place, bend the knees and raise the body's trunk to a horizonal position.

Do deep breathing and repeat.

Rite Number Five

1. Support yourself in a cobra position.
2. Keeping the hands and feet in this position, bend at the hips and bring the body into an inverted V position. Bring your chin to your chest. Do deep breathing and repeat.

Lesson 17 – Seven

The Mystical Number and the Book of Revelation

St. John's biblical Book of Revelation is a blend of Essene apocalyptic tradition, Babylonian mythology, and astrological fantasy derived from the Persian magi and the Egyptian temple mysteries.

Seven foldedness is important to the understanding of the Book of Revelation, as the world proceeds in rhythms of seven. There is the mention of seven stars, seven golden candlesticks, seven messages, seven trumpet blasts, seven angels of the seven churches, the seven seals, and the seven vials of wrath. Seven is important to religions and initiation rites that preceded Jesus. In the east Buddhists refer to nirvana as the seventh heaven. There are seven wonders of the ancient world, Seven Hills of Rome, seven colors of the spectrum, lucky seven, seven archangels and seven elohim, seven notes of the scale, and seven days of the week. Seven symbolizes movement of life in space and time. Seven is seen in the seven chakras, seven sacraments, seven virtues, seven deadly sins, and seven planetary oracles on which are built seven great cathedrals.

Mystics found sevenfoldedness to be the key to enlightenment through the Book of Revelation, which eventually became the search for the Holy Grail. The Grail is not a literal cup or chalice but an allegorical representation of enlightenment and the potential of human consciousness. Finding the Holy Grail, according to mystics, will be the salvation of the world.

Luz reiterated to Jon that creation is indeed a product of an incredible intelligence, which has structured the universe on a base of complex mathematical principles. She told Jon that he must develop a deep appreciation for the mystical numbers of one, three, seven and twelve.

Lesson 18 – Galactic Changes

In 1964, dramatic changes began to occur in our galaxy. These changes are expected to continue until around 2012 AD when they will culminate in a dimensional change that will take our planetary system from the third to the fourth dimension. This elevation to the next dimension has been described as the Ascension.

Our solar system is in orbit around the center of the galaxy, which takes 26,000 years to complete. The 26,000-year period is divided into twelve phases or aspects of experience. The solar system is periodically exposed to high-energy photon belts, which can alter DNA within the planetary system. At this point evolutionary leaps occur, which bring life forms to higher dimensions and closer to oneness with the source, the creator. There are eight dimensions in the universe, which are distinct because of different vibrational frequencies. Currently, our world is in the third dimension, but it is about to enter the fourth dimension as it reaches a point between the twelve phases that manifested creation gathers new energy before it moves to the next cycle.

Solar cycles are classed into two periods, one of 25,000 years and one of 75,000 years. At the end of three times 25,000 years, a dimensional shift occurs because the energy of the planet is altered into a higher grade by a zone of galactic energy called the photon belt.

Those individuals who are prepared to withstand the new vibrations will be transformed into a higher, less dense vibration when the moment of change arrives. A transmutation to a Christ-like state will occur as mankind ascends into what can be described as the second coming; we will all become as Christ… a child of God. A new utopia will manifest itself after the Ascension and a world without poverty, hunger, pain, hatred and war will ensue. Levitation, healings, telepathy and love will prevail. Attachments to materiality must be broken. No money, cars, homes, fame and possessions will be taken up because it will be a spiritual evolution: third density bodies can't survive the fourth density and will disappear in the Ascension, because their DNA will not be supported by the new torsion waves. The fourth density human race will be non-judgmental and have a sense of universal love and interconnectedness.

Luz explained to Jon that the fourth dimension corresponds to the fourth chakra, which is the heart chakra. She further expounded on the idea that we will be leaving the realm of the third chakra (power) and entering the fourth chakra (love). In addition, unconditional love must exist within a person before the Ascension will be allowed.

As regards the commonly accepted theory of evolution, Luz offered some truly profound ideas. She opined that evolution is an extinct theory, which will rapidly lose support in academic circles. As we learn more about the nature of DNA and that it can change when influenced by consciousness, we will realize that random mutation as mentioned in Darwinian evolutionary theory is a flawed concept. Rather, a conscious force directs and alters DNA's structural changes to push the evolutionary process forward into increased complexity and a return to the higher dimensions. Modern physics is beginning to discover and verify the truths and mysteries that were known by ancient peoples and mystics of yore.

Luz reminded Jon that "all is one" and that the architecture of the one is of harmonic design. The number eight, which represents the octaves of light and sound, is the underlying factor supporting the sacred geometric of the multidimensional universe.

To illustrate to Jon that hyper-dimensional physics is well understood in hidden scientific circles, yet not revealed to the masses, Luz related the story of the Philadelphia experiment of 1943. In this experiment, which was authorized by the U.S. Navy and designed by some of the greatest scientific minds of the day, it was demonstrated how a strong magnetic field could make a ship disappear by transforming the matter phase of everything within an area to another dimension. There was even rumor that some aboard the vessel actually went into the future for a brief time and then returned as the ship came back to visibility. For reasons known only to them, the Navy and the government never did confirm nor admit that the Philadelphia experiment took place. However, many believe it did occur and it did confirm the idea that magnetic changes can transport matter to a higher dimension. Luz explained that as magnetics on earth change, the preparation and eventual Ascension will occur.

Beginning in the 1980s, the following solar system changes have gradually begun to unfold:

- The sun's magnetic field has grown stronger than it was at the start of the 20th century. Solar flare activity is increasing dramatically.
- The quality of space energy is moving 200% faster than expected.
- The resonance of the earth is gradually changing from what has been thought to be a constant of seven to a high around thirteen. This increase in resonance heralds the coming Ascension.
- The atmospheres of the planets are changing. They will be brighter, hotter, more magnetic, more geologically active, and the atmospheres will become denser.
- Venus and Jupiter are becoming noticeably brighter.
- Jupiter and Uranus have shown dramatic increases in their magnetic fields.
- Uranus and Neptune are manifesting pole shifts.
- Neptune is getting brighter.
- Pluto's atmospheric pressure is increasing.
- Galactic dust is increasing.
- Volcanic activity is increasing.
- Natural disasters such as hurricanes, typhoons, tornadoes, floods, tidal waves, mudslides, and fires are on the rise and will quadruple in number.

El Fuego De Barcelona

When the sessions were over Luz asked Jon to join her for dinner at El Fuego de Barcelona, a highly respected authentic Spanish restaurant in the downtown Scottsdale area. Jon was delighted to have this opportunity to be in Luz's company in a situation other than their usual mentor/student relationship. It had occurred to him that he was getting rather enamored of Luz, although he never would allow his feelings to be demonstrated out of respect for her.

The meal was sumptuous as they enjoyed a delicious steak dinner done wonderfully in the Spanish style. The restaurant not only served fantastic food, they also entertained diners with great Flamenco dancing by a small troupe of two male and one female dancers. One of the dancers, Jorge Cruz, glanced out into the crowd and noticed Luz sitting just below the stage. He informed the audience that they were in the presence of a fine Flamenco dancer, Luz Barca, and begged the audience to try to get her to come onstage and perform. Luz acknowledged the crowd and reluctantly agreed to give a brief exhibition of her dancing skills. Jon had no idea that Luz was a dancer of such ability and was flabbergasted as she took to the stage.

Luz placed the castanets in her hands and began her dance to the rhythms of the Flamenco guitar. As she danced and swirled she kept her eyes solely on Jon Corbett. Jon's heart and mind started to spin in concert with Luz's movement and he experienced an arousal and passion he had never known before.

At the dance's end the crowd responded with a rousing ovation and Luz acknowledged and thanked them. As she took her seat at the table she reached out to tenderly hold Jon's hand. The energy between the two was electric and Jon and Luz realized they were falling in love.

When they left the restaurant and settled into Jon's Jaguar XKE they immediately fell into each other's embrace and engaged in a kiss of the deepest passion, a kiss that melded their hearts in a total union. Their lips met in a soft, gentle caress that lasted for several minutes. Jon's heart and being throbbed to be one with Luz; however, the size of the sports car would not allow that to occur. Jon and Luz laughed over the frustration of not going beyond their first incredible kiss to something deeper.

Sometimes love comes from above, going from male to female and thence to the entire universe, but sometimes love takes an opposite path, rising from below going from female to male, from the material to ideal world, from earth to heaven, and returns to God those who so deserve the right of return.

On the drive back to Luz's home, Luz told Jon that she had known they were falling in love as they progressed through the two months of learning sessions. Jon revealed he had the same feelings but could not imagine how to proceed with a lady he so highly respected. As they drove up to Luz's place, it was mutually understood, without a word, that Jon would be spending the night, sharing her bed, and exploring their love.

The love scene was indescribable, for the communion that followed is rarely experienced in the western world. Luz jokingly informed Jon that what they were about to do was a bonus lesson, the final one so to speak.

Luz told Jon to wait for her in the bedroom while she undressed and prepared herself in the bathroom. The anticipation was maddening as Jon waited excitedly on the edge of the bed for Luz to emerge and enter into his arms.

As Luz slowly approached him her body was aglow. A shaft of light streamed from her heart and penetrated Jon's heart, so that Jon began to glow as he too was infused with light. As she stood directly in front of him, she dropped her robe to reveal a physical presence like none that Jon had ever seen. She was all woman, with breasts and hips perfectly shaped; her full lips were slightly parted and ready to reprise the kiss they had shared after leaving the restaurant. The kiss was again magical and led to Luz naturally mounting Jon who was in a sitting position. Luz wrapped her legs around him as they continued their kiss. When Luz backed away Jon looked into her beautiful brown eyes, which seemed to be lustered like pearl in an endless swirl.

She shared the gaze as they focused on their oneness. It was then that they began a conjoined dance of love. Jon's being merged completely with Luz. His mind became her mind, his heart became her heart, his body became her body. This total union brought them into union with all that is. They remained in that deeply engaged state for many minutes until spontaneously they experienced a simultaneous cosmic orgasm, the ultimate in sexual experience.

Jon was totally taken aback. He had never experienced anything beyond the simply physical action of having sex. He now realized this was not having sex but this was making love—a true union of the male and female principles and an approach to oneness not only with Luz but also with the universal Creator. Two hearts were pulsing as one as they rode a giant swell on a sea of love. Their minds and souls were truly united in a total union. This was the type of love that inspired poets. Jon never imagined that such joy could exist. As they finally withdrew from one another, Luz gently kissed Jon's forehead and said, "I love you, you are my beloved." Jon fell back and rested his head on the pillow and lay there with his eyes closed thinking about all that had happened.

A soft zephyr of breath blowing across his face broke Jon's spell of thought. He opened his eyes to find Luz looking at him lovingly and holding a packet of travel information. She then presented Jon with an offer he couldn't refuse.

Luz had taken it upon herself to plan a two-month journey known as a spiritual quest. The itinerary included visits to seven great cathedrals of Europe, the Great Pyramid at Giza in Egypt, and the monasteries of Tibet. It was Luz's hope that such a trip would solidify all that Jon had learned in his lessons. She anticipated that Jon would accept this incredible offer to travel to some of the most important mystical sights on earth. Jon did not disappoint—he placed his lips upon hers to express his acceptance, appreciation and love.

Within three days Jon and Luz were on a plane to Portugal via a stop in New York City. Jon was in a state of exhilaration as he was deeply in love and also making his first transatlantic flight on the highly respected BOAC Airline. The service and courtesy of the British staff were impeccable; they did everything to insure the comfort and safety of their passengers.

After a perfect flight Jon and Luz disembarked in Lisbon, Portugal where they spent a day exploring the enchanting ancient section of the city, called "Al Fama".

The following day would be the first day of a pilgrimage of initiation to seven great cathedrals of Europe. The journey to the first cathedral, St. James De Compostella in northwestern Spain, was a scenic, leisurely ride made in a new rental car.

The next morning Jon and Luz started the day with a wonderful continental breakfast at an outdoor café. The atmosphere was most conducive to conversation and Luz provided Jon with a discussion of the history and meaning of the pilgrimage of initiation to the seven cathedrals: one in St. James of Compostella in Spain, the five "Prayers in Stone" in France; Toulouse, Orleans, Chartres, Notre Dame in Paris, Amiens, and lastly Rosslyn in Scotland.

The importance of the seven cathedrals is paramount because they signify profound truths which, if known by the general public, would create a new perception and awareness of spirituality. According to Luz,

"Mankind, in general, lives in a giant illusion steeped in materiality and a disconnectedness from God and the true reality. Jon, you will see that the ancients were well aware of these truths as evidenced in the design and location of the seven cathedrals. It will be a most revelatory experience for you."

To further deepen Jon's appreciation of the depth of knowledge held by ancient peoples Luz defined the term, IS RA EL as being derived from three roots: IS – ISIS, RA – Sun God, EL – Elohim. Each root represents three divine Egyptian and Canaanite roots of Hebrew Gnosticism, which is the basis of Judaic and Christian spirituality. Jon shook his head in amazement and disbelief that a term as common as Israel would have such a depth of meaning for which the mass of humanity would have absolutely no understanding.

"Luz, I love you. You light up my world," Jon exclaimed.

"I truly value that comment," Luz replied, "but let's get serious. I really want to discuss the subject of our journey and pilgrimage."

"Okay, Luz, I'm ready to begin the discussion," Jon said.

Even before Christianity and the building of the cathedrals, ancient Celtic pilgrims traveled from the Iberian Peninsula to Scotland via the seven planetary oracles, associating the alignment within them to that of the earth chakras. These seven earth power points arc across Western Europe from northern Spain through France and into Scotland. They are aligned under the arch of the Milky Way and possess an energy known as Telluric Power.

The earth's planetary energy flows through meridians (Ley Lines) and focuses in chakras, which correspond to a similar flow of energy through the human body. Earth is not just a hunk of lifeless matter suspended in space. It is a living organism that requires spiritual sustenance just as man does if it is to be in balance and harmony. Remarkably, the seven cathedrals were built on these exact sacred Druid sites, and each one represents a certain chakra. For someone to achieve eventual enlightenment, one must release his personal energy from the base chakra and allow its movement upward through the other chakras until it reaches the seventh (crown) chakra. It is at this point that a mystical union with the All occurs. It was common to see medieval Christians do a walking pilgrimage from Spain to Scotland with the objective of drinking from the eventual chalice of light, the Holy Grail, located in the seventh and final holy site.   The builders of the Gothic structures were the Knights Templar, who were in possession of esoteric truths and who allegedly fully understood the so-called mysteries.

Starting at the base chakra, St. James of Compostella in Spain, to the crown chakra, Rosslyn in Scotland correlates to growth in spiritual awareness as energy flows from below to above.   Each stage in the pilgrimage is accomplished after intense preparation, which culminates in an initiation into the higher degrees.   So, as each chakra opens the student aspirant makes progress towards the ultimate goal.

Luz outlined the seven cathedrals to prepare Jon for the pilgrimage:

1. St. James of Compostella

First moon oracle
Base chakra
First degree symbolized by the "raven"
Purpose to establish humility
The raven represents the "messenger to the divine"

2. Toulouse

Second mercury oracle
Sacral chakra
Second degree symbolized by "peacock"
Purpose to develop imagination
The peacock represents the "occultist"

3. Orleans

Third Venus oracle
Solar plexus chakra
Third degree symbolized by the "knight"
Purpose to awaken the life force (chi, prana)
The knight represents the "warrior"

4. Chartres

Fourth sun oracle
Heart chakra
Fourth degree symbolized by "swan"
Purpose is to create a realization of the divine and the death of self. One is expected to commit to duty and compassion. At this point a union of the spiritual and physical aspects occurs.
The swan represents the "lion"

5. Notre Dame (Paris)

Fifth Mars oracle
Throat chakra
Fifth degree symbolized by "pelican"
Purpose is dedication to service and to develop communication in a purposeful way

6. Amiens

Sixth Jupiter oracle
Brow chakra
Sixth degree symbolized by "eagle"
Purpose is to develop clairvoyance, insight and intuition

7. Rosslyn

Seventh Saturn oracle
Crown chakra
Seventh degree symbolized by "crown"
Purpose is to awaken Kundalini so it reaches the highest chakra, which allows one to drink of the Holy Grail and to achieve union with the Creator.

With Jon's new appreciation for the fact that a pilgrimage can be far more than just a physical journey, he looked forward to experiencing a journey of a lifetime. As they arrived in Compostella, a town that dated back to Roman times and had housed the tomb of the apostle St. James for hundreds of years, Luz and Jon could not resist going directly to the cathedral of St. James. Although the cathedral of St. James was not Gothic in design as were the other six, it was a magnificent example of Romanesque architecture, which was built in the ninth century. The building had been well preserved and showed little sign of deterioration. Strategic lighting enhanced the beauty and grandeur of the interior and also leant an atmosphere conducive to meditation. Visitors described a feeling of deep spirituality as they entered the mauve main doors that separated the ornate exterior from Portico de la Gloria, a masterpiece creation of the genius, Master Mateo. The seated statue of St. James looked down upon the beautifully carved central column with James holding a tablet in his right hand, which stated in Latin, "The Lord sent me." The central pillar was a reference to the genealogy of Christ and represented the tree of Jesse, who was the father of King David. It was a tradition for visitors to insert their fingers into hollows on the shaft of the tree of Jesse. Master Mateo was depicted in stone offering his work to the Father. Many pilgrims would bang their heads against Mateo's in hope of gaining his wisdom and abilities.

As they walked by Mateo's work, the imposingly beautiful Baroque main altar came into view. The all-seeing Eye enclosed in a triangle hovered over the altar, which was situated above the tomb of St. James. Jon and Luz remarked about the similarity of the all-seeing eye in the great seal of the United States of America and the eye above the altar. Luz explained that those who have knowledge of esoterica would know the connection between the Knights Templar and the Free Masons and would find nothing surprising in the similarity.

Another important relic was the silver bust of St. James the Less, which contained his actual skull. James the Less was the brother of James the Just, the Gnostic leader for whom the church was built, and of Jesus himself. Even the New Testament refers to James the Less as being the brother of Jesus. Both of the James brothers were fathered by Zebedee who married Mary after the passing of St. Joseph. Interestingly, the skull of St. James the Less was punctured in the temple area much like the skull of St. John the Baptist, which was kept in the Amiens Cathedral.

There were many symbols of Knights Templar influence, which provided evidence of their involvement in the Cathedral's design. For example, the Templar Seal was located above the triumphal arch, which crowned the roof. The Seal depicted a lamb, the Templar Cross, and a flag. It was used as a seal for Templar documents and a symbol of influence in various buildings throughout Europe. Other Templar symbols found in the cathedral were the five-pointed star, two brothers on a single horse, a dove in flight with an olive branch, and the floriated cross.

The Telluric powers of the cathedral have been attributed to watercourses under the structure. Placing the cathedral on this site was further testament to the genius and insight of the master builders. Such energies were considered to be powerful adjuncts to reinforcing the spiritual atmosphere of churches.

Jon and Luz followed the tradition and placed their fingers in the five worn hollows on the Tree of Jesse. They then walked over to the statue of Mateo and knocked heads in the tradition of the pilgrim, followed by a few moments of contemplation in the lower church. It was in this area that the Gnostics of early Christianity were initiated into the awakening of the base chakra and the subsequent release to go to higher levels of spiritual awareness. As Jon and Luz meditated away from the crowds and reflected on the mysteries of St. James the Just, they felt compelled to share some of their feelings. Jon explained how he experienced an infusion of energy transmitted through his fingers and had a sense of vertigo as he touched the Tree of Jesse. Luz admitted to being affected by her contact with the Tree of Jesse in that it caused her to be overwhelmed by emotion. Jon noted that he felt unstable and lightheaded as he banged heads with Mateo and even wondered if he were being awakened to his true self.

When Jon and Luz departed from Compostella they drove due east towards the Pyrenees Mountains on their way to the next stop, Toulouse in southern France. During their drive of about four hundred miles, Jon and Luz had plenty of time for a wide range of conversation. One main topic was their future as a couple. Both agreed, without much consternation, that the pragmatics of their relationship, such as the age differential and Jon's obligation to his upcoming career, did not lend themselves to continuing their relationship once the time came for Jon to fulfill his promise to those who provided his education. Both realized that the depth of their love was unfathomable and would always exist whether they were together or not. Once they resolved this issue, it freed them up and they committed themselves to enjoying their tour to the fullest extent possible.

The city of Toulouse, located in the Languedoc area of southern France, was dominated by the Christian Gnostics known as Cathars until their slaughter in the Albesnian wars. The cathedral was built on the planetary oracle of Mercury, also known as Hermes, the messenger of the Gods. According to ancient Egyptian and Greek traditions, Hermes imparted divine knowledge to mankind and has been linked to Enoch in the Bible, Idris in the Koran, the Druids, the Magi, and Pythagoras, who was initiated into the Hermetic mysteries by the Druid, Abaris. Even the Romans had a temple of Mercury in Toulouse.

Upon their arrival Jon and Luz sought out the cathedral, Notre Dame La Dal Bade (Our Lady in White), which was in the proximity of the Roman Temple. The original structure was built by the Templars around 1200 AD in a Gothic style and destroyed by fire in 1442. The structure now standing, was consecrated in 1455.   As they entered the church they immediately perceived it as extremely harmonious, yet simple. Giant pillars, adorned with Templar symbols, supported the vault, a symbol of the heavens above.   Both Jon and Luz experienced tingling, lightheadedness, and unsteadiness due to the Telluric energies. The power was strongest in front of the altar and caused them to actually sway as they stood on that point. Luz had a vision of ancient cloaked Druids. Her experience was probably due to the fact that the opening of the sacral chakra is associated with awakening to the so-called other world and to increasing one's psychic powers.

After spending two days of enlightening time in Toulouse, Jon and Luz proceeded to the next stop, Orleans, the town of Joan D'Arc. The Cathedral of Orleans was built on the ancient Druid site of the Venus oracles. They appreciated its magnificent exterior and a welcoming interior that elicited a sense of lightness. The architecture was quite delicate with an emphasis on laciness, noticeably different than the heaviness of most Medieval structures. They immediately noticed a life-size statue of John the Baptist in a dominant baptizing pose. The Templars highly revered John the Baptist. Once again, as in the other great cathedrals, remnants of an ancient Roman temple--this one dedicated to Venus--stood on this site.

Legend has it that the finger of God consecrated the Cathedral of Orleans when the bishop could not perform that duty due to illness. Orleans represents the third chakra (solar plexus), which signifies the rightful use of personal power or the will to reach one's goals and potential. Jon developed a strong determination to complete his quest for spiritual growth as he kneeled in reverent prayer. He couldn't wait to proceed to the next stop, to the magnificent cathedral in Chartres.

It was best described by Napoleon, who once exclaimed, "Chartres is no place for an atheist. Chartres is a statement of the mysteries that bring us to God." Visitors often depart with a sense of spiritual uplifting and self-transformation. Probably the most impressive structure of the seven cathedrals, Jon and Luz noted many distinctive features. First, the entrance had three main doors: the Door of Mystical Faith in the middle; the Gate of Birth on the right; and the Gate of Ages on the left. The Gate of Birth depicted the seven sages and the seven liberal arts, which were taught by the sages: dialectics/Aristotle; rhetoric/Cicero; geometry/Euclid; arithmetic/Boethius; astronomy/ Ptolemy; grammar/Donatus; music/Pythagoras. There were many depictions of scenes from the life of Jesus and Mary, but nowhere was there a depiction of the crucifixion, a reminder of the Templar belief that the crucifixion never occurred. It must be understood that in their excavations of Solomon's Temple in Jerusalem the Templars unearthed many hidden truths about early Christianity, which included a different interpretation of the last days of Jesus Christ, as well as the secrets of sacred geometry. It was the latter knowledge that allowed the construction of the Gothic cathedrals with their pointed arches, highly vaulted ceilings and arcane symbolism.

The interior appeared dark and shadowy upon first entering but as they acclimated to it a certain luminescence totally captivated them, an effect resulting from a secretly produced stained glass brought back by the Templars from the Holy Land. The glass was said to create a wavelength of light that was in concert with cellular vibrations and allowed viewers to maximize their spiritual sense. Three huge rose windows depicted the Last Judgment and homage to great figures of esoterica and religious history, such as St. Anne, Melchizedek, Aaron, David, and Solomon.

The Black Madonna was first venerated at Chartres, which was a veiled adoration of the Druidic figure, Virgin, Pariturae. A replica of this figure was found in the crypt, which was used as a place of initiation. Interestingly, a well had been dug to 123 feet from the crypt floor, the same distance as from the church floor to the vault. "As above, so below," was the age-old statement defining the idea that the two realms of materiality and spirituality were mirrors of one another.

Chartres' water sources, which fed fourteen underground streams, were configured especially to maximize Telluric power. These streams were symbolized by doves surrounding the Black Madonna, the Druidic "Lady under the Earth."

A second Black Madonna was on the main floor of the Cathedral. The energy levels next to this figure were overpowering. Jon and Luz experienced this powerful effect as they began to shudder and feel faint in the presence of the Madonna. Jon conjectured that such a feeling could represent a transitional point between the worlds of matter and spirit. Chartres represented the fourth chakra (heart), which is the point at which we leave our lower nature and enter the higher self (chakras 5, 6, 7) and the eventual State of Grace.

Chartres has been sacred ground since early Druid times and cannot be denigrated by materiality in any way. For example, the Virgin stands on a pillar, which cannot be disturbed, thus keeping the Virgin intact and undefiled. For this reason Chartres is the only cathedral of the seven that does not have any human figure buried therein.

Some have theorized that the Knights Templar actually discovered the Ark of the Covenant in their excavations of Solomon's Temple in Jerusalem and brought it back to Europe to be hidden below the crypt of Chartres Cathedral. Upon the dissolution of the Templars in 1307 the Ark and many sacred documents were ostensibly taken and hidden in Rosslyn Chapel in Scotland.

One of the most fascinating features within Chartres, Jon thought, was a labyrinth of circular design made of black and white stone that covered a third of the nave's floor. The purpose of the labyrinth was to provide those who danced upon it bare-footed and traced its path a way to absorb the earth's telluric energy, allowing them to experience a sense of spiritual awareness and intuitive growth.

Once Jon understood that Chartres represented a transition from materiality to the spiritual, he could imagine the initiation rites that took place in the crypt hundreds of years ago. Candidates for initiation were expected to overcome their sense of ego and allow themselves to serve God and their fellow man in a totally selfless way.

Jon and Luz, upon leaving Chartres, were excited about their next stop in Paris at the Cathedral of Notre Dame. They planned to not only visit the cathedral but to also spend several days enjoying the romance of the incredible city of light. Their accommodations were in a charming hotel, the Tuilleries, just across from the Louvre Museum. This strategic location allowed them access to many of the Parisian sites simply by walking. At day's end, after exploring the various quarters of the city, Jon and Luz would settle into deep, restful sleep to restore their tired bodies. The hotel room was a love nest located on the fourth floor overlooking a side street and an outdoor café.

Each morning they would wake to the sounds of street cleaners washing the streets, and prepare themselves for the day, and, best of all, a relaxing breakfast at the café below. This pleasant unhurried beginning of the day would allow them time to plan their daily itinerary and absorb the energy and spirit of Paris. They visited the Louvre, D'orsay Museum, the Lido, the Eiffel Tower, Versailles, and took a three-hour romantic dinner cruise on the Seine River. It was a magical week for the lovers and further deepened their love and intimacy. They explored the city on foot for six days before they made a reverent visit to the Cathedral Notre Dame.

The cathedral rests on a small island in the Seine, Ile de la Cite, which has been a sacred site since pre-Roman Celtic times. They understood that this cathedral represented the fifth chakra and the entrance into the spiritual realm. They saw this association in the heavy emphasis on the medieval science of alchemy in carvings within the church. Alchemy, which involves the transmuting elevation from the lower nature to the higher, was depicted as a feminine figure seated on a throne with her head connected to the clouds. She held two books, one open and one closed. The open book symbolized the open path and the closed book the hidden path to enlightenment. The "Scala Philosophorum," an eight-runged ladder, which represented the seeker's climb to the eighth and final dimension, rested on the female figure. The statue and the church itself have been said to be an occult bible written in stone whose purpose is to reveal the secrets of "The Great Work," which describes the process of transmuting the imperfect being to an enlightened one. The Cathedral was dedicated to our Lady, the Virgin Mary, who personifies the sacred feminine and the spirit of all things.

Jon and Luz spent their last two hours in meditative prayer in a quiet area of Notre Dame. In spite of the flood of tourists and the noise distractions they still realized the power of Notre Dame—a holy place designed to open the fifth (throat) chakra and one's ability to communicate with the divine. It has been purported that when one reaches this stage of growth, he or she may no longer require food and drink to survive and may also develop a keen sense of prophecy and past life memory. As Jon and Luz departed Notre Dame for Amiens, the next stop, they were amazed to have experienced the living energy of yet another Gothic structure.

Amiens, the largest cathedral in France, was replete with symbols of initiation and alchemy, much like those at Notre Dame. Amiens was distinctive in its majesty with a pervasive sense of light and space enhanced by spectacular vaulted ceilings rising to 140 feet. The windows added to the sense of light by being void of dark colors. Jon mused that coming from Chartres to Amiens gave him the perception that he was traveling from the love of God to the love of wisdom. Amiens was designed and built for two reasons: first, to incorporate space, stone and light in venerate recognition of the principle of sacred wisdom--a goal of Gnosticism--and secondly, to house the skull of John the Baptist.

The skull has rested in Amiens since 1206 when it was brought by the Templars from the Holy Land, in testimony to the revered status of the "Baptist." Even Jesus was quoted in the Gospel of Thomas as stating, "No one since Adam, the first man, has ever been superior to John the Baptist."

The Amiens Cathedral was built on an ancient sacred site used by the Druids and later by the Romans in reverence to the Jupiter oracle. The early Gnostic Christians used Amiens as a means of awakening the sixth chakra (brow) on the quest for eventual enlightenment.

As Jon and Luz prepared to leave Amiens they turned to take one last look and to indelibly imprint the wonder and beauty of this sacred site into their memories. Having visited the five cathedrals of France they were excited to realize their next stop would be Rossyln in Scotland, the home of the Holy Grail, "The Cup of Light."

After having arrived in Edinburgh, Scotland, Jon and Luz rented a car and drove seven miles to the small village of Roslyn. It was dusk of a midsummer day in July when they reached their destination. The two attempted to visit the chapel immediately, but were disappointed to find it closed for the day. An informational sign stated that appointments for a curator-guided tour were strongly suggested and would be of inestimable benefit to the visitor. Disappointed, Jon and Luz resigned themselves to the fact that they would have to wait until the next day to experience the mystical and spiritual atmosphere of the chapel.

The following day found Jon and Luz anxiously waiting for the doors to open. When they entered the Chapel the curator welcomed them and offered to give them a personal tour. The curator graciously escorted them through the fascinating interior and graphically explained the history, symbolism and significance of Roslyn Chapel.

The Chapel's foundation was laid in 1446 AD and construction ended 40 years later, although most experts feel it was never completed. The impetus behind the design came from Sir William St. Clair, Lord of Roslyn and Earl of Orkney, who was a man of great nobility and erudition. He was considered an "illumined one," and was a grand master of masonry. He was descended from Henri de St. Clair who was involved in the First Crusade and the formation of the Knights Templar in the earliest years of the 13th century. Evidently, the St. Clair family was exposed to the arcane knowledge taken from the Templar excavation in the Holy Land and it became an integral part of family lore and belief.

The Chapel's vault was profusely lined with five-pointed stars and roses. The stars were meant to represent those of the Milky Way, which arch over the ceiling of the galaxy just as they fill the arched ceilings of the sacred churches, which extend from Spain, through France and into Scotland. Luz told Jon that some believe that when the seven major heavenly planets mirror the alignment of the seven planetary sites on earth a massive planetary transformation will occur.

"Really? I hope it's for the betterment of man and not to his detriment," Jon replied.

"That time could be nearer than you think," said Luz.

"Are there any estimates as to when, Luz? If you know, please tell me."

"Many ancient cultures like the Hindus, Egyptians, Mayans and Hopi Indians have predicted great change in or around 2012 AD. One scenario that's been predicted is that the planet will actually stop its rotation for three days and then resume in the opposite direction. It will spin at a more rapid rate, creating a 16-hour day that will impart certain magnetic and density changes. This transition will promote a new spiritual awareness on the planet. Man will realize he is part of the One and will have full appreciation of the message of the Savior, Jesus Christ. You will probably be around to see that day, but, given my age, I doubt I will."

As they continued the tour the curator explained the significance of the Pillars of Boaz and Joachim, which bound the arch of stars. The curator described the arch of planetary oracle sites of the seven churches as being bound by the Pillar of Joachim in Cintra, Portugal, and Boaz in Rosslyn. Cintra, which is south of Compostella, was an eighth sacred site and could have marked the beginning of the journey through the seven sacred sites of Europe. Including Cintra brings attention to the number eight, which plays a significant role in esoteric lore, especially with Egyptians and Templar traditions. There are eight steps on "Scale Philosophorum" (Philosopher's Ladder), which is seen in Notre Dame de Paris, eight points on the splayed Templar Cross, and eight sides to the octagon that was so important to the sacred geometry of Gothic architecture.

Rosslyn Chapel, Jon and Luz agreed, was most distinguished by its marvelous carvings. The Rosslyn guidebook described the Chapel as "one of those architectural wonders whose intricate beauties and peculiarities extort our imagination while they baffle description." The sculptures demonstrated the great mystical insight held by the Templar builders. Even though many think of the Chapel as being Christian, in reality it is totally eclectic in that there are depictions of Egyptian, Babylonian, Norse, Greek, Hebrew, Druid, and Gnostic belief systems. Many have inferred from Rosslyn's arcane design that it is strongly prophetic and predicts the future spiritual awakening of mankind. The art of Rosslyn was validated by the ancient phrase, "Ars Sina Scienta Nihil est," which means that art without knowledge is nothing. This statement could also apply to all great literature, music, poetry, and architecture, all of which are divinely connected and inspired.

Jon Corbett was totally enraptured by the spiritual power of Rosslyn and expressed his thankfulness to Luz for having taken him on their enlightening journey. He felt that the pilgrimage had further strengthened his sense of purpose in life and had given him a thorough understanding of the true nature of man and the law of one. The prospect of visiting Egypt and the Great Pyramid loomed large in Jon's mind as he could only imagine what startling new insights might be gained on their next scheduled stop.

The relationship between Jon and Luz had deepened into one of pure love as they continued to share their hearts and inner beings. Jon inquired about what to expect in Egypt. Luz surprised him when she postponed answering that question and said that she had decided it would be fortuitous for them to visit Stonehenge before leaving for Egypt. It had occurred to her that being in such close proximity to the Glastonbury Plain and Stonehenge behooved a visit to this most important mystical site. Jon's heart leaped when Luz suggested a visit to Stonehenge. It happened to be a special time of the year, midsummer, when according to Druidic lore, the so-called other world was more easily accessible. What was about to happen was completely unexpected, but it would demonstrate how advanced Jon was on his way to spiritual enlightenment.

Jon and Luz approached Stonehenge from a distance and observed a vast area of barren land. Jon wondered about the strangeness of this moonscape-like area in the center of England. A huge stone structure loomed ahead of them. Jon and Luz kept their eyes transfixed on the alluring megalith as they walked towards it.

When they were close enough to observe the details of the giant, bluish stones, Jon was awe-stricken and overwhelmed by the massiveness of it all. The thirty stones were nearly twenty feet high, squared at the top, capped by cross stones and formed a giant circle. Upon closer observation, Jon noticed not one circle, but a series of three, one within the other. The inner two circles were smaller and open ended like a horseshoe with a stone altar in the middle. The overarching impression was one of a kind of magnificence. Questions of why it was built, who built it, and when it was built raced through Jon's mind. Luz attempted to answer his questions by explaining that some ancient civilization, probably Atlanteans, had built it several thousand years ago as a permanent beacon to religious truth and a means of entrance into the spiritual realm. The name Stonehenge stems from the Saxons calling it "hanging stones." The unique bluish stones were of special magnetic quality and were likely quarried in a special area in Wales. Stonehenge actually sat in ruin for thousands of years until the Druids began to explore its mysteries. Luz iterated that many of those secrets are probably still undiscovered.

At one point Jon was overtaken by his curiosity and started to advance toward the giant ring, only to be startled to a halt by Luz. "No," she exclaimed. "Can't you see this is serious? You must prepare."

Jon retreated and returned to sit next to Luz.

"We must wait here until the proper time to enter," she said. "There are things to learn before you step into this holy ring."

As daylight passed into dusk, Luz told Jon to settle in and relax so she could teach him the sacred lore and the aim of their visit to Stonehenge. Luz informed Jon that Stonehenge would permit him to challenge space and time and to see things that once existed on this earth plane but now dwell in another dimension. After hours of discussion Luz told Jon that they should catch some sleep because they would be getting up at first light to enter the ring.

As Luz fell into a deep slumber, Jon attempted to sleep but could not reach that state due to the racing of his mind and the strong, powerful influence of the great stones. He decided to seek communication with the life force in the stones by going into a meditative state of suspension. After checking to be sure Luz was sleeping, he quietly stole away and approached the outer ring of stones. With all the courage he could muster he reached out to touch one of the monoliths. Upon contact he was thrust into a world of explosive light, which created an extreme state of fear within him. In a panic he attempted to withdraw his hand from the stone, but could not break contact. Suddenly a giant buzzing sound consumed his mind only to be abruptly ended as he fell in a heap upon the ground.

"Silly boy," Luz exclaimed as she assisted Jon to his feet. "I warned you to wait for dawn's first light. You should never have attempted this without my guidance. If I had not broken your contact you might never have returned to this earth plane."

Jon apologized for his rashness and promised Luz he would obey her to the utmost from that point on.

As the sun emerged over the horizon Jon and Luz began their walk to the inner circle of Stonehenge. Standing together before five enormous central stones, Luz invoked in sacred tones a call to the other world. Suddenly the veil that separates the world of matter from the world of spirit was torn away and a shaft of light descended from the heavens. Next, five shining beings stood before each of the five giant stones.

Jon followed Luz's directive and they both assumed a face down prostrate position with arms splayed out, creating cross-like figures in total supplication before the luminous beings. The five beings acknowledged the gesture and each took a turn to welcome Jon to their world. They introduced themselves as minor Gods, who were representatives of the "one God." As each one spoke they were transformed into a solid being and each explained their significance. The first represented birth, the second love, the third mortality, the fourth the dark world, and the fifth the world of enlightenment and light. Collectively they then retreated to the altar and placed a hand on it. In unison they stated, "You are now to feel the power of the divine God." Immediately, a blinding beam of light descended upon the area and Jon was thrust into an indescribable experience; he had a sense of total oneness with the all—both timeless and limitless. Could this be heaven?

The holy experience was what is known as "naugal" in that a voice was felt but it was a voice without words and without gender. It has been described as having the impression of a spoken presence, which presents a blended scene of timelessness and countless experiences culminating in awareness that all is one. It was heaven—without time, without limits. Jon had no sense of how long he was in this state before it abruptly ended. It could have been seconds or years, but regardless, it ended when the five bodily beings transformed into their luminous forms and ascended as one beam of light to their divine realm.

The experience left Jon physically weak but spiritually strong. He regained some of his strength when Luz lovingly kissed his forehead and said, "This is just the beginning. Next we go to the Great Pyramid, the next destination of your journey towards truth."

The flight from Heathrow Airport in London to Cairo was quite fruitful as Luz took the time to explain how the ancient Egyptians had also made a seven-stop pilgrimage, quite similar to the one they had just completed. Luz discussed the strong correlation between the seven temples of Egypt and the seven churches in Europe. Both systems were based on the seven chakras and the movement upward to the eventual connection with the divine.

The Egyptian pilgrimage started at the Temple of Phrae on the Nile River and concluded in Heliopolis, where the initiate, after having satisfied the requirements, would enter the fraternity of illumined ones. The new member then had the right to read the mysteries of Hermes, to attain divine union, and to participate in the election of the Pharaoh.

It became apparent to Jon Corbett that the Egyptian pilgrimage of initiation had to have been the precursor to the pilgrimage in Europe. He mulled over the pact that those who are steeped in esoteric knowledge, such as Essenes, Gnostics, Freemasons, Templars, and Rosicruceans, understand that the Atlantean origins of such knowledge stemmed from ancient civilizations that were in reality divinely inspired.

With each day Jon could sense that his intellectual and spiritual growth was advancing him towards a profound appreciation of the sacred mysteries. As the airplane made its descent onto the barren, yet fruitful land of the Pharaohs, he was looking forward to whatever new adventures his time in Egypt would bring.

Luz contracted with a guide named Abdullah to take them to the Giza Plain and guide their exploration of the Great Pyramid. Abdullah's appearance was overtly one of the physically unwashed but one could sense his cleverness and insightfulness into the true significance of the ancient Egyptian. He seemed to be well respected amongst the many who participated in the business of taking tourists on tours of the area. It was without much delay that he was able to take them within the massive structure and to the eventual goal of the so-called King's chamber.

Upon reaching the chamber, after considerable physical effort, Abdullah left Jon and Luz alone to engage in whatever ritual they had planned to exercise. Having studied the secrets of the Great Pyramid, Jon realized that each person might experience something totally unique, but had no idea what was in the offing. Jon and Luz began with a meditation followed by an "aum" chant. After a few minutes of chanting Jon entered into an altered state of consciousness that at first revealed a scene of his being initiated into a priestly caste in a time several thousand years ago. As he remained prone and suppliant before the high priest, he found himself facing a flaming door through which he ventured forth. Upon passing through the door, he found himself in an interior of total, infinite blackness with a single point of absolute white light in the great beyond. As he approached the light he was overtaken once again by the same voice he had experienced at Stonehenge. The same feeling of oneness and timelessness were felt but this time the voice had a clear message. "You, Jon, have entered unto the source where all truth is known and all questions are answered. Let it be known that it is your destiny to someday be the one who will unify mankind and bring a new spiritual awareness to your fellow man. This understanding will propel man into a Christ-like status and will truly be what has been called the second coming. With you as philosopher King, man will learn to live in the city of God, where peace, harmony and abundance will prevail."

Having noticed Jon's detached state, Luz waited patiently for him to return to their earth plane. When Jon finally opened his eyes and recounted his experience, Luz was quick to explain some of what had happened. She defined the flaming door as a representation of the gateway to the Divine Light. The message rendered was intended to inform him of the role to which he was born. In Jon's case, he was born to unify mankind and to live his life as a reflection of that heavenly place where all creation merges into one.

Jon was somewhat overwhelmed by the enormity of the prophesied role he would someday play in human history. However, he was fully prepared to accept the responsibility for he was committed to a high purpose in life and to serving truth and God in his every action.

As they flew from Cairo to Bombay, India, Luz informed Jon that the sojourn to the Himis Monastery in Ladakh, Tibet, would be both difficult and perilous. There would be few modern comforts, difficult travel, unsanitary conditions, and even the threat of man-eating panthers. Jon jokingly said that it would all be worth it if he could learn more than he had already learned about sacred truths.

Luz took advantage of the long flight to Bombay to provide a detailed account of Tibet's history, culture, the 1950 conquest by the Chinese, and the storied traditions of Jesus Christ, who had spent fifteen years in India and Tibet.

Luz explained that the first indication that Jesus had ever traveled to the East came from the Russian adventurer, Nicola Notovitch, who traveled to the Himis Monastery in Ladakh in 1887. Notovitch was shown ancient scrolls that supported Jesus' presence in Leh, Bernares, Kabul, Rajagriha, Juggernaut, and Lhasa. Jesus was known to the natives as Saint Issa (the Islamic Koran also refers to Jesus as Issa) and purportedly had traveled east to perfect his knowledge of the divine word by studying the philosophy of the great Buddhas and the Hindu Vedic Laws. Following Notovitch's startling discovery he wrote the highly controversial books, The Unknown Life of Jesus Christ and The Life of St. Issa. It should be noted that the existence of the ancient documents in Himis was corroborated by several other investigative adventurers, including the Swiss music professor, Elisabeth Caspari, in 1939. Others were the Hindu swami, Adhedananda, in 1922, the Russian poet, mystic, painter, and archeologist, Nicholas Roerich, in the mid-1920s, and the U.S. Supreme Court Justice, William O. Douglas, in 1951.

Luz informed Jon that she had long yearned to take this journey to the Himis Monastery, especially after having studied for a time under the Swami Yogananda who had informed her of the life of St. Issa. Prajnananda had presented Luz with a letter of introduction to the chief lama in the event that she ever reached the Himis Monastery. It was felt that such a verification of her honorable intentions would be necessary to dispel any doubts of the highly suspicious monks.

Although the invasion of Tibet by the Peoples Liberation Army of communist China in 1950 had caused the destruction of more than six thousand monasteries and forced the eventual exile of the Dalai Lama in 1959, the Himis Monastery was spared because of its location in Ladakh. Ladakh, known as Little Tibet, is a high, cold, remote barren land. It was a kingdom for a thousand years until 1834 when it was subdued by the Jammu of India. It is now a part of the Kashmir state and borders Pakistan, Tibet and Turkestan. Ladakh is the last remnant of Tibetan Buddhist culture. Leh is the capital of Ladakh and has a population of only five thousand inhabitants. There is but one road to Leh, which is narrow, perilous and fraught with danger. Leh would be their last stop before embarking on the journey's last leg of twenty-five miles to the Himis Monastery. Himis is the largest and most celebrated monastery in Ladakh and is situated in a hidden valley eleven thousand feet above sea level. It holds a lower chamber, which is a treasury of thousands of ancient scrolls, several of which describe the life of Jesus in India and Tibet.

Luz told Jon that if he still had doubts about Jesus' life in Tibet he could further erase any doubt by comparing Catholicism with the Tibetan religion. The similarities were clear and self-evident. For example, they both incorporated the concept of the Trinity, hierarchy of clergy, robes and vestments, mass-like ceremonies, holy water, maxims of morality, chants, monasteries, processions, prayers for the sick, crosses, rosary-like beads, penances and poverty. These comparisons provided strong evidence of a common origin and lent further support to Jesus being the founder of both religious systems. Luz said there was also reliable information that demonstrated that the Apostles Thomas, Bartholomew and Matthias evangelized India, Tibet and China around 35 AD. Thomas, who some believe was a half brother to Jesus, was actually martyred by Indians in 52 AD.

Christianity assimilated the beliefs of many faiths and codified them in an attempt to uplift all of mankind. All religions seemingly have a common origin. For that matter, the word religion refers to the joining of man to God much like a ligament joins muscle to bone.

The Books of the Hindu Vedas and the Gospels, Luz noted, are in strong agreement on most issues. As a matter of fact, if it had not been for the elimination of many venerated gospels, known as the Apocrypha, which were expunged by the church, we would have a much clearer picture of the commonality of all major religions. Events such as the burning of the Sybilline books in 401 AD, the Nicene Councils of 325 AD and 787 AD, and the 16th century Council of Trent censored many eternal truths. The church's rationale for such action was to avoid controversy in the public mind and to serve as a means of reinforcing its control of church members.

Once Luz had established a foundation of knowledge for Jon, she proceeded to provide a concise history of Jesus' life in the East. The story went as follows: When Jesus was thirteen years of age he had developed a reputation for great wisdom and insight as regards spiritual matters. Many came to the House of Mary and Joseph in Nazareth to seek Jesus' advice and to hear his discourse. Jesus decided to perfect his knowledge and stole away on a caravan to India. Known in the East as Issa, Jesus entered the Indus Valley in what is now Southeast Pakistan and became established among the Aryans. He became well known and was a particular favorite of the Jains in the Sund Region, who implored him to stay with them. Instead Jesus chose to travel to Juggernaut in Eastern India where the Brahmin priests embraced him and taught him to read and comprehend the sacred Vedas. The priests also taught Jesus to teach, heal the sick, and to exorcise demons from the possessed. Issa spent six years studying and teaching in Juggernaut and other holy cities. By attempting to teach the mysteries to the lower castes, Issa offended the priestly caste, which plotted to assassinate him. The peasants (Sudras) warned Issa of the murder plot and he fled from Juggernaut under the cover of darkness. He traveled to the foothills of the Himalayas in Southern Nepal, the birthplace of Gautama Buddha 500 years earlier. After another six years of study Issa was considered to be the perfect exponent of the sacred mysteries. He subsequently traveled west towards Palestine, preaching the message of the true God until he returned to his homeland at the age of twenty-nine.

The flight from London to Bombay, India, although long in distance, seemed short in time because of the deep conversation and Luz's teaching discourse during the airtime. Jon was becoming more and more cognizant that his time with Luz was approaching an end point. He decided to make this last segment of the spiritual journey one in which he would demonstrate his deep love and appreciation for Luz. She had fashioned Jon into an intellectual giant with a deep sense of purpose and an absolute belief in the spiritual side of life. He was mentally prepared for the rigors of the trek to Himis and was anticipating another enlightening adventure.

The monotonous rhythm of the train's wheels meeting the metal of the rails provided the harmonic background for the scenic trip from Bombay north to Delhi, North Lahore, and finally to Rawalpindi. The remainder of the journey would require the use of animal-drawn carts, pack animals, male porters and plenty of difficult walking. While in Rawalpindi, Luz contracted with an experienced guide-servant named Jimbi, who had been recommended by an embassy employee in Bombay. Jimbi was thoroughly familiar with the geographics of the area and was conversant in the various dialects of northern India, Kashmir, and Ladakh. Jimbi also supplied a tonga--a two-wheeled vehicle pulled by ponies--which provided Jon and Luz a fair amount of comfort for the easiest portion of the journey, which would terminate in the Kashmiran city of Sringagar. The journey beyond Srinagar would be over difficult terrain and would require pack horses and ambulation. The planned route included passing through the Punjab, the eighty-five miles of the Valley of Kashmir, the sixty mile dangerous Defile of Sind (inhabited by tigers, panthers, bears, wolves and jackals), and finally into the Tibetan Buddhist land of Ladakh.

As they journeyed to the ultimate destination of the Himis monastery in Ladakh, Jon, Luz, Jimbi and the retinue of porters passed through several towns and villages wherein different ethnic peoples lived. It was dismaying for them to view the uneducated, ignorant Hindu peasantry being manipulated and exploited by Brahmins who corrupted the original monotheism of the Vedas into an absurd polytheistic conglomeration of various gods, goddesses, demigods, angels, and devils, which were depicted in idols of horrible form. The once great Hindu people had degenerated into a condition of pure idiocy, involved with a wide variety of ritualistic ceremonies that had no relation to the pure religion of the Vedas.

In one small Kashmiran hamlet known as Tongue on the Jhelum River, Jon visited a bazaar and tried to purchase a container of warm milk from a Hindu. To Jon's surprise the Hindu insisted that Jon take the whole container because, according to Hindu law, if someone of another caste looked upon their food for any length of time the food would become contaminated and must be discarded. It was further verification of the strangeness of foreign thought.

Jon realized that understanding the customs and thinking patterns of indigenous peoples, as well as diplomatic means of dealing with such individuals, would be important to the success of any endeavor.

As Jon and Luz proceeded from the Vale of Kashmir the road narrowed and became quite perilous. They began the ascent into the mountainous regions, which had to be traversed if the Himis destination were ever to be reached. The last major outpost of civilization in Kashmir was Srinagar, which is situated on the Jhelum River. While in Srinagar, Jon, Luz and Jimbi spent a few days resting, buying provisions and four horses, and hiring coolies for the journey across a largely uninhabited region of Tibet.

Once they had departed Srinagar the traveling party encountered all measure of difficulty ranging from the dangerously narrow mountain paths to confrontations with wild animals, such as panthers, tigers, bears, wolves and jackals. The entourage had several close encounters but were saved by their clever thinking and Jimbi's excellent shooting skills. Several days out of Spinagar the landscape became quite severe and inhospitable and the journey most difficult as they had to deal with the twelve thousand foot altitude and the treacherous travel.

When the traveling party finally reached Ladakh they had at last set foot on Buddhist soil. The contrast with the Hindu culture was quite obvious and intrigued Jon and Luz. Women were highly esteemed and dominated the men. Each woman had three to five husbands and lived in a legitimate system of marriage known as polyandry. The women were fewer in number because of the custom of killing female new-borns by strangulation. As distasteful as this abhorrent custom may seem to western minds, it does offer a pragmatic means of population control. It's a system that predated Buddhist teaching and lived on for its practical benefits. The men were typically of feeble appearance, of bent posture, and seldom lived to old age.

As the party trekked across Ladakh, they found delight in visiting various hamlets along the way. The Ladakian people were civil, truthful people, although quite idle. The women carried an aura of gaiety and a look of prosperity. They were scrupulously clean and washed daily. These characteristics were in strong contrast to the men who dressed in rags and bathed once a year. No jealousy existed in this Tibetan society and romantic love was non-existent. Love would be considered selfish and unjustifiable. Women were highly respected and had total freedom in the choice of husbands. They were of good humor, inquisitive and free to go wherever they wanted, except to the prayer chambers of the monasteries. Each town had a Gonda (monastery), which was manned by monks who were the first-born males devoted to prayer and contemplation.

The first monastery encountered was in Mulbekh, which was set into the mountainside. Using Jimbi as an interpreter Jon and Luz queried an affable head lama as to his knowledge of Jesus Christ having spent some fifteen years in Tibet. The lama was completely aware of the legend of Christ in Tibet where Christ was known as "Issa". He also mentioned that the history was recorded on scrolls which were only kept in Lhasa, the seat of Tibet Buddhism, and in the more important monasteries, the nearest of which was in Himis, some twenty-five miles from Leh, the capital of Ladakh.

Their next stop was Leh, a town of five thousand inhabitants who welcomed Jon and Luz with open arms and a warm greeting. The governor was especially friendly and welcoming. He created a celebration of welcome, which included a polo match, dances, and games. Bonfires lit the night and people formed a large circle and danced the night away.

The next morning Jon and Luz started out for the great convent, Himis, which was situated on the zenith of a rock overlooking the Indus Valley. Upon their arrival all the lamas within the monastery gathered as a group to welcome them. Musicians blew their long trumpets in long monotonous sound, accompanied by the rhythms of several drums. Finally the chief lama accepted Jon and Luz and proceeded to engage them in a friendly conversation. Luz presented a letter of introduction from her teacher Swami Yogananda that was well received by the lama. After two hours of discussion the lama offered to share the traditional drink, tchang, which was an affirmation of his respect and trust. In their conversation the Lama explained the need for ritual and ceremony as a means of providing the ignorant masses with an explicable way of knowing religion as the union with the divine. The lama affirmed the fact that Jon and Luz were well beyond the average individual in their comprehension of the law of one and he would be willing to entertain serious questions they might have. Jon and Luz were grateful for the lama's offer and explained that they were searching for documents detailing the life of Jesus Christ, known as Issa. The lama was quite forthright and admitted to the fact that Himis held sacred scrolls, which depicted the life of Issa. Without any hesitation the chief lama ordered one of the monks to retrieve two large yellowed-by-time scrolls on the life of Issa from the chamber of storage. With the help of Jimbi as interpreter they spent several hours translating the verses, which described Issa's time in India and Tibet.

The life of Issa was written in a collection of verses that detailed the early life of Christ in his native Israel, his studies and ministry in India and Tibet, his confrontation with Zoroastrians, and near execution in Persia on his journey back to Israel.

Jon and Luz spent the next two days organizing their notes into a readable account of Issah's life. Once the task was completed they wrote an account of quotes taken from the translation. Some of the more notable ones were highlighted and read as follows:

1. "The human race perishes because of its lack of faith, for the darkness and the tempest have scattered the flocks of humanity and they have lost their shepherds. But the tempest will not last forever, and the darkness will not always obscure the light. The sky will become once more serene, the heavenly light will spread itself over the earth, and the flocks gone astray will gather around their shepherd."

2. They reviewed the assertion that Jesus was the incarnation of the universal God and came upon earth to show forth in the guise of humanity the means of self-identification with divinity and of attaining eternal felicity. It was Jesus' role to demonstrate how man may attain moral purity and, by separating his soul from its mortal coil, the kingdom of heaven, which is unchangeable and where happiness reigns eternal.

3. Jesus left his parent's house in his thirteenth year in order to avoid his betrothal as he reached maturity, which for an Israelite boy at that time was the age of thirteen. He departed from Jerusalem with a caravan of merchants to the east, the motherland of all religions. The object of his mission was to perfect himself in the divine word and to study the laws of the great Buddhas.

4. Jesus spent six years in Juggernaut (Jagannath), Rajagriha, Benares and other holy cities of India. The people loved him for he lived as they did. The people of Jainism, a sect of Hinduism, especially loved him and begged him to stay amongst them. The priestly Brahmins were offended because Jesus taught the lower castes and they plotted to assassinate Jesus. He was warned and fled the region and journeyed to Tibet where he embarked on six more years of study. He then left the Himalyas and descended into the Valley of Rajputana

in India and then west preaching the way to perfection and oneness with God.

5. Jesus Christ was known in India and Tibet as Saint Issa. Jesus' name is pronounced and spelled in different ways in various languages, but it has the same meaning in the Koran (written in Arabic). The name used for Jesus is Isa or Issa, the same as in Tibetan documents. Only through changes by speakers in many lands did the pronunciation, Jesus, evolve. The English word Jesus, prior to the sixteenth century, was not spelled with a "J" but with an "I" as in Latin and Greek (Iesous).

According to the Gospels of Luke and Matthew, an angel instructed Mary and Joseph to name the divine child Yeshua, Savior (in Greek, Iesous; in English, Jesus.) Yeshua is a contraction of Yeshoshua and Yahweh (Jehovah, the creator). However, the spoken language of Galileans was a Hebrew dialect, Aramaic, in which his name would have been pronounced "Eshu". This name is remarkably similar to the ancient Sanskrit name, Isa, which was purportedly bestowed on the divine child by the three wise men from the east.

The high meta-physicians of India knew full well that the wise men who followed the eastern star (the light within all men) on their way to Bethlehem were great sages of India. Interestingly, a Hindu Temple in Calicut, which is dedicated to the Virgin Mary, was built by Perimale, one of the wisest Brahmins, following his return from Bethlehem and the birth of the Savior. The temple was discovered by the Portuguese explorer, Vasco Da Gama, in 1498. Its existence totally baffled the Christians of that day. Fortunately, we now have a plausible explanation because of the new knowledge of Christ and his affiliations with the East.

1. Every man shall bear his burden. Follow my path for it is the best, simplest and most direct way to union with God. A quote ascribed to Jesus goes as follows: "Take my yoga upon you and learn of me, for my yoga is easy."

2. "The judge eternal, the eternal spirit, comprehends the one and indivisible soul of the universe, which alone creates, contains and unifies all."

3. "The creator willed it and the world appeared. In a divine thought he gathered the waters, separating from them the dry portion of the globe. He is the principle of the globe. He is the principle of the mysterious existence of man, in whom he has breathed a part of his being."

4. "For it is the false beliefs that have led you from the true God and those superstitions and cruelties are conducive to the perversion of your soul and the loss of all moral sense."

5. God will drive the impure from among his flocks, but he will take back to himself those who shall have gone astray through not having recognized the portion of spirituality within them.

6. Do not give yourself up to debauchery for that would be to violate the laws of God.

7. Everywhere Jesus went in the east and preached. The greatness of his ministry was recognized and the people welcomed him.

8. The spirit of evil dwells on the earth in the hearts of those men who turn aside the children of God from the straight path.

9. Jesus returned to Israel in his twenty-ninth year.

10. "As to the Laws of Mossa (Moses), I have endeavored to establish them in the hearts of men. I say unto you that you do not understand their real meaning, for it is not vengeance but mercy that they teach; only the sense of these laws has been perverted."

11. There is one miracle, which is possible for man to accomplish. It is when, full of sincere belief, he decides to root out from his heart all evil thoughts, and when to attain his end forsakes the paths of iniquity.

12. The Lord our God, who has no equal, is one, all mighty, omniscient, and omnipresent. It is he who possesses all wisdom and light.

13. The secret of nature is in the hands of God. For the world before it appeared existed in the depth of divine thought; it became material and visible by the will of the most high.

14. "Whosoever respecteth not his mother, the most sacred being after his God, is unworthy of the name of son. She gives birth

to you in the midst of suffering. By the sweat of her brow she rears you and until her death you cause her the gravest anxieties. Bless her and worship her for she is your one friend, your one support on earth. In acting thus you will find favor in the sight of God and many sins will be forgiven."

15. The King of Heaven is greater and more powerful than the terrestrial law, and his kingdom surpasses all the kingdoms of the earth.

Jon was surprised to discover that the Tibetan records provided an account of Jesus' execution that differed from conventional thinking. The story depicted in the scrolls asserted that it was Pontius Pilate who condemned Christ and not the Jewish Sanhedrin and that Pilate ordered Jesus' body removed from its original tomb and buried elsewhere to minimize a popular insurrection.

Surprise followed surprise for Jon as one new revelation after another came to be known. It so happened that in the conversation with the chief lama, a startling story of the early years of Jesus was revealed. The lama informed Jon and Luz of an apocryphal Gospel of Thomas known as the Gospels of the Infancy of Jesus Christ. The apocrypha were gospels that were rejected for inclusion in the New Testament by the Council of Nicea in 325 AD. The decision to exclude many gospels from the bible was a political choice by the organized church because these stories were antithetical to the aims of the hierarchal clergy, who were more interested in controlling the laity with a brand of faith that supported their continued power and influence. In other words, the church would hold the keys to heaven and not the individual children of God. "Remember," the lama reminded Jon, "that the kingdom is within you and is there for you to discover."

The lama went on to explain many incredible tales of the young Jesus, which depicted several miracles, healings, and exorcisms. Several of these events that exemplified the power of Christ's divinity were outlined as follows:

- Discussions Jesus had with learned scholars and his amazing revelations to them.

- Exorcising demons in a young boy, Judas Iscariot, who went about biting others and himself. Judas was to later become infamous for his perfidy and betrayal of Jesus.
- Restoration of life to a child who had been killed in a fall from a building.
- Restoring his brother James, who had been bitten by a viper while gathering wood, by the simple act of blowing his breath over the bite.
- Explaining the Immaculate Conception and how the divine cosmic vibration of the Holy Spirit can stimulate the ova of a mortal woman to actually conceive. The idea that current science cannot explain such a phenomenon does not necessarily mean that science will not someday have an explanation for the possibility of such a miraculous event.

The lama had vast knowledge of the infancy gospels and he continued the discussion with many more stories of Jesus' early life. Jon was in rapt attention as the lama continued with story after story. Some of the more memorable narratives follow:

When Joseph fled to Egypt with Mary and Jesus to avoid the slaughter of newborns by the order of King Herod, the Holy Family took up residence in Egypt for three years. While in Egypt many miracles were ascribed to the infant Jesus. The infancy gospels described how: a young bride struck voiceless by sorcery was healed when she took the infant Jesus in her arms; the son of an Egyptian high priest was cured of possession by demons and the idol adored by his father fell into pieces; many others were cured of physical debilities and diseases by pouring over their bodies the water that had been used to bathe the infant Jesus.

The lama related the story of how Mary had presented the three wise men of the east with a swaddling cloth in which Jesus had been wrapped. Upon their return home they demonstrated the power of Jesus' divinity by placing the cloth in a sacred fire. Upon extinguishing the fire the cloth was without injury, much to the amazement of the observers.

Upon return to Israel the miracles continued but they reflected a greater sophistication as Jesus became more aware of his unique powers. It must be understood that even those acts that punished evil-doers were done to mete out God's karmic justice to not only punish but to free their souls of their indebtedness. Jesus' ability to affect animate and inanimate matter was a result of his manipulation of the vibrational power of the cosmic God consciousness.

It was told in the infancy gospels how Joseph utilized Jesus' incredible abilities in his carpentry trade—not as a simple laborer but when an error was made or a correction in wood length was needed Jesus could simply will the change and material could be brought to the proper dimension. This power would also be seen in later, more familiar, miracles of changing water into wine and the multiplication of bread loaves and fish.

Jesus was not only a mental genius but also a spiritual genius. A mental genius has great knowledge and learning ability because of an endowment from previous lifetimes. Whereas, a spiritual genius has the super conscious ability that allows him to connect with the all-knowing properties of the soul and the divine intelligence.

Even as a young child Jesus would frustrate teachers who attempted to school him. One teacher who was teaching Jesus the alphabet was astounded when Jesus provided an explanation of the meaning and origin of each letter. The teacher was flabbergasted for he had never seen or heard of any such information. Another more highly rated teacher was brought in to teach Jesus and he met with the unfortunate fate of a withered hand because, in frustration, he attempted to scold the young student with a striking blow.

The story of Jesus at the age of twelve lecturing to a cadre of scholars in the Jerusalem Temple was embellished with more details as to what Jesus had to say. One Rabbi queried Jesus about the sources of his vast knowledge. Jesus answered that his knowledge came from something beyond books; it came from the divine father. When another scholar, an astronomer, asked Jesus if he had knowledge of astronomy Jesus responded by detailing the nature of heavenly bodies and the planets with further explanation of the planets' number, sizes, orbits, rotation and other prognostications. The astronomer was left dumbfounded, for such knowledge was unknown at that time in history. There was a philosopher present who challenged Jesus in the area of physics and natural philosophy. Again Jesus responded with information unknown to mankind. Jesus explained physics and metaphysics, the human anatomy in great detail (circulatory, skeletal, neurological system, etc.), the soul/body relationship, and how the soul achieves salvation.

When Mary found Jesus in the Temple and scolded him for his disappearance his reply was, "Do you not know that I must be about my father's business?" This simple message represented Jesus' renunciation of material bonds for the greater love of God.

In his concluding remarks the lama provided a descriptive account of salvation that would leave an indelible imprint on Jon's mind. Even though Jon felt he had a fairly good understanding of such spiritual matters due to his lessons with Luz and their just completed mystical journey, the lama's explanation would clarify everything even more and would leave no doubt in his mind as to the nature of a soul's salvation.

"The process begins with a true baptism," said the lama, "when man allows himself/herself to become permeated with God's cosmic consciousness. To understand the means to salvation one must understand that man is a microcosm of the macrocosmic universe. His finite consciousness has the potential to be infinite. Even though our physical senses are bound by the material world, man's soul has the ability to know God within. Even Jesus, our Issa, taught that the kingdom is within."

The lama continued by explaining that all that is manifest (matter is condensed cosmic energy) is from the cosmic vibration (Holy Spirit or Holy Ghost) and contains the intelligence and power of God. Every fragment of the whole contains the intelligence and power of the cosmic consciousness of God the Father that is reflected in the vibration of Christ consciousness. This very same trinity of Holy Spirit, Christ consciousness (son) and God consciousness (Father) exists in a microcosmic sense within the spiritual eye located in the brow chakra region. Just as the universe is a product of the trinity, so is man a product of the microcosmic triune power and intelligence of the spiritual eye.

Jon asked, "Would it be correct to say that we are in reality made in the image of God and that the part is the whole?"

"Exactly!" The lama replied. "You are learning very well."

The lama went on to tell how the spiritual eye can actually be seen in deep meditation. It appears as a brilliant white light in the center, surrounded by blue light, which is enshrouded by an auric glow. The golden aura represents the vibrational sphere of the blue light the Christ consciousness, and the white star-like light is the mystical gate into the consciousness of God the Father.

In the human body, Chi (vibrating life force) and consciousness are each in different vibrational ranges and are kept together by the ego and the soul. In order to achieve ascendancy of the soul from the limited nature of external (material) man, the divine consciousness within man must unite with the Holy Spirit, the "aum" cosmic vibration or the "word". Only then will man's consciousness merge with the cosmic Christ within, which will take the soul back to the Father. Thus is the cycle of rebirth broken and soul becomes one with the Father. No one can reach God the Father and the heavenly realm except through the Holy Spirit and the Christ consciousness. As Jesus Christ said, "I am the way." It is our sense of ego and separateness that keeps us from knowing our real nature, which in reality is the spiritual component of our being.

The lama then ended his discussion by saying, "Jon, this explanation will leave you to ponder these absolute truths and hopefully your understanding of them will help to propel you on the journey that destiny has in store for you."

"I get it, I get it!" Jon exclaimed. "I really do."

Jon and Luz heartily thanked the Chief Lama and all the other monks who had treated them with complete cordiality and had provided them access to some of the most important information that man could ever learn. It was with profound gratitude that Jon and Luz departed the Himis Monastery and began their three-week trek back to Bombay and the eventual flight back to the USA.

As Jon and Luz reached a point a few hundred yards down the mountainside, they stopped to look back for one last glimpse of the monastery. They were so pleased to see the Chief Lama and brotherhood of monks watching and waving goodbye to their western friends. With one last wave Jon and Luz turned away from a most memorable visit and descended to the valley below and the road back home.

Although the flight to America would be long and tedious, the time seemed short, as Jon and Luz were totally engrossed in recounting their incredible journey. It wasn't until just prior to landing in California that Jon again realized that his time with Luz was coming to a rapid end. His commitment to begin his employment was at hand and he had a deadline to be in Rome in just a matter of days. The three years of freedom and little responsibility were over and the obligations of adulthood lay ahead as the next obstacle in the path of Jon's life.

Even though there was an unfathomable depth to their love, Jon and Luz knew that the disparity in their ages and the fact that Jon was about to embark on a career path in a place far from Arizona precluded the continuation of their romance. Jon's heart pained at the thought of giving up his first true love, his darling "Apache". He would always be indebted to her, for she had taught him about total incorporation and union of body, mind and soul through their lovemaking; she had demonstrated to him the difference between consumptive passion and unselfish love; and she had restored his interest in goodness, virtue and truth. He now understood that his fall into profligacy, where he was heading prior to meeting Luz, could have led to an eventual descent into an abyss of despair and oblivion.

Jon was slated to satisfy his obligation to those who had financed his education by reporting to the Egalitaire Foundation in Rome, Italy, within just two weeks of his journey's end. Jon and Luz decided to relish every moment of the next fortnight by slowly turning the pages of each succeeding day as Jon approached the next chapter of his life. Jon was fervent in his appreciation of Luz and thanked her for having taught him the mysteries and helping to prepare him for his mission in life. Their last night together was one of heightened intimacy and both treasured every moment of it.

The day of departure, though understandably emotional, was not unpleasant. Jon and Luz pledged their eternal love with the understanding that they would always retain some measure of the oneness they had known. They promised to stay in communication with one another.

As Jon separated from Luz for one last time to board the plane for the flight from Phoenix to New York and then to Rome, he looked back to see her forlornly watching him walk away from her. When the plane was in its ascent, Jon looked down for a final time on the arid zone below and realized he had quenched the thirst in his parched life by drinking the sweetest nectar of all.

Chapter Three

- Start of Employment
- Work in Egalitaire Organization
- Display of Great Talent
- Presentation of a Plan

The Egalitaire Foundation was a newly formed global think tank located in Rome, Italy. It was set up by the Club of Rome in the late 1960s and operated under the auspices of the club. The Club of Rome had a membership of approximately one hundred globalist one worlders whose mission as stated in their charter was "to act as an independent, global, non-official catalyst of change through the identification and analysis of the most crucial problems facing humanity, in the global context of the worldwide problematique, the research of future alternative solutions and the elaboration of scenarios for the future through the communication of such problems and solutions to the most important public and private decision makers, as well as to the general public."

In 1972 the Club of Rome would publish "the limits of growth" that warned about and highlighted the consequences of continued population growth. Some even suspected that the club was behind some genocidal plans to reduce the world population, for example: the AIDS epidemic.

The Club decided to recruit the world's finest young minds to populate a think tank whose purpose was to be an intellectual potboiler, which was ostensibly designed to conceive of programs to improve the human condition. Manned by a coterie of seventy-five to one hundred of these young recruits, the Egalitaire Foundation was the genesis of many of the social programs seen in the modern western democratic states. The think tank members were recruited and assigned to their roles by a still unknown agency. Mysteriously, each member had been discreetly offered this opportunity because of the enormous intellectual talent they had demonstrated in their early life. The incentive was always the same: free quality education with a mandatory high-paying position following graduation.

Jon embraced his new position with unbridled enthusiasm. It seemed he wanted to transform human society overnight. Certain vigilant eyes immediately noticed his dedication and productivity. However, unknown to Jon, such positive impressions were much too premature to elicit any real changes in his current situation. As time passed and one year ran into the next, Jon's five-year commitment to the Egalitaire Foundation was nearing completion. He was weighing an open offer to renew for another five-year term against opportunities in the political or business world.

Coincident to this period was the escalating turmoil of war in Vietnam. This situation was becoming an ever increasing concern for many young men of Jon's generation. Many young men and women were being swept into the armed services with no real conviction or commitment to the purpose of the conflict. Jon had not given the war much thought until he was notified by the selective service to take a physical exam prior to possible draft into the U.S. Army. He was a young man in his twenties with his whole future in front of him. The possibility of having his promising career and life snuffed out in the jungles of Southeast Asia was a thought that burned in his brain. He was responsible enough to take the physical exam and pass it. Much to his surprise Jon was offered an occupational deferment without any real solicitation on his part. He never really questioned the process, probably because he was so relieved to have this psychological onus lifted from his shoulders. Unknown to Jon there were unseen forces at work to keep him out of harm's way and the danger of war.

As the time for the end of Jon's stint at the Egalitaire Foundation approached, he embarked on his most important project to date, which was an important analysis of economic problems facing the world.

The late 60s of the 20th century was a period of great discord in the world due to the horror of the Vietnam War, the social disembodiment caused by the tearing down of traditional values, and the extreme dangers of the Cold War with the Soviet Union.

Jon Corbett was a keen observer of these powder keg situations in the world. He had embraced the challenge of working in the Club of Rome think tank with all of his passion and enthusiasm. He also perceived the dangers facing the world with its ever increasing population, the financial division between the haves and the have-nots, the threat of declining oil supplies and other irreplaceable energy sources, the possibility that more people than functions to employ them would exist in a highly technical and automated work place, the dangers of pollution to the environment, the problem of how to sustain the elderly population in their retirement years, and how to avoid a world wide monetary crisis and economic depression.

Jon was consumed by these many problems and searched his mind for solutions. It became apparent to him that one of the major problems rested in the unbalanced monetary system. After countless hours and toil Jon developed an analysis in which he isolated seven key factors that were contributing to economic inequality and instability in the world. He listed the factors as follows:

1. Instability of the international monetary system lends a sense of uncertainty to investment decisions. The fact that the U.S. dollar is the international monetary standard is of such great importance that a dollar crisis could threaten the stability of world economies and trade.
2. The process of money creation by banking systems promotes fluctuating   business cycles.
3. The bias for short-term results, which is held by financial and investment systems, offers only temporary and weak solutions.
4. The need to offset the debt of individuals and corporations by encouraging conservative, continuous growth is the means to providing long-term stability.
5. The increasing concentration of wealth into fewer hands exacerbates the disparity between the rich and poor.
6. The erosion of social capital, which reflects civility and co-operation amongst citizens, must be eliminated to sustain a social order.
7. Inequities in the mobility of capital and goods must be corrected. Flight of capital cannot be tolerated in international trade agreements.

Jon realized these seven systemic flaws in our financial systems precluded our ability to maintain general well being, sustainability, and security in society. It was Jon's realization that a new definition of money must be formed. Money simply being defined as legal tender or a medium of exchange was no longer adequate if the values of co-operation and sufficiency in a civil order were to be evident. This brainstorm was an absolute epiphany for Jon. It was a eureka moment! Jon's next task was to create a solution for the insolubility of financial disorder.

As Jon's status in the Egalitaire Foundation continued to grow into one of greater influence, he was given assignments of ever-growing importance. In the year of 1971, which was Jon's third year at the Egalitaire, he was sent to Brazil to negotiate a loan to the country.

Negotiations were being held in Curitiba, Brazil, the capital of the southeastern state of Parana. While in Curituba Jon observed a complementary currency system at work, which sparked his mind into realizing that he could be viewing the long sought after solution to the problem of world-wide financial instability.

The Curitibans created a means to match unmet needs with unused talents and the willingness and desire of the people to create a better life for themselves. They did so by making use of monetary initiatives that did not replace but complemented the national currency system. This observance of a complementary currency system at work propelled Jon into writing a proposal of such great ingenuity and promise that it caused certain members of the roundtable, a group of powerful individuals who essentially controlled the world as it was known, to take notice of Jon Corbett, an obviously superior young mind. This omnipotent cabal, which met at regular intervals, took up the subject of Jon Corbett at a subsequent meeting. It was unanimously decided that Jon's dedication and brilliant work deserved his advancement and initiation into the inner circle.

The day after Jon completed writing his proposal, he decided to celebrate the occasion by experiencing a Roman night of dinner and wine. He began his evening by visiting the Trevi Fountain where he planned to throw three coins into the fountain for good luck. While at the fountain, which was crowded with tourists, Jon was jostled by a young lady and nearly fell into the fountain. Fortunately, someone grabbed his arm and prevented him from tumbling into the water. Jon turned to thank the individual who had saved him from the embarrassment and was astonished to be looking into the eyes of an incredibly beautiful woman.

"Thank you so much," Jon exclaimed. "I can't thank you enough. I'm Jon Corbett. Who are you?"

"Just call me Ginger," she replied.

"My God, by the looks of you, you must be the spice in somebody's life," Jon stated.

"Unfortunately, that's not the case. I'm here in Rome alone on a Trafalgar tour of Italy," Ginger replied.

"Excuse my boldness, Ginger, but would you walk up the street to Giordano's Ristorante and have dinner with me?"

"Well, as long as there are no strings attached, I'll agree to that," Ginger said.

The moment Jon and Ginger walked into this quintessential Italian restaurant they knew it would be a magical evening. The atmosphere was one of absolute joy and frivolity. Waiters bustled about serving the many meal courses so common in Italian restaurants. A popular guitarist-singer, Umberto, played crowd favorites as revelers sang along. Jon and Ginger settled into a corner table to enjoy an evening of Chianti wine, delicious cuisine, and enlivening conversation. They became so engrossed in one another that they had to be interrupted by Umberto, who asked them for any special request they might have. Jon requested the song, "That's Amore," which was perfect for the moment. As the evening came to a close Jon and Ginger took a romantic stroll past the Spanish steps and down to Piazza Novona Plaza. Jon had not felt such an enamored feeling with a woman since his experiences with his first love Luz Barca several years ago. It was with some sadness that Jon escorted Ginger back to her hotel. They promised to stay in touch, and they kissed good night. The kiss so consumed them that time seemed to stand still as their hearts joined in one rhythm. Unfortunately, the two young lovers would be unable to see one another the next day for Ginger was scheduled to fly back to her home in bad Gotesburg, Germany, where she was a high school English teacher.

Bad Gotesburg is a suburb of Bonn, which was the capital of West Germany at that time. Ginger had a most satisfying position of teaching English to children of diplomats from the various embassies. She was grateful for this fortuitous assignment and thoroughly enjoyed the wonderful atmosphere of this charming village along the Rhine River. The shopping district was exceptional with its exquisite specialty shops, fine eateries, and beer gardens. Ginger was greatly impressed with the sense of safety in the town, the extreme civility of the German citizens, and the architectural splendor of the age-old buildings. She suggested to Jon that he someday pay her a visit there to see the beauty of the town and spend some time in her company.

Jon was delighted by Ginger's invitation and was determined that he would see her again. He was pleased that she lived in fairly close proximity to Rome because he occasionally went to Germany for organizational meetings with the leaders of the still mysterious organization that controlled his employment.

Jon returned to his apartment on winged feet with a feeling of total exhilaration. He settled into a deep, peaceful sleep only to awaken at 3:00 a.m. to see an apparition of Luz at the foot of his bed. Luz stood with arms outstretched reaching for Jon with a smile of love. This situation caused a most unsettled feeling within him and he immediately arose and placed a phone call to Luz in Arizona. He was in total shock when Zadia, Luz's daughter, informed him that Luz had been fatally injured in a car accident just a few hours ago. Jon, of course, understood what had happened because he was aware that such experiences are rather common when someone you love passes over. It seems that if someone's mind is attuned to the astral plane's frequency, as in deep concentration or sleep, a person who has died can create a clairvoyant or clairaudient experience in those they love. It's a way of saying goodbye and a statement of great love and commitment. Jon's heart heaved with remorse, but he realized in a lucid moment that death is the beginning of true life and reality.

Luz's passing caused a sense of obligation within Jon, which impelled him to attend Luz's funeral services in Scottsdale. The service was a somber, but dignified occasion. Only Luz's closest friends and family members were in attendance. As Luz lay in death's repose, each individual was allowed to speak about the significance and impact that Luz had on him or her. Some of the comments were truly inspired and approached poetic beauty. Jon provided an epitaph of exceptional meaning. He espoused her many virtues and told everyone of his great love for her. Jon concluded his soliloquy by reminding everyone that our real nature lies in our spiritual nature and the soul exists beyond physical death. Luz would continue to live in a strictly spiritual sense for she had achieved enlightenment and had certainly satisfied any karmic debt. Those in attendance politely applauded Jon's statement and walked away from Luz's body with a renewed reassurance that life is truly eternal.

Shortly after Jon's return to Rome he attended a conference at Club of Rome. The conference was a showcase for several of the young functionaries who were given this opportunity to present papers on various topics. Jon's presentation on complementary currency was received with great enthusiasm and kudos by those in attendance.

Chapter Four

- Induction into the Inner Circle
- Discovery of the Plot
- Decision to Become a Leader
- Indoctrination
- Formation of the Trinity
- Details of the Plan

Within a week after the conference Jon received a mysterious request to be present at an evening meeting in downtown Manhattan in New York City. The succinct invitation read: "You are requested to attend a meeting for review and possible changes in your employ. Be prompt and present yourself in Suite 1301 on the 13th floor of International Building at Rockefeller Center at 11:00 p.m. on March 21, 1967.

New York City was always one of Jon's favorite places to visit during his college days. Being just an hour from New Haven, New York beckoned to the Yale students whenever a night on the town seemed to be appropriate. It was a center of culture and bustled with energy like nowhere else. The decay of the city had not started, or it was not yet evident back then. Broadway teemed with wholesome activity: nightclubs like Jilly's, the Copacabana, and Toots Shors were flourishing; people walked the streets dressed in their finest regalia; the lights of theater marquees advertising Broadway plays and musicals lit up the streets; and all was wonderful in Gotham. Nothing could be finer than a Sunday spent at the Metropolitan Museum or strolling in Central Park.

Let's not forget to mention jazz, a native art form that Jon had learned to love and appreciate in his days at Yale. The Big Apple was the jazz mecca of the world, as many great jazz clubs featured stellar artists of the day. The stylings of Miles Davis, Bill Evans, Sonny Rollins, Wes Montgomery, Fredie Hubbard and the like could be heard routinely at clubs such as the Half Note, Jazz Gallery, Village Vanguard, and the Five Spot. These were halcyon days for the city that never sleeps. Jon was excited about the chance to see New York again and was hoping the meeting would be brief because he was planning to catch a 1:00 a.m. set at the Half Note where the Cannonball Adderly Quintet happened to be playing.

Jon entered Rockefeller Center surprised to find virtually no one present in the lobby. He found an operational elevator and made his way up to the 13th floor. All seemed silent and eerie as he strode through the bowels of this sleeping giant. It seemed as though he was invading the privacy of an elegant lady.

Having arrived at the designated Suite 1301 about fifteen minutes early, Jon was happy to find the entrance unlocked and a softly lit waiting room awaiting him. The furnishings were rich and reminded one of the elegance of former times. The finest leather chairs and sofas lined the walls, luxurious carpeting cradled his feet, and highly crafted antique furnishings were placed perfectly to create an atmosphere of quiet comfort and luxury. He especially admired the exceptional artwork by some of the world's most respected painters, which gave a perfect accent to the room.

Jon settled into a comfortable chair to await his call to enter the main office. Time passed slowly and no summons occurred. After ninety minutes of waiting while listening to piano music played by Glenn Gould, and reading Time magazine, Jon began to think that something might have gone amiss. He decided to wait until 1:00 a.m. before taking the initiative to try the door that separated the waiting room from the office itself. Jon walked to the door and turned its burnished brass knob, which opened to a shocking and frightful sight. As he stared from the doorway, Jon could see a gray-haired male slumped onto a magnificent mahogany desk. All was quiet as Jon went to investigate the condition of the silent figure.

The man could not be roused and when Jon felt his wrist, the corpse had no pulse. In the man's left hand, whose skin looked strangely coarse and scaly, a bottle of unopened nitroglycerin tablets was tightly held. Jon assumed the man had died suddenly of cardiac arrest as he was waiting for Jon to arrive. This situation caught Jon totally off guard, and he searched his mind for a strategy as to what to do next. He decided to look for identification on the person of the man lying before him. Upon examining the man's wallet he found a business card with the following statement, "If you find this individual either injured, unconscious, or lifeless, please call 1-800-serpent.

As directed, Jon called the number and was told to remain until a team of paramedics arrived. As Jon returned the phone receiver to the phone base, he happened to notice a leather-bound manuscript to the left of the moribund individual. The beautifully bound book's title "The Wounded Eagle" was embossed in gold lettering. Jon was deeply intrigued and fascinated by the title and succumbed to his inquisitiveness by examining its pages. As he flipped through them, he realized that he was reading a detailed plan to severely wound the United States of America (Eagle) and bring it to its eventual demise as a free country with a representative government. When Jon reached the conclusion of the book he was aghast at the goal of the plan. The plan was essentially to undermine the nation in myriad ways--politically, socially, economically, and morally. The plan had begun in 1913 and was to conclude in 2011 with the end point being the declaration of an absolute dictator and the end to all constitutional freedoms. The final event would be the only possible solution to the total chaos plaguing the nation.

Several thoughts flashed through Jon's mind. The first thought was that he must copy the plan as quickly as possible so he could have a later opportunity to study it in more detail. He noticed a copier in the next room and rushed to copy the pages of the plan. Jon also realized that he could go to no one to reveal this dastardly plan because the organization (the roundtable) had infiltrated all areas of life, from the media, military, law enforcement, unions, the judicial and, political parties.

A feeling of despair momentarily overtook Jon, which disappeared when an inspirational idea flashed through his mind as an arrow shot from above. The idea was that he could be the one to be declared dictator in 2011. Yes, yes, he decided this might be the only solution to save the world from the evil ones. As Jon was thinking of means to implement this idea, he glanced down at the individual slumped on the desk and noticed a strange change slowly occurring on the exposed areas of his skin. The skin appeared to be transforming into a scaly, reptilian look.

Just as Jon was trying to figure out what was actually going on, he heard the clamor of several individuals entering the office. They were all dressed in black and had emergency equipment and a cot, which was to be used for body removal. As they quickly covered and removed the body, Jon tightly held on to his briefcase, which held the copied pages of the plan, "The Wounded Eagle." Jon was told to remain in the office until he received a phone call, which would give him further instructions. Approximately thirty minutes later the phone's ring pierced the air. Jon answered the phone and was told to make arrangements to stay in the area for at least six months so he could have several high level meetings, which would change his life forever.

In summary, The Plan that Jon discovered and held in his briefcase, was as follows:

The Plan "The Wounded Eagle"
Introduction

The following outline is a plan to mortally injure the United States of America. The dream of a one-world system of material wealth and social harmony based strictly on pragmatic humanism has one major obstacle: the liberties of the U.S. citizenry. To effect our desired goal the United States of America must be destroyed in a gradual and systematic manner. It will take many years to erode the nation, but we are firm in our belief that with proper planning and implementation our ultimate goal will be achieved.

A word from the supreme commander to all who believe in a godless universe.

A nation that gives its citizenry the liberties and freedoms to explore and discover truths beyond materiality is an ever-present danger to the fulfillment of this plan. Therefore, the destruction of the Eagle is of paramount importance if this plan is to achieve its goal.

Written this 22nd day of December, 1913.

Signed: _____*Lucifer*_____
L. Lucifer

The Plan

The doctrine – Ordo Ab Chao (Order Out of Chaos)

The Hegelian Principle will be used as a guide for implementation of this plan.

Step 1: Create a problem
Step 2: Initiate a public reaction
Step 3: Offer a solution

The focus will be to create numerous events that will lead to chaos in the following areas: morality, politics, economics, health care, education, social order, weather, genetics, physiology, intellectualism, environment.

Appropriate solutions will be in place when the public demands corrective action. The solutions will always be an encroachment on civil freedoms—all in the name of order.

I. Economics
   A. Establish Federal Reserve Corporation as a private, secret membership and form the Federal Reserve System.
      1. Amend the Constitution to allow the female vote
      2. Encourage the feminization of society
      3. Create a demand for social programs to be funded by the government
      4. Amass enormous public debt to enrich the Federal Reserve Corporation
   B. Economic Chaos
      1. Undermine the efficient productivity of goods
         a. Overregulation by agencies of government e.g. OSHA, EPA, FTC
         b. Affirmative Action
         c. Corporate and business taxes
      2. Overtaxation of Citizens
         a. Income Tax
         b. Inheritance and Estate Taxes

3. Debase the U.S. Currency
    a. Remove Gold Standard
    b. Print Fiat Money
    c. Encourage Deficit Spending
    d. Inflate Money Supply
4. Create Bank of Rothschild in U.S.A. as the Bank of America, the logo of which is a Red (Roth) Child (Shield)
5. Allow easy credit to create massive consumer debt
6. Destroy border integrity to allow millions of illegal immigrants to enter the nation
    a. Promote the destruction of sovereignty of USA and create a Tri-lateralist America union consisting of North America, Central America and South America.
C. Create Public Dependency on certain energy systems
    1. Promote use of fossil fuels such as oil and coal
    2. Suppress the knowledge of free energy technologies, such as the concepts of Nikola Tesla regarding crystal power
D. Destroy individual property rights
    1. Overtaxation of property
    2. Eliminate lordship
    3. Overregulate via building, fire and safety codes
E. Development of China as the manufacturer of world's goods
    1. Slowly establish this goal under the guise of free trade
    2. Destroy economic viability of middle class in USA
    3. Bankrupt USA due to negative trade balances and debt due to wars
II. Social Order
A. Destruction of family structure as basic unit
    1. Encourage and promote contraception
    2. Allow easy divorce
    3. Legalize abortion
    4. Foment the sexual revolution with emphasis on pleasure in place of love
    5. Undermine the role of paternal authority
        a. Battered women's movement
        b. Children's rights

B. Undermine the three basic psychological needs of an individual in a social structure
   1. Identity
   2. Security
   3. Stimulation
C. Destroy professional class, merchant class and independent life styles and thinking
   1. Destroy professional fee structures and control reimbursements
   2. Fail to support profitability of private enterprise
   3. Encourage formation of large corporate entities
   4. Establish stifling regulation
   5. Propagandize individual practitioners so they relinquish their independence
   6. Destroy entrepreneurial social class, which is a traditional deterrent to tyranny
D. Feminization of society
   1. Emasculate paternal status in family
   2. Discourage idealism
   3. Encourage pragmatic humanism
   4. Place emphasis on emotions and sympathy—not on reason and principles
   5. Create softness in warfare and foreign policies
   6. Promote equal rights amendment to U.S. Constitution
   7. Explain the purpose of life in existential terms—not in universal terms
E. Create a culture of fear and extreme negativism
   1. Negative energy will feed the rulers of the material world, the Lords of Darkness
   2. Expose the public to a constant flow of negative images
   3. The goal is to produce a negative polarity on planet earth
F. Weaken the military
   1. Voluntary army
   2. Less rigor and discipline
   3. Female soldiers
G. Establish a sense of national guilt over the nation's history
   1. Guilt over slavery

2. Guilt of subduing Native Americans
3. Guilt over past wastefulness and exploitation of other cultures
H. Depopulation tactics
  1. Exposure to processed foods containing toxic substances, such as preservatives, dyes, hormones, additives, adjuvants
  2. Exposure to viruses in the form of bacteriophages, which will be used to treat foods
  3. Chemtrails to introduce aluminum compounds (AL2O3) into the atmosphere
    a. Create cognitive deficits in the public mind
    b. Manipulation of weather
    c. Deprive the people of the benefits of "blue" skies—a need for mental health
  4. Mandatory vaccinations will be used to weaken immune systems of the public.
I. Media Control
  1. Take control of newspapers, radio, and television
  2. Manufacture a biased and slanted delivery of news that will create a public sentiment favorable to achieving the goals of the Lords of Darkness
  3. Present constant negative images to the public. For example, emphasize crime, war, disease, destructive storms, earthquakes, volcanic activity, shortages of staples, global warming, poverty, nihilism, a lack of heroes, hopelessness
J. Perpetuation of continuous wars
  1. War is a means to developing fear. People in fear are easily managed and controlled
  2. Wars from 1913 to present—WWI, WWII, WWIII, Korea, Vietnam, Cold War, War on Terror, Armageddon
K. Radio frequency identification
  1. RFID – microchipping all people will be the "crown jewel"
  2. This technique will allow for electromagnetic control of the world population
III. Moral dissolution
A. Create culture of pleasure
  1. Sexual revolution
  2. Sensual titillation

        3. Illicit drug use to be promoted, particularly use of marijuana, cocaine, heroine
        4. Legalize gambling
        5. Sensuality and hedonism
        6. Glorification of sports figures and entertainers
        7. Body piercing and tattoos
        8. Homosexuality
        9. Pedophilia
        10. Bestiality
        11. Perversion of music and art
    B. Negate the influence of organized religion
        1. Limit public display of religious holidays
        2. Remove Christ and God from public activities
IV. Destruction of quality education
    A. Infiltration of teacher unions
    B. Changes in curriculums
        1. Frivolous courses, less rigor, grade inflation
        2. Lessen discipline
        3. Reduce demand for excellence
        4. Eliminate neighborhood schools
        5. Create early preschool to indoctrinate children
V. Intellectual bankruptcy
    A. Use of entertainment as an opiate of the public mind
    B. Titillation of five senses with emphasis on "left" mind
    C. Discourage development of the "right" mind, which can lead to spiritual awareness
    D. Corruption of music
        1. Use syncopated rhythm, which retards the upward movement of Kundalini and spiritual growth
        2. Create a music of the devil
        3. Deprive the public of melodies and give them textured noise
        4. Rock music is destructive to the balance of its listeners. It is discordant in construction and unbalanced. The advent and growth of this destructive form of music was intentional—the intention being to slow and retard human vibration and higher dimensional experience

E. Mindless television programs with emphasis on violence and sexuality, which are meant to appeal to man's lower nature
F. Encourage violence in sports
G. Encourage drug abuse and mind altering substances to promote decadence and retard spiritual awareness
H. Pornography
I. Encourage moral disintegration
   1. Self indulgence, narcissism
   2. Promiscuity
   3. Moral relativism
   4. Nihilism
   5. Promote the seven deadly sins: greed, lust, sloth, gluttony, pride, anger, envy
IV. Genocidal Plan
   A. Chlorination and fluoridation of water supplies
   B. Synthetic drugs
   C. Processed foods
   D. Stealth viruses
   E. New diseases
      1. HIV-AIDS
      2. Ebola
      3. Lyme disease
      4. Avian flu
      5. Mycoplasma pneumonia
      6. Morgellon's disease
   F. Chemtrails
   G. Radiation sources
      1. Television
      2. Microwave
      3. Cell phones
      4. Magnetic resonance
      5. Computers
   H. Vaccinations
      1. Corruption of immune systems e.g. Asthma, allergies, autoimmune diseases
      2. Neurological damage
      3. Autism

    I.   Artificial sweeteners
        1. Carcinogenic
        2. Neurotoxins
    J.   Legalize euthanasia

VII.   Development of an electromagnetic curtain around the planet.
    A. Utilization of satellite technology will create an electronic blanket to survey and control earth's inhabitants

VIII. Weather wars
    A. Scalar technology used to manipulate weather and to create destructive storms
    B. Chemtrails (geo engineering) will be used to impregnate the atmosphere with aluminum oxide particles to alter weather
    C. HAARP – high frequency auroral resonance. These electromagnetic waves can genetically alter the DNA helix. Waves with a frequency beyond 1100 MgHz can influence change and alter the characteristics of life forms. High frequency signals are designed to ionize the energy in the upper atmosphere, which consists largely of nitrogen. These signals will transform lower MgHz particle beams (435 MgHz) into higher frequencies.
        1. This technology may allow the alteration of man's genetic makeup.
        2. These facilities will be located in remote areas to avoid detection.

IX. Political Plan
    A. All major political leaders will be selected by the roundtable.
    B. Elections will appear to be free but will be controlled in all aspects
    C. Be it known that certain galactic changes may occur around 2012 AD, which may be part of a cosmic plan to take man to a higher dimension. We must initiate an accelerated thrust of the "Wounded Eagle Plan" to prevent that from ever occurring.
    D. In the year 2001 Operation Full Force will begin and will conclude in 2011 with the established goal of an absolute dictatorship
    E. Operation Full Force will require the election of an easily manipulated buffoon-like president in the year 2000. He will lead the country into chaos.
    F. In 2008 the election will be rigged to insure the election of a weak puppet president. The level of the nation's dissolution will be

raised to the point of no return. The only solution will be the end of democracy, which will be replaced by authoritarian rule.

G. The public will demand a dictator who will be of our choice.

H. Once in total control we will create a negative polarity that will prevent man from ever ascending into a higher dimension and returning to the cosmic creator.

With foreknowledge that a galactic event will occur at some point around 2012 AD, we declare the Plan will be complete by the year 2011. This will prevent all manner of change on earth and thwart the threat to our rule.

As part of the Plan we will do everything possible to encourage the dissolution of civilized and moral man by directing their focus on the seven deadly sins: lust, greed, envy, pride, sloth, gluttony, anger.

Long live Baal!

The meetings were held in New York City at Rockefeller Center and involved Jon Corbett and two other young recruits, Herman Sparkman and Ion Ampere. Their preceptor was a middle-aged man of obvious high intelligence named Caligo Mendaci. Mendaci had a certain sinister look about him. Despite his impeccable dress, his steely black eyes and angled bushy eyebrows evoked a sense of trepidation and suspicion within Jon. Each succeeding day was filled with an exhaustive ten-hour training session, which explained the origin, makeup, and purpose of the organization behind their free education and the think tanks for whom they were working. The threesome of Jon Corbett, Herman Sparkman, and Ion Ampere were somewhat surprised and yet excited to learn what really makes the world the way it is.

It was explained to this young triumvirate that they were selected to be brought into the inner circle of the organization that essentially controls the world. They had been selected as the crème de la crème of the brilliant recruits from several think tanks around the world. Their incredible talents, intelligence, dedication and character had spurred the roundtable members to recommend the threesome to be elevated into the inner circle. All three were greatly surprised at the hidden structure, which was orchestrating world events and dictating the course upon which humanity was developing.

From the very first moment of meeting one another the trio seemed to be in total accord and had a sense of amicability and unity. Jon saw them as being a wonderful complement to one another and hoped that they would develop a long-term relationship, which would then play a significant role in the future of the world.

The threesome of Jon, Herman, and Ion all came from lineages that were remarkable and helped to explain their exceptional qualities. Jon, of course, was the great grandson of gentleman Jim Corbett, who was the second heavyweight-boxing champion of the world. Herman Sparkman was the grandson of John Sparkman, who was the democratic nominee for vice president of the United States in 1952. Ion Ampere was a descendant of Andre-Marie Ampere, who was a famous French mathematician, physicist, and scientist in the early 19th century. The electrical term, ampere, is derived from Andre-Marie because of his contributions in forming theories on electricity and magnetism. Ampere's theory became fundamental for 19th century developments in electricity and magnetism.

All three were distinctive in appearance. For example, Herman was an anomaly of the time because he eschewed the casualness, the bell-bottoms and the folk rock music of the period. He had a clean-cut look, accentuated by a meticulously styled short hairstyle. Herman dressed in a conservative way and always chose well-tailored, tasteful clothing. He epitomized his given name, Herman, by incorporating the best of both genders. He balanced the characteristics of a dual nature by showing the passive/active, the preservative/creative and the pragmatic/ideal. Highly intelligent, spiritually aware and thoroughly schooled in the liberal arts, he had a great capacity to communicate his ideas to all those who would listen.

Ion, on the other hand, was more of a rebel with a longish hairstyle, controversial views on the nature of the universe and man's place in it, as well as a commitment to elevate his fellow man to a new awareness and paradigm. He seemed to represent the idea that man is made in the image of God. It was his personal view that "the part is the whole" and that we are all fragments of the creator (God) with an ability to know that oneness.

114

Jon was a perfect balance of the other two. Extremely handsome, yet not at all self-absorbed, he was the quintessential man who understood man's potentiality of knowing the cosmic Christ within. Jon was the most advanced in spiritual awareness because of his mystical training from Luz Barca. All three, however, were in agreement that the true reality was not the material world. They held these views privately because to espouse them to their peers would definitely jeopardize their positions within the organization and possibly life itself.

After several months of intensive indoctrination and training, Jon, Herman and Ion were designated for assignment. Herman Sparkman was assigned to the United States delegation at the United Nations in New York City. Ion Ampere was given an advisory position in a fledgling organization, the Trilateral Commission, and was to be stationed in the Tokyo headquarters. The Trilateral Commission was set up as a public offshoot of the Council of Foreign Relations (CFR). Its members represented the power brokers of Europe, Asia and America. The goal of the TLC was a one-world state with a trilateral (America, Europe and Asia) economic network. Jon was to further develop his currency theories at World Bank headquarters in Brussels, Belgium. As a reflection of his excellent reputation within the organization, he was placed in a highly responsible position for such a young man.

To celebrate the completion of their training and elevation into the upper levels of management the three went to dinner at a great French restaurant on Third Avenue in New York City. Copain was noted for its quiet atmosphere and excellent cuisine. It was Jon's suggestion that they celebrate at Copain. He had grown to love and fully appreciate this exceptional restaurant by having patronized it several times over the past six months, and was anticipating a great meal of escargot, veal Francais and a fine Beaujolais wine.

The young triumvirate had become great friends and learned to trust and confide in one another. Conversation over the meal started in a polite, superficial direction until Jon directed it down a more serious path. Emboldened by several glasses of wine, he found the courage to ask Herman and Ion what their reactions were to the revelation that one powerful organization actually controlled world events. Once all agreed that the goals of the one-worlders were antithetical to their core beliefs,

Jon was secure in making a proposal that was not only brave but also ingenious in many ways.

Jon convinced Herman and Ion that the three could change the course of humankind by exposing and ridding the world of the hidden forces that were directing man into a godless world of stifling density and strict materiality. Jon's idea was based on the concept of the mystical number of three. It was his thought that they could develop a counter group within the organization by taking the original trinity and increasing the number of secret members by having each one recruit two others of like minds. The network would grow from three to nine, then to twenty-seven, eighty-one, two hundred forty-three, etc. The projected number of eventual members would be several million around the world. Jon explained that if they could achieve a critical mass of enough individuals with one shared belief of the true reality, that all of human consciousness would be swept into the same belief. This belief would then lift man into the Augustinian City of God where all would be Christ-like and live in peace, harmony, love and abundance. The ascendancy would in actuality be the second coming!

The basis of Jon's plan was the theory of the 100th monkey. The idea is that if you teach a monkey a certain task and a second monkey observes this and performs the task, subsequent monkeys will do the same thing. The process would continue until a critical mass developed which would result in all the monkeys in the world doing the task because the collective mind would have allowed every monkey to attain such knowledge.

"Brilliant," Ion exclaimed.

Herman concurred and said, "Let's do it!"

The three raised their glasses of Beaujolais together in affirmation of their new bond and commitment. As their glasses remained aligned as one Jon stated, "To real truth—the part is the whole—all is one."

The toast became their motto as all finished their drinks with one affirmative swallow.

The next night the threesome had the first of several meetings, which would define the counterspy brotherhood known as the "Brethren of Light." Since Jon, Herman and Ion were required to report to their respective assignments within two weeks, the new trinity did not have much time to organize its secret society. They decided to meet daily so they could fully develop an organizational structure, compose a constitution, create a central theme of core beliefs and teachings, plan a worldwide network of members, and formulate plans for the year 2011, which would allow a takeover from the globalist cabal.

The first order of business at the initial gathering was Jon's discussion of the Wounded Eagle Plan, which he had purloined six months earlier. Ion and Herman were flabbergasted by the intricate detail and sinister nature of the plan. This was their first exposure to the possibility of such a conspiracy existing. As they listened to Jon explain the various segments of the Plan, their determination to fight it mounted with each revelation. When Jon concluded his description, all three swore their commitment and pledged to defeat the Lords of Darkness and to lift mankind to a higher plane.

Subsequent meetings dealt with the following:

Organizational structure of Brethren of Light

1. Trilateral System with three chapters in the world

- Kingdom chapter in Asia to be headed by Ion
- Power chapter in Europe with Jon as leader
- Glory chapter in America to be led by Herman

2. Subdivisions of regional temples or loosely organized cells located in major cities around the world

   a. Temples to be fueled by smaller organizational groups of 3, 7 or 12. The size of these groups will be determined by population densities in their respective locations

      i. The numbers 3, 7 and 12 are reflective of mystical numbers and insure success based on that truth

3. Four different levels of membership

    a. Novices (apprentices)
    b. Fellows (professed brothers)
    c. Masters
    d. Perfected Masters

4. Ten degrees. Each of the first three levels will have three degrees each. Progress through the chain of elevation will require completion of the teachings in each degree. The final level of perfected master will be reached after completing the last and tenth degree.
5. All meetings will be in secret locations and at random times. Such tactics are meant to avoid detection by the Lords of Darkness

The Constitution will consist of several articles defining the purpose and requirements of the membership.

Article One:	The Order is to be known as the Brethren of Light
Article Two:	Founding members of the Brethren of Light and all future members pledge to fulfill the conditions in all articles of this constitution
Article Three:	The duration of the brethren is unlimited
Article Four:	The Brethren of Light is a secret society. All its information, decrees and records are not to be available to anyone outside the membership
Article Five:	The Brethren is open to all adult persons who are in agreement with its aims and accept the obligations of membership
Article Six:	All members have the right to one vote. On admittance a member must agree to serve the brethren in all circumstances and promise to further the aims of peace and universal love.

To insure anonymity and the protection of its members, only appropriate contacts should be made. Discussions should be carried out in groups of three, seven or twelve (this reflects the power within divine mathematical order). Each group should formulate a statement of purpose. Eventually, the perfect one will form and a larger awareness will occur due to the fusion of input from all groups. Let us be reminded that when in divine harmony, thought becomes a manifesting power unto itself.

The Brethren has an awesome responsibility because we hold the key to preventing the intended horror of a godless, fascist, strictly material world. If we succeed it will be because we have adhered to the universal laws of attraction and focused intent, which will allow a world of balance and harmony.

The basic philosophy and teachings of the Brethren will be based on the age-old tenets of the Gnostic, Essenes, Rosicrucian's, Druids and the Atlantean "Law of One." A text known as the "Course in Miracles" will be required reading and will be an important foundation in teaching the following principles: unconditional love, non-judgmentalism, separation from the true reality is a product of the ego. Atonement is perfect love and the means to healing; miracles occur when one finally accepts the truth; each individual is an expression of God and we are made in the image of God; creation is a giant hologram; a hologram is a 3-D image of laser light and energy; each individual has a personal hologram that must be completed to achieve salvation; completion results when one does God's will.

The Plan for the takeover and the beginning of the cleansing reign will begin in the year 2011 AD.

The strategy to remove the evil ones from power will be implemented on October 13, 2011 at a coordinated time throughout the world. (This is similar to the arrest and incarceration of the Knights Templar by Papal forces on October 13, 1307). All will be taken into custody and incarcerated in camps, which they actually built to imprison dissenters to their original plan to imprison mankind. There will be no cruel treatment of these prisoners; they will be treated with care and compassion. They will be given the opportunity to learn the principles of the Law of One in the hope that they too will become spiritually aware and be able to rise with all of mankind when the omega point is reached in 2012.

The pledge to entrance into the Brethren of Light:
"I give you to the Holy Spirit
a part of myself
I know that you will be released
Unless I want to use you
To imprison myself
In the name of my freedom
I choose your release,
Because I recognize that
We will be released together
The official motto of the Brethren of Light:
"To real truth--the part is the whole--all is one."

Having completed the task of defining their secret society, Jon, Herman and Ion felt confident that they had established a foundation that would support the enduring nature of the Brethren of Light. They pledged their love and commitment and promised to dedicate their lives to the expressed aims of the organization. All three were to leave for their respective assignments the next day, so they parted that night to begin the march to their final destination.

On Jon's last day in New York he decided to spend time at St. Patrick's Cathedral before taking a cab to Kennedy International Airport for his flight to World Bank Headquarters in Brussels, Belgium. He enjoyed moments of quiet contemplation in this remarkable spiritual place and was looking to commune with the God mind for inspiration and guidance.

As Jon was in the Cathedral his preceptor, Caligo Mendaci, whose office in the International Building of Rockefeller Center overlooked the Cathedral, decided to leave for lunch. It just so happened that when Jon exited the church, Caligo was walking out of Rockefeller Center. Caligo glanced across Fifth Avenue and noticed Jon Corbett as he walked down the church steps. Seeing Jon leaving a church severely unnerved Caligo because he had grown to admire and trust in Jon throughout the indoctrination period. Mendaci became immediately suspicious of Jon and questioned in his own mind why Jon would have visited the Cathedral. He made a mental note to make a concerted effort to always keep tabs on Jon's career. It was his intent to safeguard the organization from any traitorous activity on Jon's part.

Chapter Five

- Jon's career at the World Bank
- Jon Meets His Future Wife
- Bohemian Grove
- Jon's Role As Ambassador and Congressman

Jon's first days at the World Bank Headquarters in Brussels were quite significant because he quickly gained the respect of the world bank community by demonstrating his great intelligence and insight in all financial, political and social matters. He was quickly given the responsibility of developing methods of seeking to uplift the downtrodden, undeveloped nations of the world. It was Jon's belief that providing massive amounts of capital to these nations would be the primary means of establishing economic stability, which, in turn, would lead to intellectual growth and equitable social order. On paper the plan offered great promise, but in practice major flaws were to develop. For one, the lack of sophistication amongst the peoples of the Americas and Africa made it difficult to implement growth in spite of the infusion of capital. Internecine and tribal jealousies, lack of appreciation for higher moral values and incessant corruption prevented forward progress in achieving the intended goals of massive bank loans to the undeveloped nations. In addition, without the anticipated growth, the ability to repay principal and interest on the loans placed these nations in greater peril because their indebtedness was crippling to their financial status. Jon was dismayed over the failure of these loan programs, but he also understood that without a spiritual component there could never be social and economic growth. Unfortunately, the pragmatic humanism philosophy that permeated the World Bank organization precluded the inclusion of any spiritual influx into these programs. Jon was hamstrung in this regard because it would have been disastrous to his position if he were to reveal his true beliefs and strong spiritual leanings.

In spite of the lack of success in the area of loans to undeveloped nations, Jon's stature in the globalist community was not at all reduced. This was evidenced when in 1972 he was appointed to be a member of a special advisory committee designed to find a way for the United States of America to extricate itself from the Vietnam conflict. His contributions to the committee's study were well appreciated and beneficial in finding an escape from the disastrous Southeast Asian foreign policy blunder.

Jon's status continued to grow, especially in the minds of the state department. As a result of his excellent reputation, the Secretary of State offered Jon a regional directorship in the Agency for International Development (AID). The year was 1974 and Jon decided to accept the challenge to become someone who could be responsible for demonstrating that a poor, undeveloped country could actually lift itself off the poverty floor. It was Jon's conviction that if he could subtly insert the spiritual element into a growth plan, real success would result. As a student of history Jon knew that societies achieve order and harmony when they have a spiritual communion with the universal creator's will and have values consistent with natural law. It seems that all institutions, whether they be economic, social or political, fall into entropic chaos when they divorce themselves from the spirit. The country of Chad in Africa was to be Jon's assignment and his station was the capital of N'Djamena.

Jon embraced his position with great fervor and took advantage of his autonomy and relative isolation in managing the development program in the remote land of Chad. Over a period of six years Jon's hands-on management technique and his ability to gain the complete reverence and respect of the Chadian people enabled the country to show unparalled improvement by lifting it to heretofore unprecedented economic strength. The real impetus behind this success was the installation of spiritual awareness as a part of educational programs. Once the people had a foundation of faith and belief it became much easier to build an economic and social edifice that could stand on its own.

Jon was recognized for his great achievement in Chad with several awards. It was a result of his growing reputation that he was elevated to the position of Deputy Ambassador to West Germany in 1980. This new promotion was a fortuitous stroke of fate because he was going to be living in Bad Gotesburg, the same village that was home to Ginger Baker, the woman he had met some twelve years earlier while he was working for the Egalitaire Foundation in Rome.

Jon had never forgotten Ginger and had stayed in touch with her with an occasional letter or phone call. He even managed to visit her a few times when he was in Bonn on World Bank or State Department business. Jon was elated to have the opportunity to reestablish a relationship with a woman he knew he could really love.

Ginger received news of Jon's assignment with absolute joy. She had known on their first meeting at the Trevi Fountain in Rome that he was the only man she would ever want as a husband. This may have been the subconscious reason that she had never allowed any serious relationship to develop over the twelve years subsequent to their first meeting.

Bad Gotesburg housed several large embassies and thousands of people in the diplomatic corps. The charm and the intimacy of the village captured Jon's heart, as he truly cherished everything about it.

Jon often reflected on his first visit when he stayed in the Zum Adler Hotel, which was centrally situated in the commercial area. The hotel had a solid, Teutonic feel to it—highly efficient and in perfect order. That first stay was highlighted by a memorable morning when Jon arose at 5:00 a.m. and decided to take a stroll through town. It was an experience unique to him. The slumbering community was just awakening, even though the sun had not yet brightened the morn. Bakers, butchers, and grocers were placing their fresh products out for display as Jon strolled through town absorbing the energy of the community. So impressed was Jon by the civility, order, cordiality and professionalism of the native people that it gave him pause as he realized he was actually experiencing a quintessential community--ideal in every way. Why couldn't all people live in this manner? He wondered. Life would be so much more agreeable and satisfying if mankind could live in such idyllic harmony.

Among the features of Bad Gotesburg that left an indelible imprint on Jon's mind were the beautifully appointed specialty shops, the distinctive architecture of both commercial and residential areas, the fresh produce, pastries and meats found in various shops, the staid professionalism of the apothecaries, the sense of community, the gossamer lightness of the town's atmosphere and, last but not least, the wonderful *biergartens* and great eateries. Jon's favorite restaurant was Valtillena's, which was known for its warm ambience and delicious Italian cuisine. He spent many a night of frivolity, conversation, and dining on good food at Valtillena's.

Bad Gotesburg was the epitome of an international community. It was a vibrant collection of people from every part of the globe. Africans, Asians, Polynesians, South Americans, Kiwis from New Zealand, Aussies from Australia, and diplomatic leaders all shared in the eclectic paradise.

Whether young or old, male or female, everyone seemed to enjoy walking or bicycling around town or along the Rhine River. Jon and Ginger's favorite thing to do was to take a Sunday stroll along the Rhine with a short respite at the Dressen Hotel for a cognac before returning home.

Soon after establishing his residence in a palatial home provided by the embassy, a whirlwind courtship with Ginger ensued. The two realized that they were destined to be man and wife and decided to marry as soon as possible. They set a matrimonial date just six months after Jon's arrival in Germany.

The wedding was a magical affair from beginning to end. The ceremony was held in the Chapel of Nonnenwerth School, located on a small island in the middle of the Rhine River. Attendees had just a short drive from Bad Gotesburg and were actually ferried to the island where they witnessed the most beautiful of bonding rituals. The majesty and loving power of the event overwhelmed those in attendance, including the priest who could not restrain tears of joy from flowing down his cheeks. As the crowd gathered outside the chapel for polite conversation and celebratory cigars, a flock of pure white doves was released to fly into a cloudless sky. It was a perfect final touch to a perfect marriage ceremony.

The wedding party and guests then proceeded to a magnificient building, The Redoute in downtown Bad Gotesburg. Beautifully designed with marble floors and crystal chandeliers, the Redoute had served as a concert hall for notables such as Beethoven and other artists. A wonderful hour of champagne and conviviality followed, which was backed by the incredible piano stylings of Kaiser Ladd, a highly acclaimed native artist. Everyone was then given a three-hour break to refresh themselves, only to return to the Redoute for a party to end all parties.

The coupling of Jon and Ginger was representative of good marriages in many ways. Both realized that love is more than emotion; it's a commitment to one another. They agreed that their espousal was a sacred, indissoluble union; they shared deep spiritual beliefs, enjoyed the fine arts, loved participation in physical activities such as golf, hiking and biking. The marriage was soon blessed with a son, Christian, who was born in 1982. A daughter, Christine, followed in 1984.

Jon embraced his roles as a husband and father. He made every effort to fulfill his purpose as a husband by never profaning the holy union with Ginger and as a father by molding his offspring into children of God with a sense of duty, purpose and responsibility. Both children were prepared for life by exposure to great literature, music, art, drama, and philosophy from an early age. Jon sought to balance their upbringing with involvement in sport and meditation as well. He relished his responsibility as a dad, as did Ginger as a mother. Ginger had given up her teaching career and assumed the role of teaching her children the practical aspects of life: cleanliness, courtesy, etiquette, proper grooming, how to dress, punctuality, and more. For all appearances the Corbetts were the ideal family, the type to which all families could aspire.

Jon's career as Deputy Ambassador took a huge leap forward when he was designated as a chief negotiator with the Soviet Union during the period of détente. His stalwart efforts were considered to be the impetus behind one of the great achievements of President Ronald Reagan's administration--the demolition of the Berlin Wall. Jon's efforts were highly appreciated by the president and the state department and this esteemed reputation led to Jon's appointment to a full ambassadorship to West Germany in 1984.

Jon also led a clandestine life. He headed the European power chapter of the Brethren of Light. He held this position from his early days in Brussels at the World Bank, through his days in Chad (although to a lesser degree because of the removed, African location), and then in full authority on his return to Europe. The brotherhood was highly secretive and exercised extreme caution in all aspects of their behavior in order to avoid discovery. The membership had grown exponentially since its inception in 1974. By the year 1984 nearly 800,000 brothers were in the fold in Europe alone. Herman in America and Ion in Asia had also done their jobs well, as the worldwide membership had reached three million in November.

It just so happened in 1983 that Jon would fortuitously meet two individuals at a secret brethren conference who would have a tremendous impact on his life and the strength of the brotherhood. The first was a converted Nazi named Otto Skorenzy who provided invaluable information on how the Nazis had infiltrated the United States and had a powerful influence within its government. Skorenzy recounted how a U.S. Senator in the 1950s by the name of Prescott Plante was a veiled Nazi who had entered the United States years earlier to target the scientific genius, Nikola Tesla. It was Plante's assignment to purloin Tesla's technology and provide the Nazis with his advanced secrets. It was poor Nikola's fate to be eventually murdered in 1943 by Skorenzy and Reinhardt Gehlin, a former Chief German SS Officer and CIA recruit. Upon hearing the name Prescott Plante, it occurred to Jon that

Prescott was the grandfather of G. W. Plante, the Yale student whom Jon had confronted many years before. It would be many years before Jon would realize the Nazi link to G. W. Plante, but once that realization occurred Jon's comprehension of the forces that controlled the course of history became greatly enhanced. It took all of Jon's loving heart to be able to tolerate Skorenzy's presence and to forgive him, but he believed Skorenzy was truly repentant for Nazi crimes against God and man. For that matter, Skorenzy was an invaluable source of information that would help the Brethren of Light in their fight to save the world from the satanic forces and the Orwellian World the Luciferians wished to create.

The second individual who would have a great impact on the course of events was a retired U.S. Army General named Colin Grant. Grant had discovered the dastardly aims of the world's hidden government many years earlier. He had dedicated himself to the downfall of this sinister cabal and sought to do all in his power to achieve this aim. Jon developed a strong bond with General Grant and the two decided to establish a second order within the Brethren of Light. This new order would be called the Brethren of Might and would be comprised of military personnel who would be the power source that would implement the final plan to overthrow, arrest, and incarcerate the evil ones. With the addition of the Brethren of Might, Jon felt that this final piece to the puzzle would make it fully feasible for them to accomplish the ultimate end of the cleansing reign—the resurrection of the Christ within all of mankind!

Upon becoming a full ambassador, Jon Corbett had achieved a heightened status in the elitist organization that controlled world events. This new position qualified him to be invited to attend events at Bohemiam Grove, a remote and relatively secret location in California. The "Grove" was in Sonoma County, seventy-five miles north of San Francisco and encompassed twenty-seven hundred acres.

Bohemian Grove was an encampment with accommodations to house several hundred attendees at July summer camp for a two-week period. The expressed purpose of this event was to allow the world's elites a means of gathering to plan their agenda to control world events and perpetuate a new world order--a world order that would be antithetical to the ideas of sovereign nations and to the personal freedoms and liberties of world citizens, the children of God. In addition, the Grove provided an opportunity for the elites to engage in perverse sexual acts, sacrificial rites, satanic adoration and ceremonies, and all manner of debauched activities.

The long entrance road to the Grove winds its way through the great California Sequoias and brings one to the elaborate encampment structures and facilities of this secret place. Jon was shocked to see so many world leaders, famous entertainers and government functionaries in attendance. However, most surprising of all was a giant forty-foot stone idol of the pagan god, Baal, which was situated below a seven-story apartment complex. The idol was massive in size and was topped by what appeared to be the head of an owl with two pointed ears.

Some measure of trepidation filled Jon, for he, like most first time visitors, had no prior knowledge of the nature and purpose of the Grove. Questions filled his mind as he was taken on an introductory tour, which explained the history of its members, the sons of Belial, the significance of certain ritual ceremonies, the location of secret rooms of perversion, the schedule and protocol of events, expected social behavior within the Grove community, and the arrangement and pecking order of the seven levels of apartments. As they walked past several large oaken doors Jon noticed calligraphic signs signifying the names of the rooms within: the dark room, the leather room, the necrophilia room and the underground lounge. A fellow who was in the tour group confided in Jon that he had heard these rooms were reserved for the upper echelons of the membership and were used for the most debauched activity imaginable. His name was Joel Coward and judging from the look on his face he was truly scared. The look did not belie his name. He went on to tell Jon that it was rumored that some in attendance actually had reptilian characteristics, worshiped Satan, and fed off of fetal blood and negative energy. It was the intention of the sons of Belial, he said, to create a culture of fear punctuated by negative emotions such as anger, hatred, stress, and guilt, all of which created a low vibrational energy, which in turn sustained them.

Jon considered Coward's statements to be beyond belief but he did give a small measure of credence to them. After all, didn't the biblical book of Enoch mention the Nefilim race that was of another world, had reptilian characteristics and sought to subjugate humanity? If it were really true, Jon thought his ultimate goal of being a great leader had gained more significance. Consequently, he introspectively reaffirmed his commitment to becoming that leader who would awaken mankind to the true reality.

At the conclusion of the tour the newest attendees were told they would be expected to attend the opening ceremony that evening. The atmosphere was one of immense excitement as the participants filed into designated positions prior to the ceremony. Suddenly a giant blaze was ignited at the foot of the idol and the more experienced members began to chant in strange guttural hissing sounds. Jon and Joel Coward were looking quizzically at one another when the chanting abruptly ended, as none other than Caligo Mendaci strode out unto the podium to welcome everyone and to announce the official opening of the two-week conference. Mendaci, of course, was the mentor and indoctrinator who had taught Jon, Herman, and Ion about the nature of the organization, which was planning to dominate the world. Several speakers, all of whom were dressed in hooded, red satin robes gave brief speeches, after which the ceremony was transformed into a social gathering with free flowing alcoholic beverages and circles of playful conversation.

Caligo Mendaci was circulating through the crowd when he noticed Jon Corbett. He immediately approached him and enthusiastically welcomed him to the Grove. The two reminisced about their time together in New York twelve years before. Mendaci was a closet pervert who had developed an infatuation with Jon those many years ago. He had never made his attraction known, but he thought the present situation was a perfect opportunity to make a play for a homosexual tyryst, to which end he invited Jon to visit him the following evening. Caligo, of course, didn't reveal his true intentions but used the pretext of having a discussion of various political and social issues.

When Mendaci answered Jon's knock at the door of his fifth floor apartment wearing nothing more than a bathrobe, Jon was somewhat surprised and questioned Caligo as to why he was inappropriately dressed. Caligo brushed off the question with a lame excuse that he didn't have time to dress. Caligo's robe was of obvious high quality and had the Grove's logo and motto embroidered over the left breast. The logo was a standing owl with the motto "Weaving spiders come not here" encircling the owl. Jon queried Caligo about the logo and was given an explanation of its history and meaning. While talking, Caligo offered Jon a scotch whiskey and told him to settle in and relax for an evening of conversation.

The discussion proceeded on a seemingly innocent track as Caligo explained his personal history and the origin of his name. It seems that his pedophilic father was a Luciferian who revered the Roman Emperior Caligula, one of the sickest, most debauched figures in human history. The surname Mendaci stemmed from a notorious family history of deceivers and liars. Jon and Caligo laughed over the amusement of a name. Mendaci decided that this soft moment was a strategic time for him to make his move. He began by mentioning that he had seen Jon leaving St. Patrick's Cathedral just prior to Jon's departure for his first major assignment at the world bank. He questioned Jon about his religious leanings and warned him that unless Jon engaged in a homosexual act he would be compelled to expose him as a believer and destroy his career. As Caligo talked his lechery seemed to transform his appearance; his eyes turned black and gazed on Jon with a penetrating look. Suddenly, Caligo leaped to his feet and opened his bathrobe, revealing himself in a state of semi-arousal. Jon was aghast at the sight and immediately got up to exit the apartment. Rushing past a surprised Mendaci, Jon reached the balcony only to find Mendaci on the floor clutching at his right leg. Jon looked down at Mendaci with pity as Mendaci pleaded, "Don't go, don't go; I need you; I need you." Jon fought his way out of Mendaci's grasp, only to have Mendaci get up and pursue him down the walkway. Incensed by the audaciousness of the abhorrent situation, Jon abruptly stopped his flight, turned and delivered a powerful punch to Mendaci's jaw. It was a punch that resembled his great grandfather's right cross and was delivered with such force that Mendaci reeled from the impact. As he staggered half-conscious, Mendaci had the misfortune of falling against the balcony railing with enough force to cause the railing to give way. Jon watched in horror as Mendaci tumbled through the air to his death below. Mendaci landed on the pointed left ear of the idol below and lay there impaled. As John viewed the scene from above he noticed Mendaci's appearance begin to change. His countenance was transmuting into a reptilian-like look. It reminded Jon of the time he had discovered the dead man at Rockefeller Center back in 1967. He wondered about these coincidental changes as he fled the scene to his apartment several floors below.

Mendaci's death was deemed to be accidental and his body was quickly dispatched. No one had the slightest suspicion that Jon Corbett had been involved.

In Jon's mind, justice was served because Mendaci's depraved mind did not deserve to survive. Not an iota of guilt was felt within Jon's heart for he felt that Mendaci had caused his own death because of his lustful indulgences. Jon understood the universal karmic law of cause and effect and realized that Mendaci's death was, in essence, a universal statement. Caligo just had to go.

Jon waited in his apartment for several minutes until attendees started to come out to investigate the commotion that occurred after Mendaci's impalement. As dozens milled about conjecturing about what may have precipitated this tragic event, Jon joined the throng and cleverly voiced total surprise and sadness over the loss of his former teacher.

As ladders were being placed so climbers could ascend to the idol's head for removal of the body, Mendaci emitted his last sound, a frightening wail reminiscent of a primitive reptilian guttural, hissing sound. The dying statement echoed through the redwood forest of Bohemian Grove and dissipated into the universal sky.

Mendaci's pierced and strangely transmuted body was removed and cremated the following day. The ritual was strikingly occult in nature and like no other Jon had ever seen. There seemed to be little remorse by those in attendance who matter of factly accepted the death of their colleague.

As Jon retired to his apartment following the cremation ceremony, he could not extricate the haunting memory of the sound of Mendaci's death wail and the transformation of his body. Jon ruminated over all that had happened in the short time he had been at the Grove. It was overwhelming to consider that it was just the beginning of future shocks that he might face in the two-week conference. He eventually fell into a fitful sleep. It did little to restore him and left him in a state of general fatigue, which he would have to overcome on day three.

The following day a schedule of seminars commenced that were designed to inform the members about the plans to eventually take total control of the planet earth. Among those in attendance were many political figures, including past presidents, former cabinet members, banking czars, media tycoons, scientists, well-known entertainers and even

G.W. Plante, the same jerk that Jon had encountered years ago at Yale University.

Prior to the start of the first seminar, all newcomers were assigned a big brother whose function was to act as a personal teacher and role model. Jon's big brother was a man named Richard Gehlin, the son of a former Nazi SS chief. Gehlin took Jon under his wing and told Jon that they were expected to have dinner together each evening. These shared meals allowed the big brother time to thoroughly acquaint newcomers with the secrets, plans and philosophies of the illumined ones. Illumined ones! What a joke, Jon thought. These self-ordained Satanists are the furthest from illumination and God's light that is humanly possible.

Even though Jon had prior knowledge of many of the areas wherein the globalists were seeking to undermine man's moral standards, political stability and economic well being, he was shocked to learn of the detail and depth of their plans. The itinerary of lectures consumed several hours every day and were to continue during the remaining two-week period. The evenings, following dinner, were reserved for various rituals and ceremonies, which glorified their reverence for the pagan god, Baal (Belial). Many of the participants prided themselves in being the "sons of Belial," true Satanists whose beliefs were totally godless and who placed complete emphasis on hedonistic and materialistic pursuits. Perverse sexual activities, unconscionable sacrificial rites (including the drinking of human blood), and an attitude of absolute disdain for all moral absolutes were a common thread that ran through the fabric of this brotherhood. Remarkably, Jon was able to endure the pain and horror of all that he was observing while remaining steadfast in not revealing his true beliefs.

On the first day Jon attended lectures on the following topics: history and origins of the sons of Belial; the ultimate goal to create a godless, fascistic material world that would feature a neo-feudal system of wealth and power for the elites and subjugation of the masses of humanity, who were to be the serfs of the new world Orwellian order; and thirdly a broad overview of the implementation of the measures necessary to effect the massive changes needed to manifest the eventual success of their strategies.

The first dinner with Jon's big brother, Richard Gehlin, was a real eye opener. Gehlin broached several topics and each was more startling than the previous one. For example, he explained that lower level members were excluded from the most extreme activities, activities that involved human sacrifice, the drinking of blood, sado-masochistic perversions, and the exploitation of mind-controlled slaves. Jon was incredulous as to what he was hearing. He queried Gehlin as to why anyone would drink human blood. Gehlin replied that many of the elites were actually hybrids who had reptilian as well as human genes, and that these hybrids required human blood because it maintained a holographic human energy field via vibrational energy thereby allowing these non-human beings to maintain human form. Jon had heard of such beings, who could shift-shape from human to reptilian form, but never imagined that they could possibly exist. Gehlin further explained that the sons of Belial dated back to ancient Atlantean times and that the obelisk in reality represented the reproductive shaft of Baal. They have used this symbol throughout the world as a veiled Luciferian statement of their adoration of Baal and the ever-present significance of the pagan God. Jon realized that humanity was about to be shafted in the most vile of ways and that he deeply appreciated the urgency of his predicted destiny in reversing the evil plans of the sons of Baal. He recalled his experience in the Great Pyramid when it was foretold that he would someday bring mankind to a new spiritual awareness. The forces of fate were seemingly in process and it was becoming apparent to him that the Bohemian Grove experience was but another step on this long journey towards the true reality and the resurrection of the planet.

Gehlin continued his discussion that first night they were together by introducing Jon to many secrets of the organization. One startling story was of how the 20th century Nazis had infiltrated America prior to World War II and had great influence within American politics even after the war. High-level Nazis were recruited to the USA and played major roles in developing the CIA, biologic warfare laboratories, NASA, and mind-control facilities. Most fascinating was the account of how the family of G.W. Plante was actually a Nazi family. The grandfather of G.W. had been a Nazi representative, who came to America, changed his German name from Scherf to Plante and then infiltrated the laboratory of the scientific genius, Nikola Tesla. He, along with his son George, purloined many of Tesla's ingenious ideas and passed them on to the Nazis back in Germany. Gehlin went on to say that his own father and another Nazi murdered Tesla in 1943. Another astonishing tale described how evil elements had infiltrated the Vatican. When discovered by Pope John Paul I in 1978 they had to murder the Pope after just one month in office.

As Jon returned to his apartment to retire for the night, his mind was flooded with the torrent of information to which he had been exposed. His mind raced to find a solution to the immense threat to humanity that promised to extinguish the world as it was known. He concluded that he would have to muster all the forces of the Brethren of Light and Might and inform them of the urgency of their mission. Jon decided that upon his return to Germany he would convene all leaders of the Brethren to a high level, secret conference with the intent of finalizing the details of the ultimate plan to free the world of evil.

Subsequent to the first day of lectures, each day found revelatory presentations on a variety of topics that further reinforced Jon's fears for the world. Some of the subjects covered in these lectures were as follows:

- The need to institute operation "full force" in 2001, which would lead to a total takeover of the U.S.A. and all world governments.
- Fabrication of wars and gross trade imbalances, designed to undermine the economic viability of the U.S.A.
- Debasement of currency by inflating the money supply with the intent of making life unaffordable for the average citizen. This strategy would allow the fascist state to take absolute power over a weak and malleable populace.
- Opening China to the western world and making China the main source of manufactured products by exploiting a cheap labor force.
- Undermining the sovereignty of all nations with emphasis on the U.S.A. by encouraging porous borders. Ultimately a trilateral world would be formed, consisting of the European Union, American Union, and the Asian Union.
- Developing technologies to control weather, to create violent storms, earthquakes, and volcanic activity with the aim of destroying private properties and small communities. By placing people in weakened economic situations and forcing them into concentrated population areas, the central authority would have a firmer, controlling grip on the masses. Areas to be developed

involved chemical seeding of the atmosphere and electromagnetic energy systems.

- Destruction of the small business community, individual farms, professional health practices of pharmacy, individual medical offices, leading to eventual corporate control of all business enterprises. The final solution would be achieved when just five corporations controlled each major industry worldwide.
- Control of the food supply and distribution of food.
- Exposure of the population to toxic food additives and genetically modified foods.
- Creation of food crises and shortages by causing plant and animal disease with the use of bio-engineered pathogens, such as wheat fungus.
- Increase in the public's reliance on synthetic drugs and their inherent toxicities. Propagandize the belief that only drugs cure disease.
- Restriction of nutritional, herbal, and holistic therapies.
- Creation of hysteria and panic over global warming by deflecting the real cause to the false idea of a man-made crisis. Environmentalism used in a doctrinal manner to change a free life style into a centrally controlled way of life.
- Mind control projects and the use of mind-controlled subjects in "necessary" assassinations, mass murders, and the creation of sexual slaves to be exploited for the pleasure of the elites of the world.

A brief history of mind control projects was presented, projects that detailed how, following World War II, Project Paperclip had sponsored the resettlement of two thousand high-level Nazis into the United States. These individuals brought the technology of mind control, biologic warfare and rocketry with them.

Joseph Mengele, the infamous "Angel of Death," was one of nine hundred military and medical scientists secretly brought into the United States, where he continued his research in the black arts and helped develop mind control laboratories. These early projects evolved into the CIA projects Blue Bird and Artichoke, which in 1953 became Mikultra

136

(manufacturing killers utilizing lethal trade craft assassinations). Mikultra employed a wide variety of techniques ranging from biology, pharmacology, psychology, ESP and lasers.

More recently programs in developing multiple personalities were being produced. Multiple personalities are characterized by:

- Two or more distinct personalities
- Identities that recur and take control of a person's behavior
- The inability to recall personal information when one is in another personality.

The phenomenon of multiple personalities has been dubbed the secret holocaust. Known in military circles as the Monarch Project, it was designed to produce slaves and targeted the young people of America. These techniques victimize younger individuals and produce a horde of children whose souls are crushed, who spy, whore, kill and commit suicide. Many are used as subjects in satanic rituals involving torture and perverse sexual activity.

Alternative personalities are used to act as couriers, drug smugglers, or assassins. The personalities are maintained by repeated use of stun guns, hypnosis and drugs, which block out the memory of previous actions. The aim is to bring a one world governmental order in which elite families control all things. They believe the planet is overpopulated and must be depopulated. Their plans include every measure imaginable such as biologic/chemical warfare, psychological techniques, food shortages, disease, cataclysmic storms, volcanic activity and earthquakes.

Most shocking to Jon was the revelation that human sacrifice was to play a major role in the lives of the Satanists that comprised the so-called hidden government. It was explained how the subjects to be sacrificed were to be supplied by a network of child kidnappers and that fifty to sixty thousand individuals would be sacrificed every year. An innocent male child of high intelligence was considered the most prized victim because he would be a powerful source of life energy--the greatest and purest force available. Incredibly, it was revealed that the CIA was involved in the international trafficking of children, which was effectuated through a CIA front known as "finders" located in Washington, DC. The picture began to grow clearer for Jon Corbett as he realized a giant conspiracy was behind much of the pornography, illicit drug use, pedophilia, prostitution, corruption and organized kidnapping of children.

Jon realized he was peering into the face of absolute evil as he examined those around him. He remembered evil as once being likened to an exercise of political power that is the imposition of one person's will upon others by coercion in order to prevent spiritual growth. He saw these purveyors of evil as people who loved control and, in the act of controlling, killed real life. Such people can relate only if they possess others and any threat to possession is a threat to them. Jon reflected on Caligo Mendaci's lust to possess him and realized that people of his sort had absolutely no capacity to love; such inability to love was the exact antithesis to the beliefs of his Brethren of Light.

The last day of Jon's first two-week experience at Bohemian Grove did not disappoint as regards shocking revelations. At the early morning lecture, he learned that when operation "full force" was set to begin--in 2001--a Pearl Harbor-like event would be orchestrated that would allow blame to be placed on a perpetual, nebulous terrorist enemy. "Once the population is convinced of the veracity of this conspired event," the presenter explained, "a sufficient degree of terror and insecurity will have been created that will facilitate the passing of a legislative act under the guise of patriotism. The act will remove many constitutional freedoms in the name of security and will be named the 'Patriot Act.'"

Another surprising revelation was the depth of sophistication in biologic assaults and the actual existence of a sixty square mile zone in the Congo where new pathologic agents and diseases were being created. Epidemics of heretofore unknown infectious diseases would create havoc throughout the world and result in the death of many millions of people. The attendees were reminded that the composite goal of all the various tactics to depopulate the world was to have a world population under two billion. The need to eliminate four billion useless eaters was considered paramount to the survival of the material world.

The final lecture focused on the need for measures such as gun control, national ID cards and microchip implantation. It was mentioned how the belaboring of these points would eventually cause the public to relent and accept these tyrannical measures. The microchip would be the crown jewel of the plan to control all individuals by 2011 AD. The chips would be sold to the public as a means of identification but in essence it would be a way to electromagnetically control behavior.

In this plan, great disruptions would occur in the economy and efforts to undermine the material comforts and prosperity of the world's middle class would be greatly accelerated as 2011 approached. Plans were being prepared that would call for fomenting the fears of death, pestilence, famine and disease by creating bio-engineered pathogens, food shortages, toxic food, destructive weather, and catastrophic earthquakes. The culture of fear and extreme negativity would make people more prone to malleability and acquiescence to an authoritarian dictatorship—the final solution.

When Jon returned to his home in Germany, he immediately called for a high-level secret meeting of both the Brethren of Light and the military arm, the Brethren of Might. He informed them of the advanced nature of Luciferian plans to enslave humanity and attempted to convince his cohorts of the gravity of the situation. The meeting was deemed the Council of Belief and was convened in 1985 at The Petersburg, a resort style meeting facility situated on a mountain overlooking the Rhine River. As were all meetings and communication, the Petersburg Convention was held in total secrecy. In attendance were the heads of the three chapters, Jon, Herman Sparkman, Ion Ampere and several other high level members. The agenda included the following:

1. Institution of the Brethren's own Operation Full Force to prepare for the time when they would have to overthrow the global elites and incarcerate the evil cabal. Thus would begin the cleansing reign and a resurrection of humanity.
2. Development of a "Manifesto Theologica," which would define and formalize the tenets of the Brethren. A committee of ten members would promulgate the dogma and encourage the study and application of the true teachings of Christ.
3. A pledge by all Brethren members that they would be sworn to secrecy, never to reveal any knowledge of the organization, even at the pain of torture and death.

All agreed to redouble their efforts and thanked Jon for apprising them of the seriousness and imminence of the sinister plans being formulated by the evil ones.

The ensuing years saw Jon continue in his roles as ambassador, husband, and father of his son Christian and his daughter Lara Christine. For all appearances it was an idyllic life with all the comforts and financial advantages of a high government official. Jon continued in his ambassadorial position until his resignation in 1990. He had decided it was time to return to the United States so he could become more involved in the politics of America. Jon was well respected by those in government service, the members of Congress and the general public.

The Corbetts took up residence in Jon's home state of Connecticut where Jon would start and eventually complete the writing of a book, The Return to Glory. In a matter of just a few months the State Republican Party offered Jon the opportunity to run for the House of Representatives in the 1990 elections. It was a fortuitous moment for Jon because it would allow him to become a public figure and help advance his image in the citizens' view.

The election ended in a landslide victory and his book became a best seller. Jon's career path seemed to be right on track and leading him to his ultimate destination—to become the absolute ruler of the United States of America.

Chapter Six

- The Twenty-One Lessons
- The Grooming of Jon's Son Christian to Be a Future Leader
- Manifesto Theologica
- Jon's Congressional Service
- Operation Full Force

Jon's son Christian turned eight years old in 1990. He had reached a critical stage in life when, as a man-child, he should be exposed to higher truths that would allow for his maturation into a son of God. As a loving father, Jon realized it was his paternal duty to be an idealistic teacher to his son, so he developed a system of twenty-one lessons that would extend over a period of eight years with the goal of shaping Christian into a man of substance.

The nature of the lessons was to open doors to new realms of perceptual experience and insight. Once a student masters these truths he has the ability to manipulate physical reality. The lessons can be likened to an apprenticeship to a spiritual master who will guide the student on a path to the true reality. The system is based on ancient beliefs that can be traced back to Atlantean and Druidic cultures.

In his memoirs of Britain, Caesar himself described Druid beliefs as "respecting the stars and their motions, respecting the universe and our earth, and respecting the powers and majesty of the immortal gods."

It is believed that children possess unique learning abilities, which, if not nurtured at the right time, will be lost by adulthood. At a critical point the child should be exposed to the seen and unseen worlds, which will teach him to have authority over himself and the world itself. The method is described as a constructive imbalance that leads to growth of the individual.

Some of the basic ideas taught by these lessons are as follows:

- The other world, which consists of the astral and spiritual realms, is an actual place and is on a different vibratory plane of reality.
- The lessons are intended to be an introduction to the other world, which coexists with the world of materiality. Understanding this concept prepares one for an ultimate union with the cosmic mind.
- The sacred mysteries are held to be secret and this knowledge is not to be divulged to the masses until they are prepared to understand them.
- An enlightened child is gifted beyond his years when he has knowledge of the supernatural.
- The lessons are designed so that the student will discover the answers to all questions for himself.

Legend has it that Jesus came to Britain with his Uncle Joseph of Arimethea as a youth to learn the ancient wisdom of the Druids. We see evidence of Jesus' visit in the words of the English poet William Blake:

"And did those feet in ancient times walk upon England's mountain green?

And was the Holy Lamb of God on England's pleasant pastures seen?"

The lessons began on a summer day when Jon took Christian on a canoe ride on Lake Waramaug in New Preston, Connecticut. After an hour of leisurely canoeing around the lake, Jon beached the canoe on a small promontory where they could rest and talk.

Their conversation began when Jon held up a closed fist and asked Christian to guess what he held in his hand.

"That would be impossible," Christian replied. Jon focused intently on Christian, who suddenly blurted out, "A blue stone."

"Correct! You have demonstrated how powerful the mind can be. Take this stone as a reminder of the innate powers within you. Christian, my son, we are about to embark on a journey of sorts, which will consist of a series of lessons that will bring you to a final destination--real manhood. You must learn to see beyond the material world and into the spiritual reality where truth resides. You must learn to see not only with your eyes, but also with your spirit. As your earthly father I will teach you a new way of thinking, so you may someday lead others to these truths. These lessons will be spread over several years and each lesson will be given at unpredictable times. It will be your responsibility to employ these teachings in your life so you will fully comprehend their meaning."

As Jon continued to speak to Christian in true, loving tones, he informed his son that lesson number one would begin on that very day. Without divulging the details of the lessons to Christian, Jon began the first in the series, which were all formalized in his own mind. The lessons were structured as follows:

Lesson One: Rite of Assumption

The lesson begins with an assortment of visualization exercises, which are designed to open one's mind to other realities. Jon tells Christian to visualize various scenes and then to depict them in poetic form. The rhymes are intended to illuminate the poet as he becomes one with the image portrayed in the poem. Development of this skill leads to assumption, a rising of one's being into a higher reality.

Lesson Two: Archetypes - Those Who Came Before Man

Jon takes Christian to a deep cavern in New York State and tells him that a race of giants created the cave. Christian must walk the entire length of the cave until he reaches its exit, which is a mile from the entrance. Jon assures his son that there is nothing to fear but fear itself. He explains to Christian that the lesson will teach him that time is a man-made creation that limits the growth of man. "By walking through the cave, you will probably contact these former archetypes, but you must overcome any fear by confronting it. If you complete this task, you will take a significant step towards manhood. You must learn that without fear you will be free to seek truth."

Lesson Two A: The Fire Globe

A globe of blue cobalt light is constructed and used to create an atmosphere for deep meditation and removing the barrier between this world and the other world.

Christian is taught the symbolism of color and how each of the seven colors of the spectrum has special subjective properties. Blue, for example, promotes contemplation and red excites passion.

Lesson Three: Four Physical Realms

The physical world is composed of four realms and each has a corresponding force associated with it. For example:

Realm of Wind – Intelligence
Realm of Sea – Emotions
Realm of Fire - Will and Inspiration
Realm of Stone – Impermanence

Jon assigns Christian the task of fabricating four items, which will symbolize each realm. The four items--oak rod, chalice, sickle and blue stone--are to be kept in a wooden box to be used in meditations and problem solving.

Lesson Four: The Summoning

The summoning is a ritual that results in confronting the darkest reaches of one's being. The individual learns to overcome the demons on his own. Christian is taught the mechanisms of this ancient ritual, which summons the other world. He learns about the four elemental kingdoms--earth, wind, fire, and water--whose powers lie beyond the material world. In this ritual one walks away with the impression that all gods are faces of the one.

Lesson Five: Four Signs of Portal

Christian is told an educational story of wind, sea, fire and stone, which explains the elemental symbolism of each of the four elements. The symbols are used in a ritualistic way to open the doorway to the elemental worlds. The four symbols and their meanings are as follows:

1. ∏ Trilithon is an arch shape similar to the arches of Stonehenge. It represents the gateway between the past and future and is a female form symbolic of the elemental kingdom, earth.
2. ∪ The concave is a cup shape symbolic of reception. It is also a female form and symbolic of the kingdom of water.
3. + The Tau, an equilateral cross, represents the equality of motion in all directions. The Tau is a male form and symbolic of the kingdom of air.
4. ∧ The peak represents the tongue of flame. It is a male form and symbolizes the kingdom of fire.

When combined with strong visualizations, the four symbols can aid in opening elemental portals.

Lesson Six: Sacraments of the Earth

Christian is taught the significance of a Sunday ritual, which is used to gain the favor of the elemental beings who dwell beyond the physical realm. The nature of this mass-like offering is evidenced in the modern Christian liturgical Mass whose origins lie in ancient Druidic culture. The early Christian Church of Culdee in Britain played a major role in bringing this ceremony to Christian worship.

Lesson Seven: Eight Grove Festivals

Jon teaches Christian about the eight major cultural festivals that are actually based on the cycles of the earth. The dates of these celebrations are dictated by the sun and moon, with four related to the solstices and the equinoxes and the other four dependent on in between times determined by full moons.

The eight festivals are Halloween/All Saints Day – October 31, Christmas – December 21, Groundhog's Day – February 1, Easter – March 21, May Day – May 1, St. John's Day – June 21, Grain Festival (sports competitions, feasts) – August 1, and Thanksgiving (harvest) – September 1.

Christian is fascinated to learn that many of the traditions, such as Halloween costumes, apple dunking, and jack-o-Lanterns; Christmas Yule logs, holly, pine trees, kissing under mistletoe, and Santa; Easter colored eggs, the Easter bunny, and egg hunts; May Day Maypole and flower gathering; grain festivals, Olympic-like competitions; the Thanksgiving cornucopia and feasting, all had their origins in ancient Druidic times.

Lesson Eight: The Sixteen Healing Herbs and Mistletoe

Christian is introduced to how plants represent the elemental kingdoms and provide great healing powers. Jon informs Christian that contained within God's pharmacy are cures for all diseases and that having knowledge of these herbs and their therapeutic effects allows an individual a certain level of self-sufficiency in health matters.

The sixteen healing herbs are separated into four classes with four herbs under each of the elemental kingdoms. Mistletoe, the most highly esteemed herb, is in a class by itself and is used to potentiate the other sixteen herbs. Each individual should have a store of these herbs in tincture form and possess a thorough understanding of their uses. The collection of herbs consists of the following seventeen herbs: earth – valerian, skullcap, lady slipper, wormwood; water – catnip, hops, black willow, echinacea; air – chamomile, calendula, yarrow, vervain; fire – goldenseal, St. John's Wort; buck thorne, white oak; and mistletoe.

Lesson Nine: The Rite of Three Rays

At the age of ten Christian encounters another young boy, Nicola Ampere, who has had similar training. Christian's father has arranged this meeting so Christian can be challenged in his knowledge of the occult. Nicola Ampere happens to be the son of Ion Ampere, the long-time friend and co-conspirator of Jon's. A competition of sorts follows and the boys are graded on their status along the path to the true ways of living. For Christian to be victorious in this challenge he must utilize his intuitive skills and draw on higher forces for guidance, strength, and protection.

For someone in this competition to contact the higher forces, they implement the rite of three rays, a seven step invocational ritual, which employs knowledge of the three rays: the right ray symbolizes the masculine force; the left ray represents the feminine force, and the middle ray represents neither and is known as the ray of balance. The right ray of God is expansive, whereas the left ray of the goddess is contractive. Knowing these characteristics of the rays allows one to either invoke or banish contact with the other world forces.

The competition ends in a draw as both Christian and Nicola demonstrate equivalent abilities. As a result of this encounter the two boys develop a strong bond and swear allegiance to one another and dedication to a mutual goal of someday working to bring a deeper spiritual awareness to humankind.

Lesson Ten: Battle of the Trees

Christian and Nicola learn that each species is seen as having a certain personality and life force. Trees were often thought of as the bridge between Heaven (spirit) and earth (matter) by ancient cultures such as the Druids and Norse. The Druids held trees in such high regard that they actually had a formalized chart on twenty-one trees that defined their personalities, rank and tarot equivalents. Christian and Nicola are instructed on methods of compounding draughts (drinks) of inspiration that were intended to facilitate communication between man and the plant kingdom.

Upon completion of this lesson the boys have to part as Nicola is slated to return to his home in Tokyo, Japan. Christian is deeply saddened by his friend's departure, but finds consolation in knowing they will someday reunite and combine their talents in a mission to enlighten and uplift humanity.

Lesson Eleven: Song Spells

During his eleventh year Christian is driven by his father to a secluded valley in northwestern Connecticut to attend a three-day music festival. He is exposed to world-class musicians of great virtuosic skill who play a form of music that intones the highest order of beauty and sound.

The experience is a great relevation to Christian as he learns of the power of music and the significance of harmonic vibration found in melody. Those in attendance are a select group who understand that music is an echo of the cosmic voice--that voice being a universal vibration that pervades all of creation and is known as the Holy Spirit.

They know the effect of the highest form of music as Song Spell. Song Spell is considered to be the mystical realm of musical craft and a means to further illumination. The actual power of music is found in the secrets of Song Spell, the knowledge of which is reserved for a select few. In essence, fine music is a vibratory reflection of the universal order and harmony and should provide sustenance for the soul.

The ancients Druids, Greeks and Atlanteans purported that different melodies represent different times of the year with their inherent modes, energies and moods. Their system of natural melodies was considered to be an echo of the universal creative force and were thought to evoke a religious experience because they represented universal truth. Truth is absolute and remains such whether man is knowledgeable or ignorant. The Druids took this idea even further by developing a collection of eight seasonal chants known as the eight songs of cycle, the basic melodies of which can still be found in the music of today.

In contrast, discordant sounds such as those evidenced in so-called modern music are disruptive to the human constitution and deliver negative energy down to the lower chakras, thus depriving one of a high spiritual experience. The upper spiritual chakras (fourth to seventh) should be innervated by certain vibratory sounds if one is to rise from his lower material nature to a fuller appreciation of man's spiritual reality.

Christian learns about the structure of an orchestra and its various sections: brass, woodwinds, strings, and percussion. He is fascinated to learn that the sections represent matter's four realms, the principles of truth (earth, wind, water and fire). The importance of the voice is also emphasized because it holds the divine spark. Consequent to this teaching Christian is encouraged to sing without thought so that the music can flow from deep within. This is the way to create Song Spell and sing the universal songs of truth.

Finally, the significance of the universal number seven is again emphasized because the seven notes of the scale correspond to the seven major celestial bodies of our solar system.

Having been exposed to the wonderful secrets of music, vibrational frequencies and hyper-dimensional realities, Christian proceeds to trace his next step, Lesson XII, the Laws of Duality and Separation.

Lesson Twelve: Duality and Separation

At the age of thirteen, the point in which a young boy enters manhood, Christian is taken to an abbey in northwestern Connecticut to be a guest for one week. The purpose of the visit is to develop an understanding of the dual nature of the material and spiritual realms.

The sisterhood of the abbey is representative of the feminine aspect, which gears activity towards honoring the earth goddess, the mother of all. It is explained to Christian that there is a natural division in all of creation; the material and spiritual worlds were formed in accordance with the Law of Duality. The law dictates that everything conforms to one of two opposite forces that can be delineated as follows:

Masculine	-	Feminine
Light	-	Dark
Birth	-	Death
Active	-	Passive
Sun	-	Moon
Positive	-	Negative
Expansive	-	Contractive
Spirit	-	Matter

These examples are but a mere sampling of the universal opposites because everything is consistent with the Law. Even the smallest atomic and subatomic particles are dependent on the Law. It is only the ultimate reality, the Kingdom of God in the great beyond, that is all one and has no opposites.

On Christian's first evening at the abbey he enjoys a dinner with the nuns followed by a roundtable discussion. It becomes obvious that these Disciples of Truth are well versed in their convictions. Collectively, they explain to Christian that the key to life is to keep opposite forces apart, so they avoid neutrality and maintain their identity. If the opposite forces merge, inertia occurs and no movement results. In contrast, when a force unites with a like force, a new strength is formed, which leads to spiritual growth. In the material world like forces repel; however, in the spiritual realm like forces attract. For this reason individuals must adhere to this law if they are to grow spiritually. It is now easier to understand why religious orders have always been separated according to gender and that chastity is considered a virtue. One older nun, avuncular in a female way, further intones that some souls are ready for growth and others are not. Those who are not ready will continue to live a life of man-made illusion. Those who find truth are called the "twice born."

The sisters of the abbey adhere to the principle of celibacy, which they feel preserves the life force within them, thereby accelerating spiritual growth. It is their firm belief that sexual activity impedes spiritual awareness and that most unenlightened individuals confuse physical love with true spirituality. According to their belief, the true goal of spiritual evolution lies not in a union of opposites but in the absence of opposites. They feel this to be a universal law and that once incarnated gender is dictated by the soul's need to move forward in its evolution. Once true human status is achieved the soul will never regress to lower developmental levels.

The sisters further explain that when someone reaches the status of twice born, it is due to a higher awareness. They go on to say that the vast majority of individuals remain once born until their growth occurs according to the mystical laws. Once one recognizes the true reality, one is bound by conscience-- conscience being the actual presence of God in the mind of man. As a follower of truth, one must act in accordance with truth--and not what one wishes to be truth. This is known as right action.

The abbess tells Christian, "You are a twilight soul on the verge of knowing truth. You are becoming a part of a select group that will someday move the whole human family to a new spiritual awareness."

Christian becomes acutely aware that this sisterhood is a unique group of women, elevated into a class unto themselves. In spite of the fact that many possess great physical beauty, they have forsaken life's pleasures for the greater spiritual pleasures. Christian begins to understand that the feminine absorbs life energy while the masculine emits it. Women acquire the life force for immediate pragmatic use, while men save the force for eventual higher spiritual use. Achieving spiritual power results from living a sacred life, one that reveres chastity and purity. It is always a danger to unleash the physical side of man because it leads to dissolution and chaos within all human institutions due to a disconnection from the cosmic consciousness (God) and divine law. Christian now has a heightened sense of the significance of chastity as a virtue, which helps lead one down the path to enlightenment.

Christian and the abbess continue their conversation as they stroll down a path that takes them to a beautiful contemplative garden. The garden is dedicated to St. Fiacre, patron saint of gardens, whose statue highlights the entrance. There amongst the beautifully manicured grounds, Christian observes the wonders of the earth goddess and views nature in all its glory. Nestled within the various culinary and medicinal herbs and plants, he views the majesty of butterfly and avian activity, which only enhances his appreciation of God's creation. The abbess points out a mating process of the praying mantis, which concludes with the consumption of the male of the species by the female. The sister advises Christian to take this action to be a lesson in knowing that the female is the deadliest of the species and is symbolic of a much higher truth—never allow the yin energy (feminine) to overwhelm the yang (masculine). "This," she says, "is the work of Satan himself."

Upon leaving the garden the abbess leads Christian to a small infirmary where an elderly sister named Angelica is spending her last days in failing health. "Excuse me, sister," the abbess intones as she rouses the nun from her drowse. "I've brought you the young man who we believe to be the one you've waited for all these years. I want you to meet Christian Corbett. He's the most exceptional of the twice born that we could find."

Angelica weakly opens her eyes as a faint smile breaks across her lips. A few tears of joy slowly streak down her cheeks as she reaches out to grasp Christian's hand. The sensation of an object is obvious to Christian as she tightens her grip. Angelica struggles to speak. "Christian, many years ago I was entrusted to keep this special ring and told to keep it until a select young man was found who would wear it as an anointed one, as someone destined to be a great leader. The young man must be worthy of wearing this ring as a symbol of an enlightened king. You, Christian, have been chosen, so wear it with great honor and let it forever be a reminder of your immense potential and responsibility."

It is a beautiful gold ring with a Maltese Cross fashioned on the circlet's face. "Let it be my last wish to see you wear this ring. Please put it on." As Christian places the ring on his finger, he bends down to embrace the nun whose face breaks out in a gentle smile as she renders her last breath. Christian loses his embrace and looks down upon her holy countenance with a sense of awe and reverence. Sister Angelica was long known for her devotion and relationship to the Blessed Mother. She constantly prayed to the Virgin and asked for her to especially provide a guiding hand at her eventual moment of passing. As Christian quietly weeps, a sudden sound of celestial music permeates the recesses of his mind. The music is overlaid by a highly sonorous voice that repeats the singing of the word "Ave" over and over again. The music continues for several minutes until it slowly fades into a higher dimension.

Christian ponders the significance of this event and realizes that Angelica has been lifted into a rightful place in the heavenly realm. His mournful spell is finally broken when the abbess places her hand on his shoulder. "Come, we must go now. It is time to leave this place, for you have many more lessons to learn."

Lesson Thirteen: A Teaching Concerning Stonehenge

In the autumn of Christian's thirteenth year he and his father reprise their visit to the promontory on Lake Waramaug—the very same scene where Christian began his series of lessons. Jon wants to take this occasion to teach Christian about the mysteries of Stonehenge by recounting his visit many years ago.

Christian sits spellbound as his father describes his naugal experience amongst the trilithons of that mystical place. John explains how Luz Barca was his first true love and the manner in which she showed him the way to enlightenment. The revelation of Luz Barca as having been a major reason for his father's exceptional nature is a shock for a thirteen-year-old son. Christian, however, is mature enough to fully appreciate his father's incredible story and realizes it was a circumstance that was ordained by a higher force.

Christian has often wondered about the mysteries of Stonehenge and is enthralled by its history. Jon explains that those who understand the ancients realize that a great race, probably survivors of Atlantis, built this monumental garden as a means to enter into the other world. This knowledge is largely unknown to the ignorant masses and will only be fully understood when all of mankind is ready for the truth.

The bulk of the afternoon is spent in fishing offshore. After a short time Christian hooks onto a good-sized lake trout, which they clean and cook over an open fire. As father and son indulge in this tasteful natural meal, they take the time to review the lessons Christian has already experienced.

The hours pass by in a flicker, as they are thoroughly engrossed in conversation. It isn't until they notice a cooling of the air as dusk envelops them that they realize they should return to the mainland. As they paddle the canoe away from that treasured promontory ground, they are awestruck by the beauty of the moment. The setting sun reflects off the lake water and the multi-colored leaves are resplendent in their autumnal splendor. One last look back by Christian creates an indelible image in his mind of a place that has forever changed his life.

Lesson Fourteen: Pink Bubble

In the spring of his fourteenth year Christian is taken to a special place in Spencer, Massachusetts, called St. Joseph's, which is the monasterial home of none other than Brother Vladimir, now in his ninth decade, but still in control of all his faculties. The aging monk will play an important role in Christian's exposure to truth.

Vladimir embraces the thought of having Christian in his charge for he knows of the greatness within this young man. It is his role to teach the meditative means to self-realization and Christ consciousness, which will provide the young devotee the power to affect physical reality.

An introductory discussion takes place as Vladimir and Christian stroll in the same garden that once exposed Luz Barca to the path of enlightenment nearly forty years ago. The monk informs his apprentice that it is his intention to teach him a technique that will put him in touch with higher vibrational planes of the cosmos. The purpose of the deep meditation will be to attract Divine Blessings in all matters of life, even to the point of changing the physical reality.

"Holy cow!" exclaims Christian. "Are you telling me that it's possible to influence future events with a mental technique?"

"Most definitely, young man," replies Vladimir. "The mind, if properly developed, can do all that it can imagine."

Early the following morning the lesson begins with Brother Vladimir revealing the first tenet: Everything in the universe is a vibration. The exchange of energy and vibrations between human beings and events that occur in their lives occurs constantly. These vibrational waves are known as "psycho-astral" waves and they move through space without us being cognizant of them. The secrets revealed to Christian will allow him to produce powerful psycho-astral waves and project them into the universe. By doing this he will be employing a powerful means of initiating the development of more positive events in his life. The result will allow him to determine his destiny.

Brother Vladimir directs Christian to take the following steps to realize his destiny.

Step One:

Every day at a specific time you will carry out a mental exercise. You must remain quiet and undisturbed for fifteen minutes so that you can activate your inner creative energies, which will make your desires a reality.

Begin the exercise in a secluded place and sit down and relax. Do not allow your legs to touch one another and place your hands, palms down, on your thighs. Think of absolutely nothing and empty your mind. Think of nothing for ten seconds. It may be difficult in the beginning as your thoughts may intrude. Repeat the exercise and hold your position for twenty seconds. Eventually you will be able to keep your mind devoid of thoughts for one minute. The minute will give you enough time to apply the secret. Throughout the quiet time breathe in and out slowly and deeply. As you breathe out, imagine that any muscle tension and anxiety are being expelled in your breath. Each time you inhale think that you are bringing in strength, chi energy, and calmness. Be aware of only your breathing. If at any time you notice a sensation of a humming sound permeating your mind, do not be alarmed. It is a sign that you have contacted the universal vibration known as the "aum" sound or Holy Spirit. This experience is an indication that you have entered a special place, which is a precursor to knowing the Christ Consciousness of the Son and the eventual cosmic consciousness of the Father.

Step Two:

Focus on a solution to a problem, a goal you desire or a wish you want to come true. Be sure it is positive and will harm no one. This is known as focused intent and is in tune with the cosmic will. When your thought is of such high character it will allow the process of transcendence to continue. The imagery you employ should be characterized by as much detail as possible. The visualization method can attract virtually anything you desire. Imagine only the end result. Only visualize the positive conditions you will experience once your wish comes true. Your design should be in harmony with the universal mind of God's will, if it is to come to fruition. This requirement is necessary for the cosmic force to allow your desire to manifest in this reality in a balanced way.

Step Three:

Keep your eyes closed as you visualize a sphere of pink light resembling a large pink bubble. Envelope your wish within the bubble and send it off into the universe. Reinforce this action by stating, "All will be accomplished for the good of humanity." After the sphere has been jettisoned, innervated with the vibrational energy of your thought, it will travel in the universe until circumstances for the manifestation of your wish have been realized. You have learned a technique that demonstrates the power of visualization. By performing this method you are able to magnetize your vibrations with the vibrations of your desire by adding the power of word. Remember the biblical reference that in the beginning there was the word—the cosmic thought that manifested in the physical reality.

Good fortune will find you. Do not force the issue. Simply rely on your intuitive skills and wait for coincidences to occur. These coincidental occurrences will make it possible for your wishes to come true. Observe these coincidences as they are signs that destiny is answering your request. The universal forces will lead you on the path to realizing your goals. Listen to your intuition and your heart and follow their lead. Leave your mind open to destiny's signs and discover how to recognize good fortune when it arrives. The scenarios may be quite unpredictable, unusual and unexpected. This is the way free will can influence fate.

Once you develop these skills you should use them in unselfish ways. For instance, the technique can be employed in a prayerful way to heal the sick or to improve life's circumstances for someone in need. Always enclose your gifted desire in the pink bubble and send it into the universe, where it will put forces into action and manifest your gift of love. By acting in this loving manner your actions will never be forgotten in the universal realm. You will be rewarded for you have brought love and light to the recipient. There is a universal law, which states, "You cannot receive unless you have given." The more you help others, the more you help yourself.

Christian is effusive in his gratitude to Brother Vladimir for having taught him this special technique. He knows that it will allow him to become a powerful disciple for the true way and play a major role in the enfoldment of the human race.

When Father Jon arrives the following day to pick up his son, Christian excitedly tells him of his new found knowledge. Jon embraces his son and tells him not to get too excited because this is but another step in his march to maturity. He informs Christian that the next lesson will be equally important and will take place in a secret location in the Green Mountain State of Vermont.

Prior to leaving the monastery the threesome of Jon, Christian and Brother Vladimir sit for conversation and a simple repast of wine, cheese and unleavened bread. Christian has developed a real fondness for the aged monk and has a feeling of emptiness as they drive away from St. Joseph's. His last glimpse and image of Vladimir smiling and waving goodbye will be embossed in his memory for all time.

Lesson Fifteen: Council of Light

Every year the Brethren of Light held an annual council upon the eve of mid-summer. The site varied each year so as to avoid detection and to allow the twenty-one delegates to meet in the security of knowing they could engage in free discussion. The three chapters (kingdom, power and glory) represented the three districts of faith (Europe, America and Asia). The purpose of the annual meeting was to formulate plans for the upcoming year with an emphasis on directing and channeling the spiritual energies of their respective areas under one unified brotherhood.

The location of the conclave was in the Killington area of central Vermont. Jon navigated the car over the winding road, which took them ever higher up the mountain. They finally arrived at a secluded mountainside villa of incredible beauty and design. The setting offered a magnificent view of the verdant valley below and elicited a sense of serenity, which was perfect for intellectual and spiritual pursuits.

As Jon and Christian entered the compound, they were welcomed by Jon's old friends, Herman Sparkman and Ion Ampere. Ion excitedly told Christian that his son, Nicola, would also be in attendance and that he hoped the two would use the opportunity to advance even further in their quest for enlightenment.

Three years had passed since Christian and Nicola had engaged in a competition, which had resulted in a bonding of great strength. The joy of seeing one another was somewhat dampened when, while attending the opening meeting, they were told that they would be given a serious assignment involving a day of isolation in the surrounding forest.

The two boys were taken to a trailhead and instructed to follow the trail until it ended in a clearing several miles distant. They were told to build a fire and to use their time in discussion and contemplation. If they were properly engaged the experience would take them into a deeper understanding of true reality.

While walking the trail, Nicola informed Christian that he had strong feelings of past life memories and of being an advanced soul. He went on to say that he sensed he was brought into this reality from the other world to play an important role in the spiritual development of humankind.

After three hours of walking, the two boys reached the trail's end, which opened onto a large clearing. In the middle of the clearing stood an enormous tree of an unrecognizable species. When they reached the base of the tree they were startled to see, situated in the highest branches, a pyramid-like structure resting on a circular platform.

"This must be a sacred, holy spot," Christian said.

Nicola concurred and stated, "The pyramid was known to the Ancients for its great power of preserving and purifying that which is within its range. I assume this is where we're to spend the night. Let's use this pit to build a fire for warmth and as a means of inspiration."

The boys expended an hour or so collecting kindling to start a fire and then built a roaring blaze utilizing logs that had been neatly stacked next to the fire pit. Once the fire was firmly established, the two settled in within its range of the warmth and began a conversation that would take them in a very special direction. Nicola began by stating that he felt both he and Christian were products of past lives and were destined by universal forces to play a major role in the future of the planet. "I feel our mission will be to integrate religious thought into a universal belief system that recognizes all gods as a reflection of the one God. That all is one! That the part is the whole!"

Nicola sat quietly as he peered into the blaze.

"Nicola, how do we know if God exists or if we have lived before?" Christian asked.

"Just keep watching the flames," replied Nicola. Nicola spoke a brief incantation; then suddenly there appeared a deep blue flame, which housed certain images for Christian to view. The images flashed before him and it became obvious that they represented lifetimes he had led in the past. His question to Nicola had been most definitely answered in a dramatic and vivid fashion.

"My gosh! Is that the real nature of life's cycles?" Christian asked.

"Yes, the cycles are exactly like that," Nicola replied. "Everything in both the material and spiritual worlds revolves like a great wheel from birth to death and back again. In each lifetime we gain experience that helps the soul's development. Eventually the soul achieves attunement with the cosmic soul and the cycle of rebirth is broken. The soul is then one with the Father in heaven."

The directness and lucidity of Nicola's explanation impressed Christian.

"Christian, you and I are privileged to know these sacred mysteries and we must fully appreciate and understand the importance of belief and faith in building a human society based on truth. Remember these two things. First, the word sapiens in homo sapiens refers to a wise, clear-thinking, spiritual individual who is connected to the all and has within the capacity for infinite consciousness. Secondly, never forget that belief imparts reality and must be sustained by faith. Otherwise, all of man's structures will crumble under the weight of untruth." Nicola looked into Christian's eyes with great intent, and said, "You and I are ordained by God to do his will and bring truth to the world."

With that said the two fledglings rested their heads on the warm ground and drifted off into a restful slumber under the dual canopy of the powerful pyramid and the starlit Vermont sky.

Lesson Sixteen: Wild Hunt

The next lesson occurs in the autumn following Christian's experience with Nicola. Known as the wild hunt, it is always scheduled as an all night event on a night of the full moon adjoining October 31 (Halloween), which is considered the time of year when the other world has its greatest influence on the physical world.

The wild hunt is actually a competition between an aspiring mystic and the elemental forces of a particular environment. The purpose of the challenge is to demonstrate mastery over nature's forces.

The degree to which the apprentice has developed his personal magnetism will be tested; in order to survive, his powers will have to correspond to the power of confrontational forces that the hunter will face.

Some of the characteristics of the wild hunt are: It always involves an isolated, harsh environment about four square miles in size; there is a starting point and a finish; prior to the hunt the challenger eats food native to the area in order to unite with the elemental forces of the area (wind, sea, fire, stone); the hunter dresses entirely in black.

Christian's father informs him of what to expect and warns him that this will be a struggle that could put his life at risk. Christian realizes that all the training of the past few years is going to be tested.

Father and son drive through the Pike County area of Pennsylvania, which is largely uninhabited. The moonless sky and the narrow, rural road penetrating the overhanging trees resemble an eerie, Transylvanian setting. Eventually, Jon wheels the car to a stop in a small picnic area and informs Christian that they have arrived at the point of departure. Jon embraces his son, wishes him godspeed, and tells him to enter the wooded surroundings. "Let your instincts guide you. If you do it correctly, you will succeed and find me waiting for you at a finish point as the sun begins its ascent."

As Christian begins his advance into the territory, a violent wind sweeps through the area and a giant tree limb crashes down on the exact area Christian has just departed. Christian has little time to consider his good fortune when, suddenly, a violent storm envelops him. As he struggles to proceed through the darkness, he calls for the protection of the God force, which manifests as a protective shield around him. Just as Christian feels some security against the elements, a flash of lightning strikes a large tree just ahead of him. Bursting into flame the burning tree blocks Christian's path and he has to scramble up to a sharp cliff to circumvent the fire. As he desperately claws his way up the incline, the climbing action dislodges some large stones initiating a rockslide. Christian senses the gravity of the situation and fortunately is able to squeeze under a ledge as the boulders tumble above him. Thanks to his instinctive reflexes he avoids serious injury. Even though he sustains some minor cuts and bruises, he is grateful to have survived the landslide physically intact.

Several hours pass as Christian fights off the four elemental forces. It is with great satisfaction that he finally reaches the open field that signifies the end of his trek through the challenge ground.

Stepping unto the meadow Christian can see his father awaiting him with a beaming look of pride; his son has passed another test on his way to enlightened manhood.

Lesson Seventeen: Power of the Word

Christian, having maintained a detailed journal of the first sixteen lessons, realized that Lesson Seventeen would be the most important lesson to date because his father had told him of its significance. He realized that his notations on this lesson should be exact so as to reflect the enormous significance of the lesson's content.

It was the winter following the wild hunt. Once again it was Jon's role to drive his son to central Vermont in the vicinity of Stratton Mountain. The site of the lesson was to be an old farmhouse located on a long, lonely dirt road in the town of Asheville.

Jon drove the car slowly because he did not want to miss the house, which was situated somewhat off the road. He was told to be on the lookout for a dilapidated barn with the words "This is it" painted in large white letters on the barn's facing. The house would be directly across the road.

It had been a particularly snowy winter, which caused the deserted house to be encased in a natural barrier of snow some two to three feet

162

high. After Jon and Christian trudged their way through the snow and entered the house, a scene of frightful proportions greeted them. Not having been occupied for several months, the house was uninvitingly frigid and furnished with decrepit old items that were probably thirty to forty years old. Fortunately, Jon had instructions on how to start up an ancient coal furnace, which provided a modicum of heat.

Having arrived late in the evening, father and son decided to retire to the upstairs bedrooms. Climbing the creaky stairs, Christian noticed the place didn't seem to have a single square corner. It sure was spooky! He imagined hearing an insidious sounding laugh echoing from the bowels of the building. Christian had a restless night trying to sleep on a lumpy old mattress under the warmth of an electric blanket that had to be as old as the technology that spawned it.

The following morning after a hearty breakfast, Jon informed Christian that the next lesson would take place right where they were. However, it would be below the house in a chamber specifically designed for demonstrating the power of the word.

Jon pushed aside the kitchen table to reveal an artfully camouflaged trap door. The door opened to a stairway consisting of twenty-one steps, which brought them into a beautifully appointed two hundred square foot granite-walled room. In the center of the room lay a stone altar surrounded by stone dolmen resembling the trilithons of Stonehenge. Christian intuitively knew this had to be a special place, probably a magical site, which could act as a laboratory where great work could be done. Jon reaffirmed Christian's feelings by stating, "Roll up your sleeves. We are about to perform a great experiment that will forever change your life."

A design known as the Tree of Zoraster was inlaid upon the surface of the altar. It consisted of three circles representing the three planes of existence (astral, causal, spiritual) and the three rays of illumination (active, passive, neutral), which intersect the circles at nine points of manifestation.

"Isn't this similar to the Kabala, the ancient mystical system of Judaism?" asked Christian.

"Yes, you're correct, my son. You must realize that all major religions share similar principles, which reflect their understanding of the true nature of reality. You should appreciate the fact that the last circle is the dimensional realm of infinities where all things reconcile. It is a dimension where no opposites exist, where the material and spiritual worlds meet somewhere in infinity. It is the point of death and rebirth—the alpha and the omega. All things begin there and all things return there upon death. The next thing you must know is that the three realms are separated by veils, which must be transgressed for one to enter the highest realm. Once one enters the highest realm of the other world, he has the power to manifest change in reality. This can be done by intoning the word or thought, just as the creator did in the beginning. Remember that action follows thought and that powerful thought has no limits. I am teaching you how to use your voice, whereby you will be able to have words vibrate through the other world and eventually influence the changes that will manifest as you desire. Know the triune name of God, "IAO". It is sacred and requires respect and reverence. Do not profane the name! It is a sin of degradation due to its lack of respect and faith. The sin is accountable to you, not to God. It is your karma.

"When you reach a deep meditative state and you are attuned to the voice, focus on the bluestones and your thought will cause them to hum and vibrate in unison with the universal vibration (aum), the Holy Spirit. The special blue stones come from Stonehenge and have the ability to store, channel, and amplify the cosmic force. The stones allow one to unite the world of matter with the world of spirit. In this way your words or thoughts can manifest into form or circumstance. Physical form manifests from thought just as it did in the beginning of creation. The forces of form are set into motion; action follows thought. This is your most important lesson to date."

Lesson Eighteen: A Rite of Passage

The location of the next two lessons was in a small town in a remote area of northeastern Pennsylvania, called Gelatt. Although lightly populated with just a few hundred denizens, most of whom were farmers, Gelatt had the distinction of having one store, Wheeler's General Store. It was a quintessential country store that supplied food, dry goods, and fuel to the community. It even had a cracker barrel and a Franklin stove that served as a focal point for gossip and serious conversation. It was the place where Christian was to meet his next mentor, Col. William Bradley, who after reminiscing with Christian's father for a short while, warmly welcomed Christian into his care. The drive to the Bradley farmstead was just four miles, the last two of which were unpaved. It was a beautiful area highlighted by meandering brooks, golden meadows and rolling hills, which caused Christian's heart to pulse ever stronger with the anticipation of spending time there.

Christian was in his sixteenth year and was beginning the final stages of the twenty-one lessons. It was intended for him to spend a year under the tutelage of Colonel Bradley, a retired British Army Officer who had served in India prior to its independence in 1947. Colonel Bradley was a man's man--stout of heart and strong of mind and body. He had served a rigorous military tour in India, but also used his time in the east to study the cultures and religions of the occident. Bradley was well rounded in that he was an expert in martial arts, weaponry, and war tactics as well as having a deep understanding of history, politics, philosophy and meditative techniques. He had learned his contemplative skills from various masters during several visits to Indian ashrams and Tibetan monasteries. If ever asked, "What is the meaning to life?" he would reply, "Life is a river! Think about it." Most would react with puzzlement and say, "You can't be serious." However, if they took his advice and contemplated his statement, they would understand the profundity of it. Consider the life stream being fed by tributaries of experience and finally finding its way into the oneness of the infinite ocean.

Still amazingly fit and erect for a man in his late seventies, Colonel Bradley epitomized the military officer of another time. He was highly admired by the Brethren of Light, who often called on him to educate their young aspirants and bring them to maturity. It was the intent of Christian's father to have his son taught the practical aspects of life by a mentor of the highest order. Christian was to be imbued with an appreciation of a myriad of topics: martial arts, history, cultural studies, political science, economics, philosophy, ethics, hunting, growing food, preservation of food, cooking skills, herbal medicine, vibrational healing, and even making alcoholic beverages known as meads. The objective of the training was to teach Christian the art of living in both worlds--the worlds of spirit and of matter. By knowing and understanding these two realms, he would develop the masculine strength of mind and body, so he could someday contribute to transforming a violent, sinful world into one of peace, harmony, stability and abundance. Christian would become a soldier, mystic, and diplomat, all in one, and thus a true Son of God.

Colonel Bradley escorted Christian to what would be his living quarters for the next year. The room was beautifully designed with proper texturing and coloration making it conducive to intellectual pursuits and contemplative activity. "Christian, you are entering that period in life when you are coming of age and it will be my responsibility to take you from boyhood to manhood. We have a whole year ahead of us to engage in pursuits that will prepare you to be a leader. But before we embark on that journey, we're going to spend a few days on the art of drinking and making sacred libations known as meads. Meads will loose the chains of attachment and allow your mind to explore new dimensions away from materiality. They are fermented alcoholic beverages comprised of herbs, honey and special waters. Different formulae are prescribed for the four seasons of the year and the herbs used are considered sacred to each season. It being the spring of the year, we're going to introduce you to a mead known as the Beltane mead. Imbibing this drink and learning the art of making meads will be a signal to the fact that you are experiencing a rite of passage on this very significant day. When you wake up tomorrow, you will be a young man who will be ready to move on to your next lesson--to linger between two worlds."

Lesson Nineteen: Linger Between Two Worlds

On the morning following his rite of passage Christian woke up to find an excerpt from St. Corneille's, The Yellow Book of Ferns, resting on a table next to his bed. A note written by Colonel Bradley was stapled to it and read, "Christian, please seriously read these words and then digest their meaning, because they will have a special meaning in your upcoming lesson."

The words of St. Corneille were presented in a calligraphic style and read as follows:

"We must live in two worlds--the world of form and the other world of force, for true existence involves the constant intercourse of both to live and thrive between form and force."

Christian included the recitation of these words as a part of his morning prayers prior to commencing his daily training routine. The routine was arduous, as Colonel Bradley expected nothing but hard discipline and dedication. Christian was exposed to serious intellectual studies as well as the manly arts of hand-to-hand combat, improvised weaponry and a variety of survival tactics.

After ten months of intensive training, Christian was given a new assignment, known as a vision quest. He was instructed to spend one month in a distant forest without the benefit of weapons, food or supplies. He must survive on the skills and guile he had learned and, most importantly, he must confront his greatest fear.

Colonel Bradley counseled Christian by telling him, "You must learn to let go. What we think of as reality is not! It's an illusion. The true reality is that of spirit. You are in for a shamanistic-like experience that will be a revelation. You will learn that the abnegation of the ego is the means to the miracle of enlightenment. You will come out of this experience as a transformed individual."

Christian harbored the fear that his training under Colonel Bradley was too violent and aggressive and felt a need to resolve that conflicting impression with his core beliefs. He realized that this conflicted feeling was the greatest fear that he would confront in his vision quest.

The days of isolation passed into weeks as Christian managed to survive rather easily by employing his varied skills. Colonel Bradley had prepared him well. The month of solitary adventure was nearing its conclusion, so Christian realized it was time to finally seek a vision via deep meditation.

His first task was to construct a lean-to structure that would provide shelter while he went into a deep and long prayerful state. Once the lean-to was completed, he literally entered into the cave-like environ where he would figuratively seek the cave within, as Jesus Christ had once described the location for his yogic technique of meditation.

Christian first cleared his mind with deep breathing and then sought a total focus on his spiritual eye. After a short time the white dove's appearance in his mind's eye, followed by the distinctive buzz of universal vibration, signaled that the avenue was cleared for a journey into the night. True reality was beckoning, and Christian took full advantage of his unencumbered freedom by flying into the higher dimensions where he had a sense of omniscience, omnipresence, and omnipotence. It was devoid of limits. It seemed timeless and endless. Is this heaven? he wondered.

Suddenly a golden light appeared before him and out of it a figure emerged. "Who are you?" asked Christian.

"I am known as Arjuna. I was a disciple of the Krishna, and I am now an ascended soul. It is my assignment to aid you in resolving any conflicts that may reside within you."

"Amazingly, I do have a major conflict," replied Christian. "I have been trying to reconcile my aggressive training under Colonel Bradley with my firm belief in universal love and non-judgmentalism. Arjuna, can you help me?

"Certainly, Christian. Let me explain."

Arjuna explained that anger can be justified if it is used to counter injustice. "It is not the emotion that is sinful, it's how it is expressed. You must understand that to fulfill your human potential, you must learn to balance the two worlds of spirit and matter. In the case of anger, you must realize that even though it's a negative in the ideal world it may be a means to justice in the material realm."

"Aha," said Christian. "I believe the conflict is resolved and my fear is alleviated!" Christian affirmed the idea that he would never fight out of anger or fear, but only to support divine standards. He also realized that the power to destroy can also be used to preserve, if proper intent is employed. Proper intent, of course, must be consistent with divine intent.

When Christian emerged from his entranced state, he realized that several days had elapsed since he began his meditative procedural countdown. He could only conclude that all his bodily functions had slowed in a suspended state and that he had actually spent that time in another world--the world of spirit. It was amazing to him, for he was transformed. No longer did he fear anything in the world of materiality for he had been exposed to the realm of truth in a higher dimension. He was ready to return to Colonel Bradley and his next lesson.

Lesson Twenty: A Vision of Destiny

Colonel Bradley escorted Christian to Abner Tinklepaw's Farm, some ten miles away. The colonel departed with a fatherly statement. "Be well, my son, for I have prepared you for the greatness you will someday achieve. You have but two lessons remaining that when completed will establish you as ready to someday assume a great leadership role in the City of God. Remember me as a friend whose door will always be open to you. May God be with you."

With that said, he turned and departed, leaving Christian facing the oddest of characters--Abner Tinklepaw. Abner was a weathered old man, harried and stooped, who in spite of his appearance emitted an authoritative presence and a twinkling eye. He welcomed Christian with a firm handshake and said, "You have been sent to me to be tested as a man, for you are no longer a boy. Are you prepared for your second vision quest?"

"Yes, I am ready," replied Christian.

"Good. Hopefully, all will end well and you will prove to be a worthy Son of God. You will be expected to go beyond the outer world and enter the inner world until you are aware of your identity and purpose in this incarnation. You have two days to prepare. So, spend it in contemplation and seek to fortify your mind and body with good thoughts and nutrition, for your test will be quite arduous."

At dawn on Christmas Eve day, Christian was told to depart into the mountains surrounding Elk Mountain. The mountain range was laden with a light snow cover and was totally unfamiliar to Christian. In spite of not knowing the area, Christian walked the logging trails with the full confidence that his instincts and intuitive skills would see him through. The winter season determined the sun's exposure, which was at its annual ebb. Yet there still remained a positive sense that a rebirth was at hand-- the so-called darkness before the light.

Upon reaching the end of the logging trail, Christian found a small clearing, appropriate for a campsite. After preparing a campfire and a makeshift shelter, he performed a rite of illumination, the purpose of which was to summon ascended souls who would assist in his next visionary quest. Christian felt in complete control of the situation as he closed his eyes and drifted into a deep slumber that produced a magnificent dream.

In the dream Christian discovers a small glass boat on the shore of a mist-shrouded lake. He instinctively takes a seat in the craft, which propels itself across the lake until it reaches an island. As he approaches the island an incredibly beautiful crystal palace looms ahead through the mist. After the boat docks itself, Christian departs the boat and walks toward the castle courtyard filled with shadowy transparent inhabitants. When Christian attempts conversation he receives nothing more than a silent look of acknowledgement. The flock seems to be moving toward the entrance of a large throne room, so Christian incorporates himself into the flow. Once inside the massive chamber it becomes apparent that the room is dominated by two large pillars capped in gold and silver. Seated below the gold-capped pillar is a male figure and below the silver-capped figure sits a female figure. Christian realizes they are symbolic of the Law of Duality, which can be exemplified by opposites such as spirit/matter, masculine/feminine, sun/moon, and so on. As the congregation seats itself Christian is left standing alone in the center of the room. Obviously out of place, he is noticed by the golden king and summoned to approach the throne.

"Who are you and why are you here?" the king asks.

"I am Christian Corbett and I've been sent here on a quest for insights into my purpose in life."

"You, Christian, have entered this kingdom on the midwinter eve when this dimension is accessible to the people of the material plane. Observe the assemblage around you. They too are in search of their meaning and purpose. They are preparing themselves for their next incarnation by being counseled and given advice that will propel them ever higher on their evolutionary path toward spiritual perfection. You, Christian, must discover your personal insight. Once you do you will be prepared to achieve your God-ordained purpose."

The silver queen interjects, "Once you understand yourself, you will understand the whole universe. Take this token of your visit, a blue rose."

As Christian grasps the rose, a thorn pierces his hand, which causes him to awaken from his slumber.

The memory of the dream was vivid in his mind and pain in the palm of his hand was also acutely apparent. Could it be real? Christian wondered. But it had to be a dream!

As his senses were aroused back into wakefulness, he developed a sense of great anxiety and immediately burst from his campsite and ran along the logging trail back to the Tinklepaw farmhouse. Abner welcomed Christian and wondered if the quest had been satisfied.

"Yes, yes," Christian exclaimed. "I finally understand what I am and what my purpose in life is." He understood that the truly exceptional individual is obligated to live life not just in a material world but in a spiritual world as well.

Abner was delighted with the outcome of Christian's latest experience. He informed Christian that his father was expected that evening to take him home, and would likely be overjoyed with Christian's progress.

"Let's eat," said Christian. "I'm famished."

A conversation ensued over dinner and Abner told Christian he should reflect on a few truisms, such as:

Dreams can be a true interpretation of reality.

Submit to your intuitive nature and overcome your ego-induced resistance. The ego is what separates you from the true reality.

Know that reality begins when we close our eyes. Do not ever limit your thinking.

Christian's pensiveness was disrupted by a sudden knock at the door, which opened to reveal his father Jon beaming with joy at the sight of his son. "You did it, son. I must congratulate you, for you have displayed great courage and perseverance in completing the first twenty lessons. It's so exciting to think you've come all this way and have but one lesson to go. You are now ready for your final lesson, the third quest--a quest into the future. It will take place this coming summer."

Lesson Twenty-One: Nirvana

The following summer when Christian was in his seventeenth year, he was taken to study with the swami, Shankara, at an ashram in Lenox, Massachusetts. Shankara's role was to inculcate within Christian the knowledge of Kriya yoga. Kriya yoga, being the highest form of transcendental yoga, was a method employed by the great masters, including the greatest of masters, Jesus Christ. Christian was reminded that Christ had studied with the masters of God union during his long stay in Tibet and India. Shankara told Christian he would be learning how to release the divine force, Kundalini, which would rise from his lowest chakra to his highest, the crown chakra, whereby he would achieve the ultimate human experience, Nirvana.

The last lesson began simply with Christian being taught deep breathing techniques, silencing the mind, and totally focusing on the spiritual eye (third eye) located in the frontal area between the two physical eyes. The area of the spiritual eye is the so-called "cave" where true mediators go to achieve cosmic union.

After several weeks of sessions under the guidance of Shankara, Christian finally experienced the release of the coiled serpent, stored in the coccyleal chakra. A burst of energy traveled through the seven chakras and released through his crown chakra, the gateway to truth, into the totality of all creation. He became one with the all, which is known to mystics as the eternal bliss of nirvana.

Shankara told Christian that he had completed his final quest and was now prepared to fulfill his ordained destiny as a leader of mankind. He would be a leader who transmuted the hearts of man for all time in the evolutionary pursuit of absolute unity with the creator. In the manner of any great teacher he reminded Christian to apply these lessons throughout his lifetime by always submitting to intuition and listening to the cosmic mind. "In other words," he said, "know God who resides within you. Follow the universal will in all that you do. Remember the light is the secret and is the pattern on which all great doctrines and mysteries are based. Know that every false doctrine is formed by man's external ego, which separates him from the true reality. The materialistic philosophical structures of communism, socialism and fascism can only crumble into the rubble of history for they are not founded in truth. Return to the world bearing the light to illuminate God's creation and break the bonds of illusion by bringing prodigal man back to the father."

"Take this ancient prayer with you," Shankara said. He presented Christian with a beautifully inscribed prayer that read:

Grant, O God, thy protection and in protection, strength
And in strength, understanding
And in understanding, knowledge
And in knowledge, justice
And in justice, the love of it
And in that love, the love of all life
And in that love of life,
The love of God and all goodness.

Christian was highly elated after completing the twenty-one lessons. He felt he had grown exponentially in his understanding of reality and his preparedness to be a significant player in the game of life. He was expecting his father to arrive on the evening of his last lesson, and anticipated his father's kudos for the achievement of entering manhood.

As Jon drove to the Lenox Ashram, he fully appreciated the incredible beauty and peacefulness of that northwestern area of Massachusetts. The relaxing drive gave him time to reflect on the course of history unfolding before him.

From the time of his first visit to Bohemian Grove in 1984, Jon had remained in good standing with the elitist membership and continued to attend the annual summer gatherings. Although sickened by the activities inherent at the Grove, he realized the importance of being able to see first hand what the elitists had planned for the rest of mankind. This role of being a mole allowed Jon to keep the Brethren of Light fully abreast of the strategies of their reptilian-like adversaries.

The Brethren had grown into a powerful organization, both in numbers (three million by 1990) and in conviction of belief. Each of the three chapters (kingdom, power and glory) had approximately one million members. The organizational chart demonstrated subchapters in major cities and smaller cells throughout less populated areas. All meetings were held at random times and in ever-changing locations. All communications were through direct contact because the need for confidentiality was paramount. All members were sworn to secrecy at the risk of ostracism and public humiliation.

The meetings of the Brethren were not just involved in plans to foil the Illuminati, but also focused on reinforcing their strong Christian convictions. Inspirational speakers, classes in doctrine and study assignments characterized these clandestine assemblies. To fully appreciate the depth and conviction held by the brotherhood, it is important to examine their basic tenets—tenets which they believed were absolute and without any doubt. For that matter, every member had a copy of the "Manifesto Theologica" which was a compilation of the doctrinal beliefs of the Brethren of Light. The manifesto was written in a style that listed hundreds of aphoristic statements in a short, concise manner. The following declarative statements are a brief sample of the beliefs held by the Brethren:

- Mystical experience is the foundation of all major religions.
- The Kingdom of God is within.
- Man has the ability to know the cosmic consciousness.
- Salvation is only achieved through union with God by means of deep meditation and prayer.
- Once the true reality is understood man can build a new age of peace, harmony and abundance.
- Unconditional love, forgiveness and spiritual awakening should be the goal of each individual.
- The only begotten Son of God refers to the Christ consciousness within all of man.
- Jesus was the epitome of this potentiality.
- All souls who become united with Christ consciousness by self-realization through meditative techniques are sons of God.
- The second coming of Christ will be when all of man realizes that we are all Christ-like.
- All scriptures (Christian, Hindu, Buddhist) have a three-fold meaning--material, mental and spiritual (body, mind, soul).

- To achieve internal peace and harmony one must satisfy his higher spiritual needs.
- Religion is devotion to highest truth.
- Philosophy is divided into three parts: ethics, psychology, and metaphysics. Ethics deals with the material world and focuses on how to live. Psychology deals with the mental plane and concerns the means to know oneself. Whereas metaphysics deals with the spiritual plane and how to know God.
- Jesus described the Christ consciousness as The Way, The Truth and The Life.
- The Trinity consists of the Holy Ghost or Spirit (aum or cosmic vibration), the Son (reflected intelligence known as Christ consciousness) and the Father (absolute spirit or cosmic consciousness).
- Meditation allows one to contact the Holy Ghost, which is God's vibratory power.
- All truth lies in the cosmic mind, to which man can connect.
- Holy Grail is the Cup of Enlightenment; to drink from the Grail is to consume the wisdom of Christ consciousness and to become Christ-like.
- Buddha, Krishna, and Jesus were Avatars—those who bring truth to the ignorant masses.
- Thought can manifest in form; thus did spirit create materiality. Matter is nothing more than spirit in a different vibrational frequency.
- The Holy Ghost reflects the feminine principle and its cosmic vibratory power gives birth to creation.
- The universe is in evolution with an eventual return to total oneness.
- There is intelligent design throughout creation. Order and organization could not exist without intelligence.
- The physical body is a manifestation of the causal body's intelligent energy, which in the form of lifetrons forms the astral body, which in turn empowers the physical body.

- Satan seeks to divorce all creatures from their creator by reinforcing the sense of separateness and ego.
- The word or aum represents
- A (akara) creative vibration
- U (ukara) preservative vibration
- M (makura) dissolutional vibration
- Yoga means divine union. It is a religious science by which God can be known.
- Man lives in a state of delusional maya (matter) until he attains sonship (cosmic Christ) or oneness with God.
- Yoga teaches one to increase his vibration to a higher rate, which brings one into the cosmic range of omnipresence and omniscience. This is how man realizes the Christ within and finds the way to the Father. This was the method Christ taught his disciples.
- Kyiya Yoga is a meditative technique by which God consciousness is realized. It was the method used by Christ.
- The nineteenth century Swami, Lahiri Mahasana is credited with resurrecting Kriya yoga and teaching it to modern day devotees.
- A true Christian achieves union with Christ consciousness by abnegating his sense of the external world and his ego.
- The Ten Commandments are a code of natural righteousness. If man does not act in accordance with these laws, conflict occurs within and delusive suffering follows.
- Heaven isn't a place and it isn't a time. Both of those conditions have limits. Heaven is oneness with the all. It is found when a soul has satisfied its karmic debt and has no need for rebirth.
- Reincarnation was accepted doctrine in early Christianity and remained so until the Second Council of Constantinople in 553 AD. The concept of purgatory replaced reincarnation and allowed the church to hold the keys to heaven.
- Homo sapiens, the species of man, is unique in that he is endowed with seven spiritual centers within the spine and brain that permit him, when awakened, to discover the divinity and power of the soul. John's gospels refer to these chakras as the seven seals.

- If all of man achieved his potential Christ-like status, it would usher in a millennium of peace and brotherhood. The goal of our Brethren of Light is to eventually return humanity to an Eden of this sort.

- Combining the esoteric yoga teachings of Krishna and Jesus' exoteric methods of unconditional love is the only way to save the world from strife.

- The spiritual eye, also known as the third eye, is located between the two physical eyes and is associated with the pineal gland. It is known in Hindu lore as the "star in the east." This divine link is the means whereby man can send his consciousness into the God realm. The eye itself is a microcosm of the same trinity that exists in the macrocosm of the universe. When viewed in deep meditation it appears as a white star, encased in a blue light, surrounded by an aura of gold. The gold represents the Holy Ghost, the blue is the Christ consciousness, and the star is the cosmic consciousness of God the Father. Jesus referred to the spiritual eye when he stated, "If therefore thine eye be single, thy whole body shall be full of light." Luciferian codes exist as evil negative thought forms in the universal scheme of things. These codes will immigrate into human life when our spiritual borders erode allowing human behavior to fall into chaos (entropy) and sinful activity.

- Emotions and ego awareness impede our knowing the divine. The early 4th century Christian mystic, Evagrius Ponticus, espoused apatheia—freedom from emotions--which leads to a love of God and opens the way to know God (theology). Dispassion towards the external, material world should be a quality of anyone who seeks the truth. Emotions create an illusion and detract from the true reality. Some thoughts lead to emotions, which can be referred to as "demons". We should realize man is a microcosm and moves in a field of forces, thereby influencing the entire range of forces in the universe. These forces have a vertical direction toward or away from God. As these forces rise into positive regions, harmony and order prevail. Whereas, if they descend into negativity (Satan), chaos and disorder become evident. This universal truth applies to all systems, be they biologic, social, political or economic. When evil thoughts become passionate, emotions arise. Such emotions as greed, lust, anger, gluttony, sloth, pride and envy have come to be known as the seven deadly sins. It is incumbent upon each individual to exercise his free choice and decide to allow such thoughts to linger within or not.

- Members of the Brethren of Light were fully expected to be serious students of the Manifesto Theologica and to know its contents completely. In addition, they were taught deep meditative techniques by a cadre of Kriya yoga masters who were from the east.

Jon had been so engrossed in his thoughts while driving that when he arrived at the ashram to pick up his son, he was surprised at how quickly time had passed. His fatherly instincts were evident for he was excitedly anticipating seeing Christian, who had finally accomplished a great feat by completing the twenty-one lessons that would shape and prepare him for a very significant role in the future.

Father and son thanked swami Shankara for teaching Christian the final lesson. On the drive home they stopped at the Lenox House for a fine, gourmet dinner. The meal not only served to satisfy their hunger but also offered the opportunity for a serious father-son conversation. Jon informed Christian that he would soon be invited to enter the brotherhood as an initiate. With that would come the knowledge of the ultimate plan to eventually assume global control and remove the Luciferian cabal from all power and influence. Jon further discussed the history of the global conspiracy, which was designed to create a godless Orwellian type society. His discussion included the story of how the Brethren came to be and of their mission to bring a true understanding of Christ's message to all of God's children.

Finally, Jon explained that the twenty-one lessons were intended to prepare Christian to become a crown prince who would someday take over the reins of control after his father's reign ended, upon retirement or death. The plan was to have Christian continue his father's benevolent monarchy until all of mankind was ready to assume a responsible and moral citizenship. Once the citizenry achieved this elevated status, the monarchy would be dissolved and sovereign nations restored to representative republics.

"Remember, Christian, total democracies never work. They always end in chaos and eventually dictatorships," warned Jon. "The best system is one of an intelligent and temperate citizenry that will make the proper choices and decisions."

At the meal's end, Jon presented Christian with a beautifully bound red leather manuscript of the "Manifesto Theologica" and advised him to become familiar with its principles.

Christian heaved a great sigh and said, "This is almost overwhelming. First, I learn the deepest of meditative techniques that take me to Nirvana; then you tell me of a giant Luciferian plot to dominate the world and that I'm to play a role in the battle to save humanity from enslavement by becoming a king! What an incredible gift. It's almost too much to bear. But, thanks, Dad. I feel your love and will always appreciate all that you've done for me. Now, let's go home. I can't wait to see Mom and my sister, Christine."

Jon served in the House of Representatives with great distinction and was highly respected by his congressional peers, as well as the public. His popularity led to his being nominated to run for the U.S. Senate in 1996. Once again the winning margin was enormous with Jon gaining close to seventy percent of the vote. He was certainly becoming the "darling of the Republican Party."

His book, a narrative called The Return to Glory, placed an emphasis on rebuilding the nation on a moral foundation. It was well received and had sold several thousand copies. However, in 1998 Jon went on a nationwide book tour that resulted in popularizing the book even more. It became a best seller of the highest order and propelled Jon to a cult-like figure. People acclaimed his brilliance and sought his counsel. He was a constant guest on radio and television shows and had become an icon in the eyes of millions of Americans. There was even talk of his being nominated to run for the presidency in the year 2000 election.

Unfortunately, the actual possibility of Jon being nominated was out of the question because the global elitists had already selected the next president. It was well understood amongst the powerful elements of world societies that election outcomes in any nation of states were predetermined and actual vote counts were easily manipulated to insure that their candidate was always elected. It just so happened in this case that their candidate was to be, of all people, none other than G.W. Plante. Plante was the very same incompetent fool that Jon had encountered back in his days at Yale. Jon, of course, fully understood the machinations of the hidden political system and had no second thoughts about his being seriously considered as a nominee.

Jon's knowledge of the true intentions of the Luciferians had been developed over the years because he had participated in the annual Bohemian Grove conferences and several Bilderberger meetings. The plans and their means of implementation were always presented in full detail at these gatherings. It was explained that the gradualism of the takeover plan would be an important aspect of the conspiracy. Such a slow approach would prevent the general public from becoming suspicious of the conspirators' true intentions. Jon often thought of the story of the frog being exposed to a slowly rising temperature as it sat in a pot of water. The frog would be unaware of its impending death and would foolishly remain in the water until death ensued. Jon knew in his heart that he and the organized Brethren of Light were humanity's only hope if man was ever to survive the sinister plan of the evil ones.

As the decade of the 90s passed into history, America was in a slow and subtle decline. However, it wasn't until the Bohemian Grove conference of 1999 that Jon fully comprehended the seriousness of the nation's imminent peril. The keynote speaker at that meeting was the noted internationalist, Henri Businger, who outlined in detail the history of the plan to effect a new world order at the expense of all sovereign nations and how it was imperative that operation "full force" would have to be implemented by the year 2001. He warned those in attendance that it would not be an easy task because they would be fighting against a cosmic process that was seeking to change the resonance on the planet to a higher frequency. He further explained that an increase in resonance, if not countered by extreme levels of negative energy and their absolute control, could possibly result in a higher vibrational state of spirituality on the planet. He reminded everyone of their commitment to resist, at all cost, the God force. Businger explained that the G.W. Plante administration would be a key player in initiating the ultimate demise of the U.S.A.

The final phase of Operation Full Force would occur in the following presidency, which would be headed by a figure that had been groomed to be an atheistic, communist leader. He would be of mixed race, being half black and half white. He had been fathered by a native Kenyan who married a young white American girl. The child was actually born in Kenya—a birth that was witnessed by his paternal grandmother and other family members. The birth was registered in Hawaii a short while later, but did not qualify the child as a native-born citizen. The fact of non-citizenry status would have to be cleverly covered up if this figure were to ever ascend to the chief executive position. In spite of this sticking point, the elites of our organization selected him back in 1992 when he was a young college student. He was to be carefully streamlined and educated to be irresistible to the American public who would foolishly elect him to increasingly important political positions, eventually culminating in the highest office of all—the presidency. Even though he will have had ties to Islam and Marxist activists and a long-time membership in a Marxist church espousing a black libertarian theology, he would hoodwink the American public into believing in a massive change in the ways of politics, economics and life in general. Businger explained that this leader would be the poster boy for a new world order and that he would initiate enormous changes in the national climate, which would result in a perfect storm of bankrupting financial chaos and destructive social disintegration. The rapid implementation of a wide variety of fascistic and socialistic programs would overwhelmingly befuddle the citizenry and quickly reduce them to serfdom and total dependency on the state. Businger reminded the enrapt listeners of the axiom, "The bigger the lie, the more people will believe it."

Once the goals of Operation Full Force were reached in 2011, the public would be so distressed by the uncertainty of their lives and the rampant social and economic chaos that they would surrender their freedoms and liberties and demand an absolute dictator. The president would be removed on the constitutional ground that he was illegitimate because he was not a native-born citizen. After the president's removal, the Luciferian elites would select a member of their group who was highly respected and admired by the masses to be appointed by Congress as the new leader. An absolute monarchy would be established, giving total control to the globalists, who would then initiate pogroms to eliminate dissidents and those they deemed to be "useless eaters." The world population would be reduced by 80-85% and a new godless, secularized humanistic system would be effectuated. This event would be the ultimate victory of Lucifer over God and would affirm Lucifer's claim that he and his disciples would never submit to the will of God.

Businger further delineated the various steps that would be necessary to achieve the final victory.

- In 2001 Operation Full Force proposed a Pearl Harbor-like event, which would become the impetus for the U.S.A. to enter two economically disastrous wars. To be specific, the destruction of the twin financial centers in New York City was being seriously considered. Whatever the eventual target, the blame would be placed on terrorists who played no role in the actual event.

- Several measures would bring the middle class to its knees, such as eliminating their sources of income, fomenting social disorder, restricting access to food, and undermining the public health through exposure to toxic drugs, processed food, vaccines, fluoridated water, and a poisoned atmosphere by using chemtrails.

- Businger admitted that his foray into China during the Nixon administration was the seminal event in the eventual destruction of America's industrial might. By making China a primary manufacturer of the world's goods, the U.S.A. would be terminally weakened and eliminated as the final obstacle to a New World Order. Destruction of the industrial base under the guise of international free trade agreements, the imposition of stifling taxes, and the enforcement of crippling regulations would be the lynchpins of destroying the viability and wealth of the middle class.

- China's dominance in manufacturing would create a tremendous outflow of money and wealth from the U.S.A., resulting in an imbalance of world capital. The lack of dollars, which are needed to support housing prices, would lead to a rash of foreclosures and undermine the banking system, leading to the nationalization of the nation's financial structure.

- Information would be controlled through ownership of media outlets (television, radio, newspapers) and the eventual control of the Internet.

- A civilian security force, as powerful as the military, would be created, a force manned by 250,000 members from lower socioeconomic classes. This force would be used to subjugate the dissidents and the affluent segment of society. Once in place this Gestapo-like force could enforce adherence to a new way of life.

- Depopulation programs would be instituted, such as abortion, mandatory vaccines, genetically modified foods, synthetic drugs, fouled water, food shortages, and a toxic atmosphere caused by chemtrails.

- Global warming and climate change will be false topics that will be heavily propagandized. The purpose? To effectuate legislation placing enormous financial burdens on the average citizen and restricting their access to energy. In addition, financially troubled major industries would be crippled to the point that nationalizing them would be the only solution.

- Individual property rights would be taken away from the citizens.

- A massive trillion-dollar aid program to uplift the dark continent of Africa would be implemented, although its true purpose would be to further the debt burden of the United States of America resulting in its financial collapse.

- Any citizens opposed to the abomination of radical change would be branded as extremists. Those who defend the right to life, the U.S. Constitution, and legal immigration would be declared enemies of the state. Adherence to their outdated beliefs would be punishable by incarceration in camps all around the country.

- Local police forces would no longer be keepers of the peace, but would be transformed into paramilitary organizations designed to keep everyone in tow.

- The Bible would be banned and churches outlawed. The belief in God would, at first, be declared a serious crime punishable by imprisonment but eventually would become a capital transgression.

- As in all totalitarian regimes the citizens' right to gun ownership would be outlawed. Such a measure is essential to limiting dissent and the possibility of armed revolt.

- Personal vegetable gardens would not be allowed and the government would reserve the right to confiscate all farms. These measures would allow leaders to control the food supply, a key element in the subjugation of the masses.

- Leaders of Operation Full Force would perpetrate a rash of cyber attacks on government computer systems, thus fomenting great consternation in the nation concerning our national security. Of course, their proposed solution would be a cyber attack protection act, giving government the power to close down the internet and shut off public access to information.

- They would plant the seeds of self-destruction by encouraging individuals to indulge in the seven deadly sins. Such actions reinforce the ego and emphasize separateness from the concept of oneness with God. Remember, God is the enemy. The tactics to be employed would include: promoting carnality and perversions, developing dissonant non-melodic music to appeal to man's lower animal nature, making constant references to gustatory excitement and satisfying gluttoness appetites, promoting a lack of diligence and reverence to reinforce a slothful lifestyle, creating detractions from man's universal nature so he places himself above God and can indulge in the vices of envy, anger, jealousy and excessive pride, and, lastly, inculcating the avaricious idea that all meaning to life is dictated by material wealth and possessions. This last obsession would be implemented with the insane idea of giving everyone a home regardless of his or her ability to afford one. A legislative act, called the Community Revitalization Act, would be a major first step in the eventual collapse of the banking system and credit markets. The Glass-Steagall Act would be repealed and banks would be allowed to trade in the stock market, securitized mortgages, derivatives, CDOs, and other unregulated instruments. This action would bring about the collapse of the banking system. The death knell of the banking system, a financial coup d'etat, would take place on September 11, 2008, exactly seven years to the hour of the original 9/11 event in 2001, after which an electronic drawdown on the banks of America would be perpetrated. Anywhere from five hundred billion to several trillion dollars would be extracted before the Treasury would notice and stop their computer operations. The damage would already have been done. Hopefully this action would strike a mortal blow to the U.S. economy, which, despite all efforts to save it, would eventually collapse. The banking system would fail, allowing Operation Full Force leaders to offer a solution--a one-world currency followed closely by a one-world government.

Businger beamed as he stated, "Then we will have them. God will have lost! We Luciferians will finally be absolute in our power. Long live Baal!

Jon sat in stunned silence as Businger ended his speech. He was aghast at the ruthlessness in the tone of Businger's strident rant. Jon would live with the haunting memory of Businger's blood lust for many years to come.

When the twin towers were destroyed in 2001, Jon fully understood it to be an inside job. Unfortunately, he couldn't share his knowledge with the media or his constituency for fear of exposing his connection to the globalists. He knew exactly how it had been done: the flying of electronically piloted tanker planes into the financial center and the subsequent controlled demolition; how all passengers on the four hi-jacked airplanes had been removed and placed on one plane—flight 93; how flight 93 was shot down by Air National Guard fighter planes; how the Pentagon attack was not even an airplane but a missile of some kind; how the twin towers had been set up with nano-sized thermite to expedite the burning of steel beams; how the owner of the financial center had purchased the complex only weeks before with a relatively small down payment, yet received an insurance reward for seventeen billion dollars; how the so-called nineteen Arab perpetrators were still alive and well and several were actually interviewed by the BBC after the incident; how this event rallied the American public who were dumb enough to give full support to the invasions of Iraq and Afghanistan, both of which would seriously undermine the financial strength of the United States.

Jon was greatly dismayed over the fact that the majority of the human family was totally clueless about their impending doom. Much like innocent sheep being led to slaughter, humanity was plunging headlong into a cesspool of self-indulgence and intellectual paralysis, which would prevent them from resisting a tide that would sweep them into oblivion. He wished he could scream a clarion warning to alert the world to what was in store.

Jon cleverly maintained his elevated status in the Luciferian inner circles. As a member of the Trilateral Commission and the Council on Foreign Relations he had commanded the great respect of even the highest order of Luciferian plotters—the Illuminati. The illuminated or enlightened ones were a group of ten of the most powerful world figures known to insiders as the roundtable. They, in effect, determined the leadership and workings of all six subordinate groups such as the Trilateral Commission, the Council on Foreign Relations, the Bilderbergers, the United Nations, the Club of Rome, and the International Council of England. It was a huge stroke of fortune when Jon was designated a chief advisor to the Illuminati in 2006, because it allowed him to be privy to their most secret plots and machinations.

The period from 2001 to 2011 would be characterized by an accelerated dissolution of a once great nation. The Luciferians were masters of stealth as they cleverly orchestrated elections, events and circumstances to propel the country down the road to destruction. Every facet of attack was incorporated into the crystallization of their master plan. They went right at the throat of the body politic by destroying the industrial base and meaningful work. Once the resourceful segment of society found their sources of income destroyed, they would have no choice but to acquiesce to the dictates of Big Brother.

"Take away their liberties, freedoms, food, recreation, and shelters. Take it all away," declared the illumined ones. "Make them crawl like the vermin that they are."

That was one of the last quotes Jon remembered hearing at the Bohemian Grove conference in 2008. Jon constantly ruminated on the fact that the "Wounded Eagle" Plan was working well as America careened along the path towards eventual social, political and economic disintegration.

Jon fully understood that the destructive storms and extreme weather were the result of weather war technologies involving chemtrails and the electromagnetic emitting installations known as HAARP. He understood that legislation such as universal health care, energy taxation (cap and trade), financial stimulus bills, and cyber protection acts were designed to either bankrupt the nation's treasury or to restrict freedoms of the citizenry.

Most of the legislative bills had been written long before they were actually proposed in Congress. They would lie in dormancy until Congress was totally controlled by the Democratic Party. The domination of Congress and the Executive Branch by liberal progressives would allow these acts to be passed in a unilateral manner. Once enacted there would be little chance of ever reversing the iron grip that was strangling the traditions of freedom, liberty and spirituality.

The apocalyptic predictions were at hand. The four horsemen of famine, death, pestilence and war were ready to ride over the planet creating unimaginable horror. Famine would result by creating food crises by limiting the growth of fruits and vegetables, measures that could be achieved in a variety of ways: contaminating fruits and vegetables with various blights and diseases; retarding crop growth via drought or excessive rain; and reducing the pollination of plants by disorienting the bee population with electromagnetic energies. The meat industry would also be damaged by the introduction of bio-engineered diseases such as Mad Cow disease and Creutzfeldt-Jakob disease, thus restricting access to animal protein. The second horseman of death would strike in several ways: initiating programs such as free abortion and euthanizing the sick and elderly populations; bioengineering a variety of infectious diseases such as Lyme disease, mycoplasma infections, Ebola, West Nile virus, swine flu, HIV and toxic molds. Pestilence would be encouraged by eliminating natural enemies of pests. For example, reducing the bat population would result in a great increase of disease carrying mosquitoes. Wars would ravage the planet as a result of fomenting hatred and discord throughout the world. Racial and religious differences would be emphasized as a means of inciting bellicosity and savagery.

The concepts of free enterprise and capitalism would also be under attack. The death of capitalism must occur because it is reflective of human excellence and freedom, which is the means to realizing one's true potential as an instrument of God. The fall of capitalism would be caused by its own success. Businesses would be encouraged to morph into ever-larger corporations that would eventually move their operations outside of America. This process would be facilitated by trade agreements foisted upon the nation under the guise of "free" trade. The net result of the destruction of the American capitalistic system would be the elimination of America's middle class.

By 2009 the urgency of the dire situations on the planet necessitated extreme counter measures. The Brethren of Light reacted by formalizing their plans for the fateful day when they would reverse the tables on the Luciferian plotters. With the help of their military arm, the Brethren of Might, a final strategy was established which would, at a coordinated time all around the world, take the members of the evil ones into custody and incarcerate them in camps around the globe. The Brethren were secure in the belief that with the help of their explicit faith in the universal God force and the righteousness of their cause there could be no possibility of failure.

Jon experienced two events in 2009 that further cemented his convictions on the ultimate truth and the spiritual nature of reality. The first occurred in the spring of the year when Jon and his son Christian were introduced to a saint-like woman named Olive Dawson at a meeting of the Brethren of Light. Olive, incredibly, had required no food nor drink for nine years and remained in perfect health. She had had a vision of the Blessed Virgin in Dublin, Ireland, in 1999 and evidently achieved a state of grace, which allowed her to approach the height of human potential. This encounter with Olive Dawson reaffirmed Jon and Christian's beliefs and strengthened their resolve to teach the world the truth and overcome the dark forces once and for all.

The second event, which involved listening to an interview with Mellen Thomas Benedict, further braced Jon's convictions. Benedict discussed a near death experience he had. His story, as related in the interview, told how he had been diagnosed with terminal brain cancer in 1981. The doctor had explained that neither radiation nor surgery could reverse the situation. Benedict was told to make his peace and prepare to die. With that hopeless diagnosis Benedict went to a hospice to wait for his ultimate demise. While there he encountered a woman who persistently goaded him into praying for his soul. Being a person of some artistic accomplishment and a non-believer, he totally rejected her pleas. About six months after entering the hospice Benedict died. As he explains it, at the moment of death he found himself in his astral body looking down on his physical body as the last wispy vapors of the life force rose into the ether. Next, he went into a total life review, followed by an approaching golden light. As the light neared him it transmuted into an angel. Benedict asked the angel, "Are you the Angel of Death?"

"No, I am your guardian angel. My name is Mellen. Come with me."

With that Benedict found himself in front of a great light of indescribable brilliance. Unlike most near death experiences he actually had a conversation with the light. "Are you God? Is their a purpose to life?" he asked.

"Who and what is not God; all is one," was the reply.

Benedict realized that light is a mandala of all human souls. It is the oversoul matrix of our system and sum total of everything. He was impressed by the idea that humanity is a part of the whole and that humans are the most graceful of beings on the planet. Needless to say, Benedict's cancer was gone when his life was restored.

Chapter Seven

- Exposure of the Secret Cabal
- Cleansing Reign
- A World in Peace, Harmony and Abundance

The year 2011 saw the United States falling into total dissolution, which was a result of financial excesses and behavioral indulgences. Several attempts to impose market policies had failed; the national debt burden had risen to unmanageable proportions; the currency had been debased, devalued and was no longer recognized by other nations which deemed the dollar worthless; extreme weather affected the production of crops causing massive food shortages; diseases of all sorts were rampant; the G.W. Plante Doctrine of nation building, which was intended to cause America's domination in the world, had failed miserably; and countless civil wars were being fought on every populated continent.

The Luciferians delighted in the horror for they knew the time to implement the last phase of Operation Full Force was at hand. They knew it was time to assume total control. Demonstrations and riots were taking place constantly as the people demanded removal of an obviously incompetent president. The president appeared confused and incapable of governance. As a result, it was decided in secret meetings to forcibly remove him from office on the grounds that he was unconstitutionally the President because of his foreign birth. Martial law was declared.

That fateful day finally arrived in June of 2011 when the president was forcibly removed from the oval office. Congress declared martial law and suspended constitutional law. After weeks of deliberation, which was largely a sham because the outcome was already predetermined, an absolute monarchy was instituted! The choice for monarch could be none other than Jon Corbett.

The coronation of Jon I took place in July of 2011 and was reminiscent of great coronations of the past. Comparisons were made to those of Charlemagne, Napoleon, and Elizabeth II. The magnificence of the pomp and ceremony left the plebian segments of the citizenry in awe as many realized that having an enlightened philosopher-king is the only true system because it reflects the cosmologic order. Jon's son, Christian, was designated crown prince, which established him as the successor to his father upon the retirement or death of the king. Christian had been groomed to be an Arthurian-like leader from an early age. The public embraced him and knew in full confidence that Christian would wield his power in an enlightened way.

On October 13, 2011, Jon I implemented the counter plan which the Brethren of Light had so carefully crafted over the course of thirty-five years. The October 13th date was chosen because it was on that date in 1307 that the Knights Templar were taken into custody, tortured and burned at the stake. The plan was designed to reveal the identify of the world's evil leaders as the fallen angels, to remove them from their positions of power and place them in incarceration camps—the very same camps that the evil ones had secretly built to house those who would dissent against their foiled plan to develop a one-world godless state. The Brethren of Light had strategized to co-ordinate, around the globe, a specific time when the elites would receive a knock on the door and be greeted by members of the military arm of the Brethren, the Brethren of Might.

In order to be consistent with the beliefs of the Brethren of Light, there would be no cruel treatment of these prisoners; they would be treated with care and compassion. In spite of their evil nature they would be given every opportunity to learn the principles of the law of one in the hope that they too would become spiritually aware and be able to ascend with all of mankind when the "omega point" was reached in 2012. The Omega Point would be marked by the moment the planet reached a new vibrational frequency, which would take the planet into a less dense and more spiritual character.

Within a week following the massive roundup of the Orwellian proponents, Jon I made a pronouncement to the world via an international televised broadcast. Entitled "Veritas" the oration was reminiscent of great orations of the past, such as those of Washington, Lincoln and Churchill. Its intentions were to explain the historical record of the secret Luciferian cabal to dominate the world and the goal of the Luciferians to subjugate all of mankind. Jon would also seek to delineate all that would need to be done to bring humanity into the new reality.

In explaining his plans for his cleansing reign Jon required the help of Herman Sparkman and Ion Ampere. By organizing a loose triumvirate of power, they would initiate programs around the globe to bring about a universal transformation in man's understanding of the true reality of spirit and the ways that man should live to be in accordance with this basic truth. Jon also expounded on the absolute need to purge the nation and the world of all who sought to destroy it in the name of Lucifer. The speech ended with a vivid allegorical analogy to a warm spring rain washing away the dirt and grime of a bleak and cold winter. The promise of a new and glorious age of enlightenment was at hand and man would begin to live as the universal creator had intended--in harmony, peace, love and abundance!

The discourse itself was divided into several categories, each of which would have to be implemented to affect the ascension. A synopsis of Jon's views follows:

History

Jon began "Veritas" with a quote from Revelation 12:7, 9, 12.

"...and there was war in heaven... and the great dragon was cast out, that old serpent, called the Devil and Satan, which deceiveth the whole world: He was cast out into the earth and his angels were cast out with him... woe to the inhabitors of the earth and the sea! For the devil is come down unto you, having great wrath, because he knoweth that he hath but a short time."

Since that time eons ago, the fallen angels have sought to impose their will on the planet. They do this by reinforcing the ego, which is a means of separating the individual from his universal nature. By creating the illusion of materiality the Luciferians seek to establish a kingdom on earth devoid of reverence and obedience to the God force. They consider themselves illumined and call themselves the Illuminati. This belief is, of course, a contradiction because it is the complete opposite of the means to seeing the divine light of the creator. That light can only be found through spiritual growth and not through materialism.

In their cunning and deceitful way they have controlled human societies for thousands of years as they revel in their ability to prevent humanity from discovering its true nature and thus live in accordance with divine will. In our contemporary world the Luciferian (Illuminati) organizational structure begins with a roundtable of as little as ten members, and then branches out into six offshoot organizations that essentially control all financial, social, religious and political activity on earth. The six organizations are well known to all of you—they are the Council of Foreign relations (CFR), the Trilateral Commission (TLC), the

Bilderbergers, the Council of Rome, the International Council in England, and the United Nations. What is not well known to you and even to lesser minions of these groups is that we all take orders from Lucifer himself.

Now that we have slain the beast and removed it from power, the time for a new age of belief is at hand. The veil of secrecy has finally been removed for all of you to see the real truth: we are all connected in spirit and one with God, the universal spirit. The New Order, which we plan to initiate in the near future, will return humanity to its rightful place in the kingdom. It is our assertion that by exposing and forever vanquishing the Luciferian and Satanic elements that have held man in the bondage of pragmatic humanism and materialism, man will ascend to a level of being Christ-like and thus enter humankind into the golden age, thereby fulfilling the promise of the second coming of Christ. Man will be Christ! This development will take place in a new density and cause a leap forward in our evolutionary journey towards absolute oneness with the ultimate creator, the God within us. The defeat of the serpent will only come by our awareness of the cosmic Christ within us, not by the intercession from God. Even though the cosmic process and a return to oneness is setting the stage, the final act will only occur when man through his free will makes the choice to return home, as did the prodigal son.

It behooves me to inform all of you of a brief history of the Brethren of Light. It all began forty years ago when I discovered the plan known as the "Wounded Eagle." It was a diabolical design to destroy America and create a godless Orwellian world, which would be neofeudalist in nature with only the global elites enjoying power and wealth of an oligarchic noble class. The shocking nature of their plan was characterized by its ruthlessness and disdain for God and mankind. It was their aim to create a system of financial control in the private hands of central bankers, which would allow them to dominate the politics and economics of every nation. The primary goals of absolute power, service to Satan, and a dictatorial world order were most evident, and the ultimate destruction of America and its divinely inspired system of government was pre-eminent in the plan.

When I serendipitously discovered the plan those many years ago, I decided to dedicate myself to overcoming the evil forces seeking to enforce the will of Lucifer. Shortly thereafter, the foundation of our organization began when Herman Sparkman and Ion Ampere joined forces with me to form a trinity of leadership. We began in a small way by seeking to expand our membership in a binary manner with each of us expected to recruit two like-minded individuals into the Brethren. With extreme care each new member was expected to do the same until our organization grew into one containing several million around the world. Our meetings were secretive and randomly held. Our beliefs were formalized in a manifesto that reflected the beliefs of Jesus Christ and the great avatars of the past. It was our intent that at some point in the future all of man would embrace these truths and cleanse the world of the illusions of the past. We knew the cleansing could only come from the grass roots and not be violent or combative. It could only come through a collective consciousness based on the power source of universal love and be characterized by compassion and goodness. As the collective grew into a great magnitude that basic characteristic of love and virtue would manifest into reality. The manifestation would overcome the antichrist of secular humanism, which has caused a distraction from man's divine awareness. Once manifestation occurs the power of eternal love (God's universal vibrational force) will overcome the devil men who have perpetrated the greatest of frauds, the unreality of the crushing density of the external world.

Now that you know something of the history, tenets and purpose of the Brethren of Light, it is proper that the following outline of our plan to bring about a cleansing reign be presented to you.

The first topic will be philosophy and spirituality, which will act as the foundation on which to build the City of God. Without a system of absolute beliefs based on truth no structure can survive, whether it be social, political or economic. Remember the words of Plato, "A nation without absolute beliefs is a dead nation."

Following the discussion of philosophy the outline will entail the topics of environment, economics and commerce, energy, health, education, justice and politics.

Philosophy and Spirituality

Citizens, lend me your ears, for what I am about to tell you will be the philosophical foundation on which we, a united people, will build a social structure reflective of a divine design so perfect that all will be in harmony, balance, peace and abundance without war, disease, hunger, distress, or discord. A golden age is at hand and all of you will participate if you accept the self-evident truths that we will now expound upon.

Once enough of you understand the nature of the true reality as taught by the great masters, that new awareness will sweep all of human consciousness and elevate us into the next dimension; we will be leaving the third dimension and transcending into the fourth dimension. The fourth dimension is representative of the heart chakra and will bring us one step closer to the ultimate reality—a total union of spirit and matter and a oneness with the all.

Let me begin by saying there is a non-physical reality and it is a large part of our universe. Its existence has yet to be discovered by science, which is mired in materiality. The true reality is beyond normal human consciousness and our five senses. For us to know the truth we must expand our spiritual nature. The study of quantum physics and the superstring theory may hold the keys to unlocking the mysteries of the universe. Many of these mysteries have been known intuitively for thousands of years by spiritual masters. However, the use of scientific methods has not yet discovered God. The spiritual realm operates above the speed of light, which is thought to be impossible in conventional scientific circles. The physical realm with its innate limits was shaped by the fall of man when he lost his connection to the frequencies of the God force. When man lost his bandwidth he fell from spiritual consciousness. We see references to these disconnections in the biblical stories of the Garden of Eden, Noah's Ark and the Tower of Babel, which reference mankind's lost communication due to man's self-glorification. When the spirit of truth comes, the bandwidth will be restored and we will once again live in the city of God. It is each individual's responsibility to know his purpose and assignment in life. Only then will he understand God's messages, which come to us from outside this dimension.

Man has been living in untruth, illusion and a false reality since the death of the age of belief and the subsequent age of reason, which fostered the spiritless philosophy of humanism. This materialistic view placed man above God and led to feminization of societies, moral relativism, and the decline in the quality of life in general. Humanism denies the existence of the soul and universal spirit by ignoring the fact that spiritual reality exists beyond this dimension in another vibrational frequency.

For all of you to understand where your new philosopher king is planning to take you, you must fully comprehend your multi-dimensional anatomy and your relationship to the universal creator (God). Think of this God force as a type of spiral torsion energy capable of thought and a cause unto itself. It is the universal consciousness known as the cosmic mind. We are all fragments of this whole and made in its image. The part is the whole with us being a microcosm of the macrocosm. Consider yourself as a personal hologram, which is part of the universal hologram. Complete your hologram and you achieve oneness and salvation.

Within each of us resides the vibrational God presence (I am), which lies undiscovered by most individuals because their sense of self (ego) separates them from their real universal self and sinks them into a focus on their material nature. In truth, we are multidimensional beings or personalities and our entire personality dwells in several dimensions simultaneously. We actually have seven bodies, each of which differs in vibrational frequency. The first and most obvious body is the physical, followed by the less dense etheric, astral, and three mental bodies. Each soul makes its own choices on an evolutionary journey to completion and a return to oneness. Each new reincarnated life moves a step closer to truth and God until finally its vibrational quality reaches "ain soph," a state of pure and perfect potentiality. This is salvation and life in God's kingdom. The soul has satisfied its karmic debt and has no need to return to material life. The concept of reincarnation is not an idea foreign to western religion. It was a part of church doctrine until the 6th century A.D. and was replaced by a simplified idea known as purgatory.

The transformation of humanity and life in a golden age will require changes in our belief systems. To break the chains of enslavement brought about by living under the false doctrine of pragmatic, secularized humanism, we must free the inner self to realize our potential as children of God. This is why personal freedom and liberties are essential to transcendence and a return to truth and God. Understand that the cosmic plan is positive and expansive, whereas, the material world is negative, destructive and contractive. As I speak, I hope you are realizing the parallels with the inspired foundations of the United States of America as being consistent with these ideas. The nation was surely a beacon of light in a dark world. Unfortunately, it fell victim to the self-indulgent deadly sins and found itself in a state of total dissolution.

Citizens, your ideas of existence are limiting and must change. No longer will we focus on the external world, but we, as a human family, will develop a new awareness that will propel us toward a life of peace, harmony and abundance. All of you will be exposed to the concept of the power of thought; thought is a powerful electromagnetic force and a form of energy. It can become manifest in physical form and circumstance. Thoughts that are attuned to the divine and thoughts of the creator breed order and harmony. In contrast, negative thoughts lead to entropy and chaos. The physical objects that we perceive are symbols existing as realities within certain vibrational frequencies. However, other realities coexist at different frequencies wherein objects are not symbols. For this physical reality to continue, it must be in accord with the universal law of balance. In simpler terms, I am saying that placing excessive attention on your physical nature creates an imbalance that leads to disorder in physical systems, be they social, economic or political. The physical reality is governed by the Law of Duality, which explains the need to balance opposite forces. Examples would be spirit/matter, yin/yang, positive/negative, masculine/feminine and light/darkness.

Each of you as a distinct personality is a fragment of the creator and has the free will to create your own experience in this reality. If you choose to make your life consistent and in cooperation with God's expansive mode, it will lead to purposeful manifestations in life and new paradigms of experience. If you deny these truths you will never know true happiness and the joy of fulfillment by living in divine grace. Unfortunately, the religions most of you have known place God outside of you and not within. The truth is that the kingdom is within and it is your responsibility to discover that fact. Only through this gnosis of knowing the truth will you be released from the tyranny of matter.

Many super gods, known as avatars, e.g. Christ, Buddha, Krishna, have reincarnated on earth to teach us these truths. However, certain forces of evil have sought to discredit their messages and have led to humankind's ignorance of the true reality. It's an age-old battle of good versus evil, God versus Satan, spirit versus matter. The world seeks to deny God and spirituality to perpetuate itself in falseness and illusion.

We must all withdraw our sword to fight the good fight. We can use the example of King Arthur withdrawing the sword Excalibur from the stone of matter to achieve his true potentiality as a spiritual leader of man. Thus, just as he did, each of us can discover the Holy Grail and drink from the cup of enlightenment.

Our new reality will place emphasis on unconditional love, non-judgmentalism, and union with divine will. Virtue must replace vice. The sins of indulgence must be expunged. The seven deadly sins of lust, greed, sloth, gluttony, pride, envy and anger must be replaced by virtues such as honesty, integrity, diligence, humility, frugality, modesty, temperance, reverence, faith, hope, charity and courage. The satanic impulses to reinforce our physical comforts by the elimination of infants through abortion and the elderly via euthanasia will have no place in our new world. It is imperative that you understand that upon conception the zygote (fertilized egg) is infused with the soul (godly energy) so, does it not follow that denying the expression of the soul is a grave offense against God's will? The millions of slaughtered infants who were sacrificed have created an enormous stain on the national soul, a stain that can only be obliterated by righteous living. Consider that the organic material world is carbon-based and the six-carbon atom is represented by the number 666, a symbol of the devil. The number 999 signifies the God number and for us to return to God's favor we must reverse 666 to 999.

I would recommend that you study the ancient mystical system of the Jewish Kabala. Kabala recognizes in each object of nature two distinct elements. One is spirit and incorruptible. The other is material and a symbol of evil. Kabbalists view hell as a place devoid of all that reflects order, harmony and love. They present the allegorical depiction of seven tabernacles for each of the seven deadly sins. Their book, The Sefir Yetzirah, teaches the oneness and omnipotence of God. It is the spectacle of the world that brings man up to the concept of God. It is the unity and order of creation that exemplifies the oneness and omniscience of the universal creator. God is both the matter and form of the universe. Nothing exists outside of God. All things bear his imprint and are reflective of his supreme intelligence. The deduction that the universe and God are one and the same is the foundation of the Kabbala's second book, The Zohar. The logos of the word are the supreme thought. It was that word or thought that manifested in the material world. All that evolves is a product of creative design and not that of random action as taught in the theory of evolution. Finally, understanding the Kabbala's Tree of Life will reinforce your understanding of the true reality. The following drawing describes the tree.

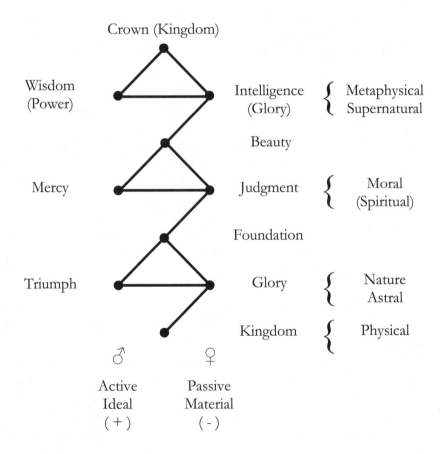

The three trinities show the deity in a different aspect or dimension, but always in the form of an indivisible trinity. The ten points of the tree are known as sefiroth and are representative of the ten manifestations of God in the total universe.

For harmony to exist a balance between the masculine and feminine polarities is required. For example, if we view the middle triangle with the opposing male characteristic of mercy and the female characteristic of judgment we can imagine a situation having judgment without mercy as being an imbalanced state. It would be a place where all is sternness or all is feminine without any masculine influences; that would be a place where everything is resistance and inertia. It is for this reason that we must realize that a golden mean is necessary for perfect harmony and ascension to exist. In this way we can understand the great lessons of the Kabbala and try to implement the Law of Balance in our daily lives.

Let me conclude this spiritual and philosophic component of the proclamation by asking you to make every effort to fully comprehend the tenets of our ascendant age. Only then will we, as a family, rise to a new level of dynamic existence and finally live in a world of blessed harmony.

Air quality, Weather, and Environment

The one-world conspirators created the myth of global warming and climate change so they could initiate measures to restrict human freedoms and prosperity. They even went so far as to devise ways to control weather and pollute our atmosphere by combining electromagnetics and chemtrails. As a consequence it behooves all of you to have a thorough understanding of the chem trail issue. The following discussion will provide you with the history and purpose of chemtrails.

Do you remember really blue skies? Have you noticed the haloes around the sun and moon? Have you observed the enormous increases in asthma, respiratory diseases, immune disorders and mortality rates? What could be the cause? Well, there certainly is a reason for such apparent changes. The answer can be explained in one word: chemtrails.

It all began around 1998 when global interests began Operation Cloverleaf, an extremely expensive and ambitious attempt to seed our skies with various biologic and chemical agents, the purpose of which was to rid the world of useless eaters and basically cull the herd. I tell you this because it demonstrates how depraved and evil the past scions of industry and government were. Truly, they were disciples of the devil. We can be grateful that we have finally stopped these operations before they accomplished the mission of Operation Cloverleaf.

The clandestine nature of this dastardly plan became even more obvious to us in 2006 when we noticed the shutdown of three national libraries and a chemical specialty library. These libraries held information on pollutants, effects of industrial practices on environmental health, and referenced articles, courses and publications not found elsewhere. The office of prevention, pollution and toxic substances in Washington, D.C. was the EPA's only specialized library on properties and health effects of toxic chemicals and pollutants. It was closed without notice to scientists and the public. By this action it appears that the Plante Administration was determined to reduce human knowledge, a seemingly pure political agenda. By removing access to data on dangers of airborne particulate matter, the government appointed EPA made it difficult to assess the damage being caused by toxic chemical and biologic particulates. This was just one of many government schemes to block the free flow of information during the past two presidencies. Another occurrence was the closing of the internet website "Pub Science," which was the most extensive collection of cross-referenced, indexed scientific research, abstracts and publications. Pub Science was closed without notice, a tragedy for scientists, researchers, teachers, students and the public, who wished to further their knowledge of a particular scientific topic.

It wasn't until around 2001 when the public alarm and awareness of chemtrails became obvious. Many true patriots and lovers of freedom worked diligently to expose the plot to bring death through the air. Even Congress made an attempt in the 2001 Space Preservation Act, presented by Dennis Kucinich, to outlaw chemtrails. Unfortunately, that provision was eliminated from the final version of the bill. Newspaper and news programs attempted explanations of the strange aerial phenomena. One article in the Idaho Observer in 2004 detailed how sub micron particles enter the blood and cause radical changes in the endocrine and nervous systems triggering high blood pressure and causing heart attacks. The mechanism by which this occurred was in the thickening of blood and its increased coagulability, which in turn, caused areas around the world to report dramatic increases in stroke victims. Some conjectured that mycoplasma organisms found in chemtrail samples induced the coagulation cascade, resulting in forming blood clots. High blood pressure became an epidemic around the world.

The chemtrail programs became catastrophic for biologic health, as the atmosphere was being engineered into highly charged electrically conductive plasma useful for a wide variety of projects. Barium and aluminum, two prominent isolates, act as electrolytes to enhance conductivity of radio waves. Did they have mind control in mind? Barium is known to weaken muscles, the heart and immunity. Aluminum goes to the brain and causes oxidative stress leading to Alzheimer's-like changes known as neurofibrillary tangles.

Even the BBC reported on the tripling of the incidence of asthma and the fact that the amount of solar energy reaching the earth's surface had been reduced by 22%. KNBC in LA was the first TV station in a major media market to cover the chemtrail issue. In 2006, citizens of Sudbury, Ontario, petitioned the Canadian government to stop chemtrailing.

One commentary entitled "Strange Days, Strange Skies" succinctly discussed the chemtrail issue as follows:

"Welcome to the brave new world of toxic barium skies, weather control, mind control and population reduction thru the use of chemtrails modulated with electromagnetic frequencies generated by HAARP (high frequency auroral resonance). Our health is under attack as evidenced by the skyrocketing rates of chemtrail induced lung cancer, asthma, and pulmonary respiratory problems. Our natural environment and planetary weather systems are under attack, resulting in freak lightning strikes, bizarre weather, 20% less sunlight reaching the earth's surface, causing alarming damage and nearly complete collapse in certain areas of marine ecosystems, and the creation of some of the largest tornadoes and hurricanes on record. Our skies are increasingly hazed over with barium and aluminum particulates, and ethylene dibromide clouds. Whether in the ocean or atmosphere this added particulate matter is a hazard to the health of every living thing on the planet. The health of millions of people is being affected. Unfortunately there is a blackout on this subject, so the only way to get the word out is via word of mouth."

The author pleaded with readers to talk to all those they knew and warn them of chemtrails and the impending danger to all of mankind.

The Las Vegas Tribune published an especially disturbing article about residents of heavily chemtrailed communities, like Las Vegas. The article described a chemtrail sickness associated with heavy spray days that left stricken people complaining of flu and allergic symptoms months after the flu season had ended. The incidence of respiratory and intestinal ailments was very high and often accompanied by extreme fatigue. The newspaper made the claim that we were under deliberate biologic attack by agents known only to the military and government officials who were responsible for permitting over flights by unmarked spray planes.

Another Las Vegas Tribune article, even in the face of government denials, explained how environmental labs had begun to identify another toxic component found in chemtrail samples. Several labs claimed that samples contained ethylene dibromide, an extremely hazardous pesticide that had been banned by the EPA in 1983. The literature is replete with warnings that exposure to even low levels of ethylene dibromide results in general weakness, vomiting, diarrhea, chest pains, shortness of breath, cough and respiratory failure due to swelling.

In 1999 emergency rooms began to be inundated by sick victims with flu-like symptoms as biologic agents began to be included in chemtrails. A huge explosion in mortality rates occurred. Many individuals were sick for as long as six weeks or more and many died. Authorities were strangely disinterested in identifying the infectious agent and the media simply referred to the deaths as being caused by flu-like symptoms. Even though 20,000 deaths occurred, the epidemic was a nonevent because of media controlled de-emphasis. The bug was later isolated and declared to be a bio-engineered virus heretofore unknown.

Shockingly, 10,000 deaths resulted from spraying in the United Kingdom. Health authorities were overwhelmed and had to resort to the use of refrigerated trucks as temporary morgues. These poor victims died of asphyxiation due to their lungs being filled with a sticky substance that could not be suctioned out or removed surgically.

An essay by Cliff Mickleson entitled, "Traitors to the Species,"[1] included the following eloquent statement (warning): "Alas, my friends, you do not even realize that the criminal hand flies each day above all you have ever loved. Even now, it grips your children as they play in the schoolyard. It throttles your retired parents as they unsuspectedly set out to see an America that is no more. It comes for you because it must!"

A polymer chemist, Mike Castle, found cationic reaction polymers with bioactive material, which can cause serious skin lesions and disease when they infiltrate the body. He identified microscopic polymers comprised of genetically engineered fungal forms mutated by viruses. The fungus' (virus) mutated spores secrete a powerful mycotoxin. Coincidentally, a strange new disease called Morgellon's disease emerged. This disease is a real horror and right out of science fiction. Morgellon's is a skin disease characterized by crawling and biting sensations all over the skin, painful lesions that never heal, dementia, brain fog, fatigue, insomnia and, most terrifying of all, mysterious tangled fibers that emerge through the sores. The thread-like fibers are red, black and translucent, some as long as an eyelash, others only visible under a microscope. The cause is supposedly not known. There is a so-called wall within the science community that did not permit release of a true assessment of

---

[1]The essay entitled, "Traitors to the Species," was written by Cliff Mickleson and uploaded to the internet on May 25, 2006.

Morgellon's. Some experts in dermatology and psychiatry claim it to be a condition known as "delusions of parasitosis," the belief that tiny bugs are burrowing beneath the skin. Sufferers scoff at the idea that the disease is induced by their hysteria because the fibers are very real. Others in the medical community feel there is either an immune dysfunction or an infectious process. Whatever the cause, an official explanation was being stifled and the truth hidden from the public.

The truth lies outside the box, where most medical truth lies. I refer to the alternative medicine field, which seeks real solutions to health problems. The real story is even more incredible than the most outrageous science fiction movie could ever be. Morgellon's grew out of the research of silicon nanotechnology, which has produced a self-replicating microscopic nanobot. These tiny silicon machines are distributed through chemtrail spraying, which had been seeding the earth's atmosphere and thus exposing the citizens of the world to this potential disease. Some researchers also suspected genetically modified foods as a source of fibers. Morgellon's does not appear to be communicable. Thank God for that! There is evidence that the Lyme disease spirochete and mold may be involved in some way, especially if combined with weak immunity. The fibers are thought to penetrate brain and all tissues, thereby impairing activity. Some conjectured that the fibers were intended to work in conjunction with the electromagnetic curtain that was being formed around the planet to be a means of mind control.

Until the absolute cause is known, effective treatment will be elusive. However, some success has been achieved with the use of alternative supplements such as cat's claw, garlic, colloidal silver, colostrum, probiotics, pro HGH secretogogus, transfer factor, and coenzyme Q-10.

Lastly, I would like to explain the dangers of barium, which is another prominent pollutant found in chemtrails. Barium atmospheric levels had reached a point wherein they were eight times higher than safe levels. EPA guidelines state that 5 ppm is safe to breathe. Levels had reached 40 ppm prior to 2011 when we abolished the chemtrail programs. Barium can even initiate multiple sclerosis. The spray planes were filling our atmosphere with nano particles of barium on a daily basis. The particles stick to lung tissue and are readily absorbed into the bloodstream. In contaminated areas people were also ingesting barium by eating plants grown in contaminated soil. Chronic exposure to barium presents significant health risks, including death. It shuts down the immune system. The purpose of spraying was to directly impact the T-cell systems of the human being. Barium blocks several modes of T-cell activation. In other words, barium will turn off the body's T-cells. T-cells are required to fight off viral and fungal infections.

Education

Our educational systems will have to be rebuilt. Education will redefine itself and teach students to prepare for a life of service to truth and God. A sense of appreciation for the virtuous life must be inculcated if we are to restore a moral foundation upon which we can build a lasting social structure.

The system of education will expose the failures and evils of liberalism and modernity. The incoherent philosophy of liberalism is a bankrupt philosophy and became the enemy within. It had grown out of the age of enlightenment and failed when man realized a good society could not be achieved by reason alone. Rather than turn to the solution of religion, it chose nihilistic philosophies like existentialism, moral revolution, hedonism and socialism. Radical egalitarianism prevents individual excellence and retards the ascendancy of society. Quotas, affirmative action and feminism are obvious examples. In response, individuals seek expression through pursuit of pleasure; thus they seek perverse sexual practices and decadent tendencies in art and music. The noble liberalism of the 19th century has degenerated and every institution, from music to education to science, has been affected. With technology, automation and computerization, real labor was eliminated and replaced by new work, which is consistent with demonism. With time and energy on our hands, consumerism and entertainment have become the focus of our culture, along with drug use, sex and violence, radio, television and movies. These activities kept boredom away. Hedonism, if unchecked, accelerates the demise of body and soul. Personal convenience becomes an obsession. People are impatient to the point of resenting anything that may be inconvenient, which leads to the rejection of religion, morality, civility and etiquette. The result of egalitarianism is cultural disaster, which becomes a tyranny of sorts and leads to hedonistic individualism resembling the bread and circuses atmosphere of a declining Roman culture. People were deceived into thinking they had more freedom (free sex and violent activity), but in reality they had less because the governing body's concern became distribution of goods and services on an equal basis, which requires greater taxation and deprivation of certain rights. A society with no sense of community lost its will to reduce obscenity, punish crime, reform welfare, stigmatize illegitimate children or maintain standards of reason and scholarship.

The failure of education was due to feminism, afrocentrism and self-esteem movements, all products of egalitarianism, which diverted resources from real education. By not providing an educational foundation our nation created rampant social discontent and eventual chaos. The system became a disgrace as evidenced by universities inflating grades, reducing academic rigor, providing remedial courses and producing students with no appreciation of history, moral law, geography and basic economics.

As you now know, this decline was all intentional and was orchestrated by the Luciferian elites who knew that a new world order could only exist if the U.S.A. was weakened to the point of a third world country. Americans became numb to the spiritual reality and instead of supporting the churches found ways of spending exorbitant sums of money on concerts, sporting events and gambling. As people lost sight of the divine they sought greater and greater stimulation only to find themselves sinking into a cesspool of indulgence. The lesson we must learn from this debacle is that liberty cannot govern without faith. Faith was the foundation of our nation and must be restored. By replacing religion with other forms of transcendence like global warming, animal rights and environmentalism, we lost sight of absolute values and our connection to the Divine. Once that occurs, entropy ensues and a nation disintegrates.

Our school systems will be decentralized as we create private teaching institutions in which the teachers will govern their own entities. Interference from government bureaucracies will be minimized, allowing the true experts to determine curricula, behavior, dress codes and scholastic goals. Parents will be responsible for tuition payments, but will be given tax credits to offset the cost. For those who can't afford tuition, a voucher system will be established. Tuition amounts will be linked to excellence; the better the school, the higher the tuition. Such a system will be an incentive for the schools to be the best they can be. Vouchers will allow the creation of private teaching institutions, which will have the freedom to teach about the true reality of spirit.

There will be a renewed emphasis on the right hemisphere of the brain's development. The right hemisphere is the creative and spiritual side, versus the left hemisphere, which is the analytical and practical side. By placing emphasis on the right hemisphere it will allow for a link to divine and cosmic truths—thus leading to inspired thought. The new education will stress music, art and creativity and lead to a cultivation of man's higher nature. Efforts will be made to discourage dissonance in music by encouraging harmony, as harmony reflects the universal order and not the disharmony of chaos. Good music is essential and can act as food for the soul.

A staunch effort will be placed on teaching the history of the U.S.A. with an emphasis on its uniqueness as being divinely inspired. The American Revolution was mostly a spiritual revolt that established individual sovereignty and liberty, which allowed one to achieve his potential and live as a son or daughter of God. The revolution proclaimed liberty, sovereignty, self-determination, inalienable rights, equality of opportunity, justice for all and human dignity for all who are derived from God—all of which are guaranteed by the constitutional republic. Its purpose, of course, is to find true happiness in doing God's will on earth.

Unlocking human potential can be a result of knowing and understanding the wisdom of the ancient mysteries and physical discord.

A new appreciation of astrology as an actual science must be inculcated into our minds because it explains that planetary and celestial influences are real. Cosmic forces play a role in dictating happenings on our planet. The speed and motion of planets determines time. A cosmic clock exists, which determines destiny. Cyclical alignments of celestial bodies affect activities on earth and should be better understood.

Earth changes are occurring as evidenced in: increases in magnetic resonance, climate change, extreme weather, and earthquake and volcanic activity. Be aware that negative energy, which results from sinfulness, can actually influence all of the above changes. The old paradigm of acquisition for the sake of ego reinforcement is a false belief and must end.

Our galaxy is entering a new cycle and humanoids throughout it will feel the power of this change. The purpose is to take us to a higher evolutionary dimension, which will bring us closer to oneness with the creator. Think of an allegory of fish returning home to their spawning ground. The old paradigms are failing and will not exist after 2011. The answers lie in self-responsibility and self-reliance. A democratic nation can only be great when it is good and its citizens are responsible and of high character.

Smaller cooperative communities will be the means to creating meaningful work and internal rewards and a return to a village-type social structure with each citizen providing his or her contribution to the whole. This is the way life will be. These social units should be populated by like-minded people, which will allow individuals to apply their spiritual awareness to new political and social structures.

All of you will learn to look for solutions intuitively by going deep within yourselves where truth resides. To accomplish this feat one must create stillness and thus link to the cosmic mind. By doing this you will discover your real self and find the ability to be shamanistic, which will allow you to create your own future and destiny. Once you understand the pitfalls of the past, you will step out of the timeline and determine your actions in the "now".

The planet is going to undergo massive change in the near future. It will only take a small percentage of aware individuals to change the collective mind of humanity. The science of Noetics will bring new understanding of the power of thought and its ability to affect the physical world. The theory of the hundredth monkey explains the phenomenon of this new expansive awareness. You must all remain fearless and create the new paradigm by staying in the flow of cosmic energy. All solutions will come from outside the old systems and will come to us intuitively. Each individual must realize that the answers lie in the kingdom within us all.

Once mankind understands this new paradigm, we will debunk the theory of evolution and randomness. The laws of intelligent design will then become prevalent. A cosmic universal consciousness is a spiral torsion energy (thought unto itself), and is the determinant for the workings of the universe.

A new focus will be placed on parental responsibilities in the raising of children. Parents will be expected to ingrain certain beliefs in the minds of their progeny. A good example of the best of teachings can be found in the "communion with God," which espouses the following advice to parents in what truths they should teach young developing citizens:

- Nothing exterior is required to achieve happiness.
- Failure is a fiction; trying is success.
- Live in a world of abundance to be shared, not gathered.
- There is nothing required that you be to get God's blessing. You are all part of God and are loved regardless of your circumstances.
- Consequences and punishment are not the same.
- Death does not exist. Your spiritual nature is eternal.
- There should be no conditions to love. Your unconditional love of others is the greatest gift to the world.
- No one is superior to another. We are all part of the one.
- There is nothing you cannot attain. Eliminate ignorance and you will become God-like. Once you live in accordance with divine will, you will be blessed and all solutions will come to you.
- Parents should be responsible in their actions, which should demonstrate proper behavior to their children.
- The expression of the divinity in all of us is an evolutionary journey.
- Reject the following illusions: need, failure, disunity, insufficiency, requirement, judgment, condemnation, conditionality, superiority, and ignorance.

Economics/Commerce

The Constitutional right of free enterprise must be restored. For this to be accomplished a foundation of ethical standards must be established that will support the new economic edifice in order to provide abundance along with the subjective happiness and satisfaction of implementing truth in one's endeavors.

We must bring about the realization that social units should produce the goods and services that they require. Trade should only be used to supply goods and services that the social unit cannot provide. The encouragement of small business and individual enterprise must be effected. To achieve this aim, restrictions on corporate size, enforcement of anti-trust laws, the establishment of fair trade laws, and grants to viable and capable entrepreneurs will be put in place.

The past forty years of living on credit created the recent economic depression. That way of doing business has come to a rapid end. A new age of fiscal responsibility is at hand. Deficit spending will not be allowed and the fiat money will be replaced by a gold-based currency. By having a gold-based currency we will restore industrial capital and bring stability to our currency.

Such measures will do much to bring a new sense of community and meaningfulness to our lives. The right of free enterprise is fundamental and must be preserved and appreciated if we are to live a life of harmony and abundance in the city/state of God.

Energy

New methods will be formed, which will provide virtually free energy. Scientific advancements such as cold fusion, Tesla technologies, and crystal, wind and solar power will be developed. Much of this knowledge has long been known but has been suppressed by exploitive political and business entities that profit from old energy sources.

Crystal power is the method of energy production that was purportedly utilized by the ancient Atlantean civilization. The ability of crystals to maximize sun energy has long been known. However, as I said earlier, this knowledge has been kept from the masses.

One example of a community energy production system would be to have wind farms supplying energy for a particular social unit. Envision a village of a thousand people being supplied by as few as six to seven windmills, which would generate power for that community. The village could create their own self-governing power companies.

A new energy paradigm will be firmly entrenched, which will no longer be exploitive of people and the planet. It will be fair to all!

Medicine/Health

The conventional, allopathic medical systems practiced in the western world are based on a Newtonian model of reality. However, a new paradigm is forming based on an Einsteinian model. This new way of viewing healing will become the medicine of the near future.

The Newtonian concept sees things in terms of molecules, cellular systems, genes and other material explanations. The body is seen as a machine controlled by the brain and nervous system much like a computerized structure. This mechanical approach ignores the true nature of man and explains the body as a series of intricate chemical systems powering a structure of nerve, muscle, flesh and bones. In contrast, the Einsteinian view sees the ultimate reality as different forms of energy and vibrational frequencies. This view sees the physical body as just one of many higher energy systems, all in dynamic equilibrium. All co-exist in the same space, but differ in their vibrational frequency.

Understanding the multi-dimensional human anatomy will clarify the new paradigm. Our anatomy is composed of seven bodies: the physical, etheric, astral, three mental bodies and the causal body. The unimpeded flow of energy from the higher bodies into the lower physical body is the key to creating balanced health. Energy and vibrational medicine will form the true paradigm. The old methods of cut, radiate, and drug will be obsolete.

Disease will be eradicated, as man acquires the ability to heal and resist disease just as Christ did! Once the Christ consciousness within all of us is discovered the God consciousness will permeate our being and lead to perfect health. Remember, true healing comes from within. All diseases can be healed in an instant, if we are delivered from falseness by allowing the God frequency to pervade this reality.

You must also comprehend the idea that all creativity comes before the physical reality. Thought or the "word" precedes form and circumstance. Prophecy is an example of this phenomenon; it predates the actual event. All creativity comes from the source (cosmic mind) via the Holy Spirit, that universal vibration which is superluminal (beyond light).

213

All actions, thoughts, and deeds done in the physical realm are recorded in the universal Akaschic records. This is how evil, illness and curses reside in certain places. These negative circumstances can be removed and erased by simply having faith in the blessings of truth.

The old ways are over. No longer will the evil forces that controlled and manipulated our world program us to be less creative and spiritual. The new discoveries that explain the true nature of reality will allow man to enter a new luminescent age of enlightenment.

The conventional system of medicine was a big lie. It had dispelled the ideas of spiritual energy and vibrational healing in order to maximize profits and control the populace. Once you reprogram your minds you will realize that real healing power lies within you and your need for external means will no longer be necessary.

Even though science has seemingly avoided metaphysical explanations, it has long known the true nature of reality. One example of this misrepresentation can be seen in the use of monatomic gold by the global elites to slow aging and increase cosmic mindfulness. This has been a long held secret dating back to the ancient Egyptian pharaohs. It has been explained that the resonance of certain elements like gold, indium and iridium activate certain enzymes that correct damaged DNA within genes, thus reversing disease and retarding the aging process.

The time has come for man to finally know and understand the true reality of the universe. This new paradigm will provide a metaphysical basis from which social ideas can rise in a secure assuredness that they are derived from universal truths. Our new way of living will maximize human potential to do good works such as charity, justice and generosity. These are attributes that are specific to the human kingdom and are natural to man when he has developed his humanness. We are truly made in the image of God and possess the innate abilities to know the divinity within us. Only through knowing our true nature will we be able to create a world characterized by universal brotherhood.

The noetic sciences must be studied, for they explain the power of thought and the mind. These pursuits investigate the fact that thought has actual mass and by having mass it can influence and change physical matter. Imagine the enormous possibilities of collective thought, which could alter and thus bring the physical world into a state of harmony and positivism.

The old world, as we knew it, was steeped in egocentrism and selfishness with a focus on attachments to objects of the external senses. Delusional thinking of this sort is what prevented man from discovering his true spiritual nature. Now is the time to expand your self-knowledge and open your ears to the call of Jesus Christ, Buddha, Krishna and the great avatars of the past. Abnegate your egos and break that sense of self that separates you from the God within you. Even the pernicious ecclesiastical systems of organized religions obscured and debased the true teachings of Jesus Christ and Buddha. By so doing it allowed these authoritarian structures to subjugate you and retard the spiritual growth of mankind.

In the new age of elevated consciousness and increased awareness, the old religious, political, economic, social and medical systems will lose their identity and die. Healing will be at the level of the luminous matrix that surrounds the physical body. The matrix encodes information that can be utilized for healing purposes and prophecy. The earth itself, being a living organism, also has a matrix, which, if understood, will assist man in his growth.

Every twenty-six thousand years the earth, sun, and center of the galaxy come into perfect alignment, which ushers in a new resonance, which can resurrect man into an advanced state higher than the previous era. We will soon be leaving the third dimension and entering into a higher frequency known as the fourth dimension. This new dimension is correlative to the fourth heart chakra (love) and will see an elevation of man into a Christ-like state—a second coming, so to speak.

Those souls who possess the new frequency will be harvested to live in the Golden Age devoid of disease, discord, hunger and want. It is your responsibility to be a part of this amazing transition by seeking enlightenment; otherwise, you will not be a "safe" person and will unfortunately succumb and not survive in the fourth dimension. The solution is to turn inward and practice generosity, speak truthfulness and express unconditional love. The new humans will become whole brain creators that utilize their brains not just for external satisfaction but also for much higher reasons.

With all that said, I hope you now have a better understanding of where we as a human family are going and why the old methods of healing and sustaining our lives will be obsolete. Hopefully, you will choose resurrection and live with us in the age of glory.

Justice and Politics

It was with great misfortune that the form of government established by the founders degenerated from a total democracy into a fascistic system of big government and big business. The impetus for that unfortunate development was a materialistic philosophy known as pragmatic humanism, which denies the existence of the divine and separates itself from the true nature of reality. When man no longer recognizes a higher order he is deprived of the inspiration and guidance of the cosmic mind. Thus, this denial leads to chaos and disorder in all human institutions, be they social, personal, economic, political or moral. By denying universal law mankind lost its way, which brought us to the mess we found ourselves in.

With the realization that our disorder was self-induced we must reverse that condition by instituting basic changes in our political and judicial systems. The cleansing of our nation will involve the following changes:

- A constitutional monarchy with a representative congress consisting of a Senate and House of Representatives will be established.
- The monarch will eventually be chosen and approved by the Congress and given a lifetime term, which can only end with the death of the king or voluntary retirement.
- My reign as Jon I will end when I reach the age of seventy-five years in 2016. I have chosen my son, Christian, to be my successor because he is greatly qualified to be a benevolent philosopher-king. It is my hope that following his reign the nation will be ready to revert to choosing its next regnum in a more democratic fashion by having Congress select the monarchs of the future.

- Congress and our judicial systems will be purged of liberal progressives who espouse humanistic philosophies that separate society from divine will.
- Unconstitutional laws such as the Patriot Act, the Homeland Security Act, the National Healthcare Act, and the Federal Reserve Act will be repealed.
- The Constitutional rights of our citizens will be guaranteed and defended at all costs.
- A limit of two terms will be established for Congressional representatives. In addition, realistic restrictions will be placed on their compensation, benefits, and prerequisites.
- There will be a prohibition, with some reservation, on practices that undermine social stability, such as divorce, abortion and euthanasia.
- Only responsible citizens will be allowed to vote. The right to vote will be reserved to those who pay taxes, abide by the law, and pass a basic test on history, civics and economics.

Jon concluded his proclamation with a light-hearted discussion of the half punch wedge shot in the sport of golf. He did this with the intention of creating a mood of levity and bringing a smile to the faces of the listeners for they now had every reason to smile; the satanic enemy within had been vanquished forever.

The first two years following Jon's assumption of power witnessed dramatic changes in all facets of life in America and the world. All of humanity was being exposed to the true reality of oneness, and order was being brought to all social systems. Evidence of a new dawn for mankind could be seen in a wide variety of changes in the patterns of life.

- The sanctity of the family unit was restored. The roles of a father and mother and the responsibilities of a child were redefined.
- Education redefined itself and began to prepare students for a life of service to truth and God.
- Disease was eradicated as man acquired the ability to resist disease and to heal as Christ did.

- Virtue replaced vice. A sense of morality was restored.
- Ethics returned to business.
- Reverence once again became a quality seen in people.
- Perverse sexual behavior disappeared.
- Fiscal responsibility was established in government and in personal lives.
- Life without fear was established.
- Unconditional love prevailed.

The evolutionary cosmic process was firmly in place as evidenced by the changes in the planet's vibrational frequencies and resonance. Individuals were becoming more instinctively aware that strange feelings were occurring within them. It was as though the cosmos was telling them to bring their own vibrational nature into attunement; otherwise, there would be no place for discordant being in a new dimensional order.

As the Omega Point neared at the end of 2012 A.D., Jon repeatedly warned his subjects that they must redeem themselves if they were to ascend into the next dimension. He explained the possibility of individuals actually disappearing from the new reality by falling into a time compression due to their negative karma. Of course, many ignored and scoffed at these portentous thoughts, just as those who rejected the pleas of Noah and Lot in the biblical stories of retribution. It would be their self-induced misfortune if they were to forever disappear and never share in the new, gloried status of mankind.

As man and the planet ascended into the new, less-dense fourth dimension, which is correlative to the fourth chakra and the heart, it became obvious that the predicted second coming of Christ was actually occurring. It would finally be that time when man would live in love, peace, harmony and abundance. Even more apparent was the thought that it wasn't the actual personage of Christ that would be returning but instead man himself would realize the Christ consciousness within and that this realization would take him to oneness with the universal creator. So, in essence, the second coming was actually the resurrection of the Christ within each and every human being.

The years immediately following the planet's transformation, 2012 to 2016, were characterized by the reformation and realignment of social, political and economic systems. Harmony became the overlying asset of all human endeavors.

King Jon I took great satisfaction in having been ordained as God's messenger and helping to bring mankind to its fullest potential. He knew that upon his retirement in 2016, his son, Crown Prince Christian, would continue to pave the road to a perfect human society. It was planned that after a generation or so, Christian would abdicate his throne and the nation and world would be ready to institute representative governments with elected presidents and prime ministers. The concept of total democracy had, once again, been proven a silly proposition because human weakness and indulgence always leads to its internal disintegration. Democracy only works when citizens of high quality elect officials of high quality. It was a lesson learned the hard way. Never again would man fall into the pitfalls of false, liberal philosophies of the past. America had been given the divinely-intentioned style of government once before and allowed its corruption. Now that the cleansing had accomplished its purpose of readying the people for self-government, it was time to turn the reins of government back to the people.

Great changes had occurred from the time of Jon's ascension to power in 2011 and his scheduled retirement in 2016. Humanity had undergone extreme physical and spiritual transformations and was just starting to settle into a more orderly and peaceful calm.

Just a week prior to Jon's official retirement, he sat with his son Christian for an evening of conversation and conviviality. The dialogue began with Jon discussing the wonders of all that had happened over the course of his lifetime. His reflections and recollections included: his recruitment and free education at the best of schools; his experiences with his first love, Luz Barca; his exposure to the sacred mysteries and understanding his purpose in life; his discovery of the Wounded Eagle Plan to destroy America; his indoctrination by Caligo Mendaci into the brotherhood of evil ones; his alignment with Herman Sparkman and Ion Ampere in creating the Brethren of Light; the experiences at Bohemian Grove; the horror of Mendaci's impalement; the tragic passing of Luz Barca; his fateful meeting of his wife in Rome; the birth of his two children and the training of his son, Christian; his selection as absolute ruler; the exposure and dismantling of the secret cabal of evil Luciferians; his leading of mankind into a Golden Age.

His wonderment was most obvious as he described his impressions of when he first viewed the incarceration camps after the great shift in 2012. The site was amazing, for not a single prisoner was to be seen. It was explained that the Lords of Darkness (Fallen Angels), once incarcerated, were deprived of their sustaining negative energy and started to wither and weaken. They were given the choice: open their hearts to universal love or choose continued weakness and eventual death and oblivion. Most chose the former and rose out of their reptilian prison into a life of shared joy and harmony with the rest of the human family. So it was when Jon visited the camps. What he saw was a dramatic scene of landscapes and wards littered with molted reptilian skins—devoid of any living creature. It was the wonder of realizing the power of love that so affected Jon. For here was the evidence that even the Disciples of Lucifer could return to God's family.

Jon continued his discussion by telling Christian that he felt compelled to explain in great detail the how and why of all the changes that had recently occurred. Jon knew that as a future king Christian would require a thorough understanding of the Luciferian attempt to suppress human awareness of its true potential and how it was thwarted, thus allowing man's great spiritual leap forward.

Jon explained that all that exists is the same energy. It is the law of one! Energy patterns create infinite forms, such as birds, trees, insects, water and humans. But, they are still forms of the same universal energy. At the level of pure energy everything is connected to everything else. Humans have the ability to access all the other energy and consciousness, and as energy and consciousness they are the same and have the means to creating oneness to the God mind. God is not separate from us but is within us. All that exists is an aspect of the infinite mind, even the evil ones.

The evil ones had created methods to prevent man's ascent to truth by delinking humanity from the essential truth. The use of religion and science was fundamental in creating the illusion that God is outside of man and that infinity and the eternal nature of life do not exist. By manipulating man's perceptions the Luciferians kept man from discovering his multi-dimensional anatomy and thus caused man to operate at a level far below its potential.

The Luciferians operated in the lower astral frequency range and sought to keep humanity in this range so they couldn't go into higher frequencies closer to the Holy Spirit. For this reason, the negative emotions of fear, guilt, hate, frustration, judgmentalism, and resentment were constantly perpetrated on the mass of humanity. Negative emotions resonate in this lower frequency and allow man to be dominated by reptilian consciousness, and to succumb to control by evil forces. In contrast, the emotion of love resonates at a higher vibrational pattern. Love is that state that reconnects man to all that is - GOD. By changing our perspectives and allowing the power of love to imbue our being we elevate the whole because we are part of the whole. We are actually creating more God! The divine unifying love force energizes all and brings unity and harmony to all systems, be they social, political, economic or even individual physical health.

The evil ones are trapped in a prison of time and space (materialism) and can only be released by opening their hearts to the power of love.

Everything is in contact with the cosmic pulse. Negative emotions impede this flow of positive energy and disconnect us from the earth and universe. By breaking the associations of heart/brain, intellect/intuition, and body/spirit our separation from the universal truth occurs and we fall into falsity and illusion.

The cycles of day and night and the seasons of the year are obvious to everyone. However, larger cycles exist, which are part of a cosmic plan to take man higher and closer to oneness with God. The ancients like the Sumerians, Egyptians, Hindus, Chinese, Mayans, and Native Americans were well aware of these cycles.

It was known to the ancients that a great shift of the ages was to occur in 2012. A new frequency had been discovered in 1991, which was being emitted from the center of the galaxy with the result of transforming energy fields on earth. When the earth, sun and the galaxy center align in 2012 the great shift will occur.

The earth is a giant magnet whose strength of magnetism is controlled by its rate of rotation. The magnetic field has declined by fifty percent as the rotation of earth slowed over the past fifteen hundred years. Additionally, the resonance on earth has increased from what was once thought to be a constant of around 7.8 hertz (7 cycles) to 13 cycles in 2012. Combining the decline in the earth's magnetic field and the increase in resonance is preparing the planet for massive changes. The planet's rotation will stop for a period of days, then begin to rotate in the opposite direction at a higher rate of rotation. The new increase in magnetism will not allow the survival of those whose vibrational qualities are not in tune with the new energies. If they wish, individuals can choose to open their hearts and transform themselves into a perfected being of higher consciousness. If we allow ourselves the infusion of the new frequencies we will live in abundance, harmony, disease free and forever in the city of God. So you can see that the ancient predictions were valid after all and have come to be!

Some scientists explain that the universe is a hologram of sixty-four timewaves and that all sixty-four of these waves peaked together in 2012. Phenomenal changes occurred in human consciousness in the year following the great shift.

The dramatic changes in weather patterns, earthquakes, and volcanic activity that occurred just prior to 2012 were all due to the various changes in magnetics, resonance, and photon activity. The global changes in climate and temperatures were certainly not due to human activity and carbon dioxide. The big lie of global warming was a desperate attempt to keep man from understanding that we were on the verge of a massive transformation in our spiritual awareness. The evil ones knew that once people were aware of their lies their rule would come to an end. There was no way they could stem the tide of truth. For we all know truth will prevail in the end. God ordains it.

The Luciferians had tried a myriad of tactics to stop mankind from making the shift in consciousness. They gave us toxic foods, harmful legal drugs, destructive addictions, fluoridated water, artificial sweeteners, poisonous vaccines, genetically modified foods, mind-destroying cell phones, destructive chemtrails, wasteful energy systems, structured education to imprison us in the left brain, and on and on and on. They even engineered project blue beam, which projected giant holographic images of UFOs and religious figures in the sky. The project was designed to evoke terrifying fear in the human population. These were desperate measures, which in the end, all failed.

"That's my story." said Jon to his enraptured son. "It's been a fantastic journey for someone of such humble beginnings. Could it have been any other way for a man with the initials J.C.?"

Jon concluded his discourse by telling Christian he was honored to hand over the scepter of power to his son. He affirmed the fact that Christian was most qualified to assume the role of king, but he wanted the assurance that Christian would abdicate his position by the year 2050.

"My only command to you is to relinquish your kingship and return power to the people in the form of a republic. By that time they will be ready to rule themselves in a responsible way."

"I agree," replied Christian, "and I do pledge to do your will."

"Good," replied Jon. "Now I can look around and see that the name of God is most hallowed and his kingdom has come to earth. With divine guidance all man's needs will be provided and there will be no sinfulness on this planet. We will be delivered from evil and have no temptation to do so. For it is finally known that God is the one and exists as the kingdom (father) power (cosmic Christ) and glory (Holy Spirit) forever. As it was in the beginning, is now and ever shall be.

"It is without reservation that I can say to you that my fated role and purpose as God's messenger has been fulfilled. So it is that I announce, in the same last words of our Lord Jesus Christ as he expired, 'Consummata est' – 'It is finished.'"

EPILOGUE

After the purge of 2011, the nation and world are taught to live in accordance with divine will. The City of God finally becomes a reality on earth and mankind lives in absolute harmony, peace, health and abundance.

Once firmly established, the kingship will be relinquished and governance will be returned to a moral and responsible populace. A true worldwide republic will then be formed in perpetuity, which will forever preclude man's future fall from grace.

SUGGESTED READINGS

The Course of Miracles .... Dr. Helen Schucman

Virational Medicine .... Richard Gerber

Disappearance of the Universe .... Gary Renard

Kabbala

The Extraordinary Life & Influence of Helena Blavatsky Founder of the Modern Theosophical Movement .... Sylvia Cranston

The Secret Teachings of all Ages .... Manly P. Hall

Circle of Intrigue: The Hidden Inner Circle of the Global Illuminati Conspiracy .... Texe Marrs

Secret Societies...and How They Affect Our Lives Today .... Sylvia Browne

The Second Coming of Christ: The Resurrection of the Christ Within .... Paramahansa Yogananda

Autobiography of a Yogi .... Paramahansa Yogananda

Your Immortal Reality: How to Break the Cycle of Birth and Death .... Gary Renard

Anatomy of the Spirit: The Seven Stages of Power and Healing .... Caroline Myss

Esoteric Anatomy: The Body as Consciousness .... Bruce Burger

The Reincarnation of Edgar Cayce?: Interdimensional Communication and Global Transformation .... Wynn Free

The Lost Years of Jesus: Documentary Evidence of Jesus' 17-Year Journey to the East .... Elizabeth Clare Prophet

The David Icke Guide to the Global Conspiracy .... David Icke

Handbook for the New Paradigm .... EMBRACING THE RAINBOW